THIRD CRIME LUCKY

A BREEZE VILLAGE COZY MYSTERY

KATE MACLEAN

For Ken

THIRD CRIME LUCKY

CHAPTER 1

$\mathcal{A}$ scream sliced through the peaceful silence in Virginia's room. She jumped, the book in her hands tumbling to land in a heap on the floor. Heart still beating fast, she crossed the room and poked her head out the door. "Can you keep it down out there?"

The horror movie marathon was in full swing, a different scary movie playing in the common spaces on the second and third floors while the staff set up for a Halloween party in the main dining room downstairs. What constituted a scary movie had been a great debate in the preceding weeks, with Ronald insisting that throat-slashing, or at least the threat of imminent throat-slashing, was required for a movie to qualify as horror, while Patricia insisted that the doll-headed spider toy in *Toy Story* put the cartoon classic on par with *The Ring*.

Beyond movie marathons of questionable spookiness, the latest phase of retirement since she'd moved into Breeze Village had brought nothing but joy to Virginia: friends she got to see every day, a room of her own to retreat to when she tired of seeing those friends, and coordinated activities to fill her time when she got bored. And, in a recent turn of events, two murders she'd very much enjoyed *not* investigating.

Six weeks ago, a woman had been found stabbed to death outside Seaview. She was in her late fifties, happily married with children and two young grandchildren, a former attorney who'd left the field and now wrote horror novels. Along with everyone else in town, Virginia read about it in the paper and talked about how awful it was over coffee and breakfast. They speculated about whether it was the husband, and then they moved on.

Interest was reignited the week before when a man turned up dead just ten minutes from Breeze Village. He'd been stabbed to death like the woman, Irene Pushton, though according to police, there was no other apparent connection between the two murders. Herman Walsh was unmarried, completely dedicated to his work as a web designer, and had moved to the area from New York five years earlier after a health scare. A colleague of his reportedly told police Herman had said, "Tomorrow's not a given, and I don't want to spend another day trudging through the snow to squeeze onto a subway train with a hundred other poor schmucks." He'd packed up and left the city the week he'd been discharged from the hospital, heading for the warmth of the South and the charm of small-town living.

And now he was dead.

Two murders in as many months was unusual. Ruth, Genie, and Byron in the spring, and then Russ and Michelle in the summer... the town had given that a pass.

Ruth was old and wasn't even a suspected homicide until Genie and Byron were murdered. And even then, all the victims lived in the old folks' home, so the town at large could mostly ignore it. And then Russ and Michelle, that all seemed nicely packaged up. Personal, contained. Not a murderer on the loose killing senselessly. But this? Seaview was starting to talk.

And for once, Virginia *loved* not being in the center of it all. Few things were as sweet as being able to read the stories in the paper, say, "That poor man, how awful," and then go to work at the Piggly Wiggly down the street without concern that the police were going to arrest her for murder, or that a murderer would walk free because the victim was elderly. No, here there was no personal connection. Virginia was well and truly an outsider and glad of it.

A knock sounded at the door just as Virginia retrieved her dropped book and settled back into her recliner. "It's open," she called, not wanting to get up and answer it.

"The party's starting." Haley, one of the longest-tenured staff members and newly promoted Director of Nursing at Breeze Village, poked her head in. Her characteristic fake eyelashes fluttered, so long they cast little shadows on her cheeks, and she tucked her blond hair behind her ear.

Virginia thanked her and Haley left, continuing down the hall, knocking on doors and inviting the residents to the Halloween party. Kim had told her earlier in the week that Diana, the new Activities Coordinator, had arranged for catering from Miss B's, and Virginia knew that would draw a crowd. No one loved Miss B's fried chicken more than the residents of Breeze Village.

Downstairs, the dining room was decked out for Halloween. Purple, orange, and black streamers dangled from the ceiling, dancing in the breeze from the air conditioner, still working hard well into the Southern fall. Black cats and jack-o'-lanterns smiled up from plastic tablecloths. The labors of the afternoon's cookie decorating class were on display: bats, pumpkins, and ghosts all covered in frosting and sprinkles. Diana was serving glittering black punch from an enormous punchbowl.

"Isn't it spooky?" She handed Virginia a cup, grinning from ear to ear. "Edible glitter!"

The Halloween party was Diana's first major endeavor since coming on board, one of Hashim's first hires after taking over Breeze Village, and she was eager to please. If there was a holiday, be it International Coffee Day, Chocolate Cupcake Day, or Read a Book Day, Diana would find a way to celebrate at Breeze Village. September 19th was National Gymnastics Day, and despite the fact that the average age of the residents of Breeze Village was over eighty, Diana had put together an accessible gymnastics class and played clips from the Olympics on the televisions.

"There you are!" Virginia hurried across the room to join Marney and Jane, who were hunkered down, Jane knitting and Manrey crocheting as far away from the speaker playing "Monster Mash" as possible. Their fingers flew across the projects pooling in their laps.

"Coming to join us?" Marney's curly hair bounced as

she lifted her head and peered over her reading glasses to smile up at her best friend.

"Only until Ronald gets down here. He promised me a rematch after he blatantly cheated in our last card game."

Jane let out a belly laugh, the sound disproportionate to her tiny frame. "He'll be a while. Last I saw, there was an hour left on that slasher film they're playing up on the third floor."

The dining room filled steadily, the conversation bustling. From what Virginia could tell, the hottest topics of the night were when the roadwork on the interstate north of town would be completed, the opening of a new Japanese restaurant downtown, and Herman Walsh's murder. She heard the words "serial killer" more than once. Then they brought out dinner from Miss B's, and all conversation halted completely while the entirety of Breeze Village busied themselves making quick work of the best fried chicken around.

"Who's that?" Virginia asked through a mouth of mashed potatoes, gesturing across the room to where a hunched man had just called one of the nurses, Kim, over to his table for the third time since the meal began.

Jane and Marney turned to look. "I think his name's Martin," Jane said.

"He has a thing for Nurse Kim," Marney said. "I asked her about it the other day after I saw him getting a bit too grabby at breakfast. Poor thing, she's just so relieved to have kept her job after her affair with Russ. She's not about to make waves." A hard glint shone in her eyes. "After she left, I went over and told him a thing or two about touching another person."

Virginia looked back over. "Seems like it stuck. His hands are planted firmly on the table in front of him."

Her next bite was interrupted by a sudden plunge into inky, impenetrable darkness. Virginia blinked, trying to comprehend her sudden blindness. It was only as silverware clattered to plates and murmurs rose around her that she realized the lights had gone out.

"What's going on?" one voice asked.

"Who turned out the lights?"

Then, from across the building, a scream cut through the chatter.

CHAPTER 2

The hair rose on Virginia's arm and a pit formed in her throat, her stomach roiling. *No, no, no.* Her hand shook. *Another murder.* She swayed in her seat, lightheaded. *Not another murder. Not here.*

The scream had hardly ended when the lights returned, brightness re-blinding the residents just as their eyes had begun to adjust to the darkness.

"Is everyone okay?" Kim and Haley had both sprung into action, Kim making the rounds and checking in on the baffled residents at the party while Haley sprinted down the hall to the source of the scream.

Virginia gripped the table, steadying herself, waiting for the news. She'd done this before; she knew the drill. It was only a matter of time before the police would be asking her questions.

But when Haley returned, her shoulders were relaxed, away from her ears, and she had a smile on. "Nothing to worry about. Janice just got a little freaked out."

The volume in the room rose as people resumed their

conversations and continued where they had left off with their meals. But Virginia couldn't ease the pit in her stomach.

"Excuse me." She avoided Marney's scrutinizing gaze as she pushed off from the table, standing and making her way to the elevator. Once inside, she leaned against the walls, and when she made it to her room she gripped the wall, holding herself upright as she stumbled toward the bathroom, where she spewed the contents of her stomach into the toilet.

"No murder," she whispered to herself as she wiped her mouth, then dabbed the sweat from her brow. "Everyone is okay. No murder." She repeated the mantra to herself until she felt her breathing deepen and her heart rate slow. "Everyone is okay. No murder."

For Virginia, the best thing about being a cashier in Seaview was that everyone knew her. Her customers were typically too busy trading gossip to care that she wasn't the speediest at her job. On her first day, she spent ten minutes trying to figure out how to replace the receipt paper in the printer, but sweet Ginny Blaker talked her ear off the whole time and didn't mind a bit. By the time she arrived home to Breeze Village after every shift, she was darn near talked out, something her kids didn't believe was possible, and she always headed straight to her room afterward to decompress.

On this day, as Virginia climbed the wooden porch steps to the front door of the main building, she found

Jane sitting in her favorite rocking chair, knitting and enjoying the fresh air in the mild November weather. She gave a friendly nod and started to make her way inside when Jane stopped her.

"Virginia!" She held up her work in progress, a fuchsia sweater with cables running down the length. "Look how it's coming along! Do you think Marney will like it?"

Virginia pasted a smile on her face. "She's going to love it." And Marney would, she knew. The classic pattern paired with the bold, anything-but-classic color was perfect for Marney. But Virginia wasn't used to someone else loving Marney as much as she did. Someone who could knit her a sweater and never put her in harm's way. Virginia did her best to tamp down her insecurity and waved goodbye to Jane, making a beeline for the elevator.

While she was waiting for the elevator, a woman she didn't recognize came popping out of the stairwell, looking flustered. "Do you know where Activity Room B is? I'm looking for the sing-along session." Virginia pointed her in the right direction and the woman smiled, relief flooding her face. "Thank you so much! I'm new here."

The woman extended a manicured hand, and Virginia took it, feeling self-conscious about the state of her own nails. "I'm Cece."

"Virginia. Welcome to Breeze Village."

The elevator dinged behind Virginia and a resident stepped out, wheeling their walker through the lobby. Before Virginia could step inside, Cece reached out and put a hand on Virginia's arm. She looked around and then, with voice lowered, asked, "Things like last night, at the Halloween party… the lights going out, you know? Do things like that happen often here?"

Virginia shook her head. "No, that was a first." She wondered if Cece knew about the murders earlier in the year. But before she could decide whether to say anything, Cece let go of Virginia's arm and headed off to the activity room. Virginia turned just in time to see the elevator doors close, the elevator heading off on its journey upstairs to retrieve another resident.

Virginia sighed, giving up on retreating to her room and instead heading through the dining room and out the French doors to the courtyard and Marney's cottage.

Even as November dawned, Seaview hadn't yet had a frost that killed off the last of the summer and early autumn blooms. Color lined the walkway of pavers leading from the main building out to the independent living cottages around back. A wreath, a gift from Lawrence, hung on Marney's door, and Virginia knocked once before turning the knob and letting herself in.

She started as she was greeted by Dylan holding a feather toy aloft while Pancake jumped for it. "Er, hi," Virginia said. Dylan gave an awkward smile. The two had rarely spoken since Virginia's last foray into crime-fighting led to Marney being kidnapped. They were civil but mostly avoided each other.

"You two, act like you love each other," Marney instructed. "After all, you love me, and I love you both, and I know you love each other deep down, once you get past the hubbub of the last nine months." Virginia and Dylan both blushed, Dylan suddenly very interested in getting Pancake to jump for his toy, and Virginia suddenly equally interested in the magnets dotting Marney's fridge.

Dylan suddenly turned to Virginia. "My team doesn't need this anymore. I thought I'd return it to you next time I saw you." She reached into her bag and pulled out a long pendant. Virginia recognized it as the one her kids had given her for Mother's Day that year, silver with her and her kids' names engraved on it. The one Liam's crony had put in Michelle's hand after murdering her. The one that had landed Virginia at the police station for questioning and made her a prime suspect in Michelle's murder.

"Thanks," Virginia said, taking it from Dylan and placing it around her neck. She wasn't sure she'd ever see it again.

"See, that's better." Marney beamed as she turned to face Virginia. "How was work?"

Virginia shrugged. "The usual." She turned to Dylan, her face lighting up. "Actually, I did hear one thing that maybe you could verify for me."

"No." Dylan shook her head. "Whatever it is, absolutely not."

Virginia continued, undeterred. "I heard that the two recent murder victims weren't just both stabbed to death. I heard they both had an initial carved into them. The letter *A*."

Marney grimaced, and Dylan's eyes grew wide. "Where did you hear that?" she hissed.

"So it's true?" Virginia couldn't hide her delight at confirming a piece of gossip. "What about how the victims got threatening letters before their murders? I heard the second victim came to the police with his letter, and the police had people keeping an eye on him, trying to protect him."

"No comment." Dylan's voice was firm, and she set down Pancake's toy forcefully. The cat rolled over and began to groom himself now that his game was over. "I actually need to head back to the station. It was good to see you, Mom."

Marney frowned. "Are we still on for lunch Sunday?"

Dylan nodded and hugged her mom before departing. When the door shut behind her, Marney turned to Virginia, glowering.

"You scared her off!"

"I did no such thing!" But Virginia flushed, hating to come between Marney and her daughter once again.

Marney flopped onto her couch, stroking Pancake's head when the cat immediately hopped up beside her. "You couldn't stay out of investigations if you tried, really. How does information like this just find you?"

"I am not involved in this investigation," Virginia insisted. "I am an entirely disinvolved bystander, content to read about the latest developments in the paper, just like everyone else. Well, except when someone comes through my line at the grocery store and gives me a hot tip. But verifying the hot tip—which I maintain any reasonable person would do and does not constitute involvement—is as far as I go. There will be no investigation here!"

Marney smirked at her friend. "I know you. And I don't believe for a second we'll get through this fiasco without your involvement."

"That's it; now you've scared me off. I'm out of here!"

Virginia gave Marney a quick kiss on the cheek before making her way back to the main building, craving the feeling of being alone in her room after a long day.

As she passed through the French doors and through the dining room on her way to the elevator, she heard a voice she didn't recognize coming from the table filled with her usual poker opponents.

"I just think someone ought to have told me before that there was a psychic living amongst us. I would have considered my options a little differently had I known that going into things, and I don't think I'm the only one." Virginia looked over to see a tall, slender, bald man waving a red ivy cap, the color a perfect match for the shade of his face.

"I assure you, you are," Patricia responded flatly. Her broad figure loomed behind the players, her photographic memory and tendency to count cards resulting in a permanent ban from playing. Instead, she circled the table, peering at everyone's cards while maintaining a face of perfect neutrality.

"Now raise, call, or fold, Ed. We're waiting on you!" Ronald tossed his cards down on the table in irritation.

"It's not safe! It's not right! Flim-flams, the lot of them, and dangerous folk, psychics."

"If they're flim-flams, how are they dangerous?" Patricia asked, the corners of her mouth tugging upward.

"It's not right!" Ed repeated. He tossed his cards down, mirroring Ronald, and stood up. The chair screeched under him as he slid it back, then shuffled over to where he'd parked his walker along the wall.

"Shame," Patricia said as he walked away. "You'd have won that hand if you stayed in the game."

Virginia continued to the elevator, raising her hand in a wave to her friends but not stopping to chat. She knew that if she did, she'd be roped into a game of cards, and one would lead to another, and then it would be dinner time and she'd have lost out on the chance to have some peaceful time to herself. Instead, she made her way to the elevator, the sounds of another game emanating from the dining room while her mind wandered back to the news that the gossip about the local murder victims was true.

Not involved. She repeated the words to herself. *Just a regular, not-at-all-involved citizen. No need to go looking for trouble.* Still, her heart raced when she thought about it: a serial killer in Seaview? It was, without a doubt, the most interesting thing that had happened since, well, at least since she'd been brought in for questioning on suspicion of two murders. She quashed the thought as soon as it arose, and after she slid her shoes off and eased herself into her recliner, she picked up her book and willed her mind to focus instead on a very fictional killer that was terrorizing a very fictional town not at all like Seaview.

CHAPTER 3

*L*uigi's Italian restaurant was a Seaview institution. Luigi, then his son Marco, then his son Luigi, had been filling Virginia's Pyrex with their pasta so she could pass it off as her own when bringing food to the sick or grieving for decades, always with a wink and a smile and a big nod of appreciation when she pressed the folded bills into their hands. But it wasn't often that Virginia dined in and enjoyed the ambiance along with the food.

The room was dimly lit, always, no matter the time of day or the weather outside. The walls hosted faded pictures of the owners' family, the grandmother and great-grandmother whose recipes the current generation faithfully stood by. Real candles adorned each table despite two separate fires that had nearly shuttered the restaurant for good.

Virginia took a seat in a booth by a window, reflex-ively holding her menu under the narrow beam of light shining in through the curtains. However, she didn't need to see the menu to know what she'd order: gnocchi alla Sorrentina with extra parmesan on top.

"Mom." Her daughter's voice made Virginia look up to see Lucy standing in front of the table. Her blond hair was pulled back in a clip and she was perched on spindly blue heels. She leaned over to hug Virginia before hanging her suit jacket on the back of her chair and taking a seat, forgoing the menu. "It's good to see you."

"You look great. Work seems to be treating you well." Lucy worked in marketing, and that was about as much as she'd say on the subject. At the start of her career, she gushed more about the day-to-day of her job, the bosses she liked or hated, and the coworkers she partnered with or competed with for promotions. But she'd long since quieted down, and Virginia had neglected to ask, and now here they were.

"Thank you. Breeze Village seems to be treating you well." She flashed a brilliant smile. She knew that Lucy and Jack were relieved to have Virginia in Breeze Village. An inkling of resentment lingered, that her kids were so thrilled she was in an assisted living facility instead of on her own, but she reminded herself that they weren't wrong about her needs, and, more importantly, that she was happy at Breeze Village.

A waiter came around to bring the pair drinks and take their orders. When he left, the two looked at each other expectantly. It had been a long time since they'd been alone. Virginia couldn't remember the last time they got a meal together. It was always *the kids*, Jack and Lucy together, usually teaming up to tell Virginia something she didn't want to hear. Now Lucy and Virginia sipped their waters, flashed each other smiles, and struggled to make conversation.

"I saw Cathy Warnsbeck at work the other day," Virginia offered.

"Oh, really?"

Virginia nodded. "She came through with her three kids. The oldest is a senior in high school."

"Already? It's hard to believe."

"Apparently, he's ears-deep in college applications. Oh, and Alana Cadence is pregnant again. Her mom came in buying sparkling grape juice and frozen appetizers for the baby shower."

Lucy smiled politely. "That's nice."

"Actually, that got me thinking. We should throw a baby shower for Jack and Stephanie. We can surprise them. It'll be sweet!"

At that exact moment, Lucy choked on her water, and the waiter returned with their food, an alarmed expression on his face as Lucy insisted through her coughs that she was fine. When she'd recovered and he'd left their plates, Virginia looked up at her expectantly. "So," she asked. "What do you think?"

Lucy took a bite of her salad and Virginia waited while she chewed. "Err, actually, Mom, that's sort of why I asked to get lunch."

Virginia lit up. "This is going to be so fun!"

"Not quite." Lucy put her fork down and stared at it as she continued. "Sam actually reached out to me the other day. She wants to throw Stephanie a baby shower."

The words rang in Virginia's ears. She tried to make sense of them. "Sam called you?"

Lucy only nodded.

Stephanie's mom hadn't been involved in her life in years. She'd had Stephanie when she was still a teenager and never really stepped up. She'd disappear for weeks or months, then reappear, excited to be the fun mom until something else exciting came along and she took off again. When Stephanie and Jack got married, Sam got too drunk and had to be escorted out of the venue. As far as Virginia knew, that was the last time Stephanie and her mom had spoken.

"Does Stephanie know?"

Lucy's head bobbed as she chewed another bite of salad. "I told Sam to get lost, actually. Then she called Jack, who told her the same thing. Then she called Stephanie, who was thrilled to hear from her. Jack says he hasn't seen Stephanie this excited since the first ultrasound."

Virginia set her fork down. Her food tasted like sand and she struggled to chew.

"The baby shower is in just under two weeks."

Virginia's mouth dropped open. "It's already planned? She didn't even ask me. And isn't it a bit early?"

"Mom," Lucy said, reaching across the table and touching Virginia's hand. Virginia yanked her hand away. "Mom, please." Lucy's voice was firm. "I know you don't like her. And believe me, Jack and I certainly don't like her, either. But Stephanie loves her. And it's not like you've always been the most involved mother, either. You screened mine and Jack's calls for ages because you didn't want us to be concerned for you, and yet you set your kitchen on fire twice and nearly lost your house because you just *had* to do everything yourself."

"I—" Virginia's stomach roiled. She tried to think of something to say but her brain whirred ineffectively.

Across the table, Lucy softened. "I'm sorry. I didn't mean that. I just meant people change. People grow." She started to reach her hand out again.

"Stop." Virginia's voice came out louder than she intended, and she fumbled as she tossed her napkin onto the table and tried to stand.

"Mom, please." Lucy stood, but Virginia brushed her off, making for the exit as quickly as she could. She wasn't even to her car before she had her phone to her ear, calling an emergency meeting with Marney and Lawrence.

CHAPTER 4

"**S**am just... called? Like, out of nowhere?" Marney was sipping sweet tea on Lawrence's sofa while Lawrence mixed up something stronger and put it in front of Virginia. She'd texted Marney, calling for an emergency meeting at Lawrence's beachside condo before she'd even made it to her car from Luigi's. They were both there waiting for her when she arrived twenty-five minutes later, the drive out to the beach having done little to calm her down.

Virginia threw her hands up. "Can you believe her? Stephanie and Jack have been married for what, eight years? Not one phone call. And now here she is, planning the baby shower. It's rude for her not to have consulted with me, right? I'm not crazy here?"

"She should have reached out to you," Lawrence said. "It's reasonable to think the other grandmother would want to be part of this."

Virginia picked her phone up from where she'd tossed it onto the couch cushion between her and Marney and resumed scrolling through Sam's Facebook. She was only two years older than Jack. He and Stephanie were fifteen years apart, an age gap that had raised Virginia's eyebrows before she saw the way they acted together. Now Sam wanted to waltz in and be Grandma after not being Mom for most of her daughter's life.

"Look at her teeth. Those can't be real." Virginia held her phone out for Marney to see. "See how they change between her Disney trip in January 2017 and her spring break posts in 2018? Veneers."

Marney nodded, though Virginia knew she hadn't really looked and didn't really care.

"And see here?" she asked, thrusting the phone toward Marney again. "She definitely had something done to her lips there in 2019."

She scrolled, eyes fixed on the screen lest she catch the disapproving looks of her friends. Lawrence and Marney let her go down the rabbit hole, chiming out as she found new information. Sam had gotten her real estate license a few years ago and had settled in Atlanta, only a few hours from Seaview. From what Virginia could tell, Sam was good at her job. She'd calmed down and grown up, established her business, and was ready to swoop back into Stephanie's life, this time for good. Ready to be a grandma. A grandma thirty years younger than Virginia, with money and fake teeth and unnaturally large lips.

The further she scrolled, the tighter her grip on the phone became, clenching in sync with her throat and stomach until her whole body felt tightly coiled. She set her phone down and forced herself to breathe out, feeling her back straighten and her stomach relax.

When she looked up at her friends, both Marney and Lawrence were looking at her with concern. Her cheeks burned as she jerked her gaze away, instinctively picking her phone back up.

"No more," Lawrence said, snatching the phone away from her. His voice was firm and his face was hard, giving a look that said, *I dare you to challenge me.*

Virginia's voice was feeble as she protested. "But—"

"No more," he repeated.

"We're on your side," Marney said. Worse than concern, her eyes held pity as she opened her mouth to continue.

"But?" Virginia cut her off.

"But you're acting crazy and you know it. You're not wrong to be upset. Sam hurt someone you love very much. She opted out of something you worked hard at—motherhood—and now she gets to reap the joys of grand-motherhood. It's not fair. And it's not fair that she's taking away from your enjoyment in doing so. Unilaterally planning the baby shower without consulting you was wrong."

"But?" Virginia asked again.

"But is she wrong for wanting to be in her daughter's life now that she's in the position to try?" Lawrence asked. "Sam clearly had her own demons, and she seems to have fought them over the past few years and come out better for it. Should she be denied a relationship with her daughter and granddaughter forever?"

Marney cut in. "If Stephanie doesn't want her around, that's one thing. But it seems like Stephanie does want to give her mom another chance."

Virginia stared at the piping running along the couch

cushion, her eyes tracing along it as tears began to sting. She bit her tongue, breathing in through her nose. Marney and Lawrence waited, giving her space until she could respond.

"I hate when you're right," she said, finally, and they both laughed. "Lawrence, I'm going to need your help picking out an outfit for the baby shower. If I'm going to be up against Sam, I need to sparkle."

"I'd be honored to help. And on another note, I heard that you two are now living in a haunted house, what with the lights-out incident on Halloween. The words Curt used to describe the scene at our bowling match were 'blood-curdling scream.'"

Marney threw up her hands. "Virginia's the one living in the haunted house. I'm only living adjacent to the haunted house, in my definitely-not-haunted cottage."

Virginia laughed, feeling the tension in her body ease. She wiped her eyes and cleared her throat before recounting the event. "I was just so relieved. When I heard that scream, I thought, 'Here we go again.' But then everyone was okay! No dead bodies, imagine that." As she spoke, her words came faster, and a smile spread across her face before she realized it.

"No dead bodies in Breeze Village is a real marvel, after the year we've had," Marney said, shaking her head.

"And the month Seaview has had!" Lawrence agreed.

Virginia leaned in. "Actually, I learned something new about that." Her excitement for gossip pushed aside the last vestiges of insecurity and jealousy, and her entire focus was on the Seaview murders as she told Lawrence what she'd heard at work and how Dylan had confirmed the story. "The police actually knew the second victim—Walsh, I think his name was?—was in danger. He'd gotten a note warning him he was next, and they were investigating, but obviously weren't able to save him."

Lawrence tried to look disinterested. "I don't know, Virginia. I don't want to gossip about the dead."

"It's not *gossip*," she asserted. "It's *news*. It's just not on the actual news yet because the police don't want the killer to know how much they know."

"You know that when I get together with Dylan Sunday I'm going to have to listen to a whole lecture on how citizens need to stay out of the way of police investigations, and it's your fault." Marney jabbed a finger at Virginia.

"I'm not investigating!"

"Uh-huh." Marney stood, grabbing her purse. "Well, can we not investigate our way back home? Diana told me that today's arts and crafts activity is making faux stained glass suncatchers to hang in our windows, and I want to get back in time."

Virginia felt lighter leaving Lawrence's condo. When her mind returned to Lucy's words, the reminders of the ways she'd failed as a mother, she pushed them aside, focusing instead on Dylan's surprise when Virginia had legitimate information on the case. On Marney's words. *You couldn't stay out of investigations if you tried, really. How does information like this just find you?*

CHAPTER 5

Marney's words stayed with Virginia through the night until the light of a new day and a quick morning plunge into the cold ocean brought with it a renewed optimism. Still, as she showered off the saltwater and dressed for work—khakis, a red polo shirt emblazoned with the store logo, and the most supportive sneakers she could find at the shoe store—she felt fragile. The emotional turmoil from the previous day had left her feeling raw. Her hand shook as she put on her earrings, and she dropped one. As the small silver hoop hit the top of the dresser and skittered to the floor, Virginia felt her throat burn and tears well up, and she chided herself for the outsize reaction.

"Pull yourself together," she whispered, bracing herself on the dresser as she bent over to fish around for the dropped earring. She stood, clasped the earring through her lobe, then straightened up and eyed her reflection.

"You're Virginia Harold Walker. You were a good wife and a good mother. And a darn good investigator. And an even better non-investigator. And heck, the best dang cashier the Piggly Wiggly has ever seen." Her voice strengthened as she went on, and by the end, she was smiling, half at the ridiculousness of the assertions and half because she truly felt better.

As she settled into her shift, the tension from the day before faded further. No matter how much she didn't want to start a shift, she always felt better afterward. Four hours straight of smiling, greeting customers, asking how they were doing and if they'd found everything okay never failed to turn her mood around. Even when the smile was forced at the start of her shift, by the end, it was authentic. Even more so when an old friend came through her line, which was almost every shift.

"There's no way!" A croak rose up, followed by the clatter of cans to the floor. Virginia turned to see Arnold, her high school prom date, standing over a fallen shelf of beans. "Virginia Walker, as I live and breathe."

Arnold was not the man for Virginia. This much was clear before they'd even made it to the prom, and was more than clear when he left with another girl, but he was a sweet man. Just a sweet man helplessly in love with someone else.

When he'd finished helping the stockers right the shelf and pick up the cans, he wheeled his cart into Virginia's line. "I almost didn't come to the store today. One of my favorite episodes of *NCIS* was on and I thought I'd just order a pizza tonight, but then I remembered I was out of oatmeal, and if I didn't get oatmeal, I'd be hungry in the morning. So I got in my car, and I figured if I got really lucky there'd be a sale on my favorite crackers or I'd be able to use this coupon that expired two weeks ago. But never—never!—did I think that here in the grocery store I'd run into an old love. Imagine!"

Virginia felt heat rise in her cheeks as she took the expired coupon he held out. "Oh, stop."

Arnold offered her a wink. "I'm still sorry about that night. How many years later, sixty? Longer?"

"Enough that you don't need to be sorry." Virginia scanned the coupon. When it didn't ring up, she manually typed in the discount, holding a finger to her lips and offering Arnold a wink in return.

"Those sure were the days." Virginia could have sworn Arnold's eyes got misty, and he busied himself bagging his groceries as Virginia finished scanning them. "Meg passed away a couple years ago. I'm not sure if you heard."

Virginia's throat caught, and she paused in the middle of scanning a box of oatmeal. "Arnie, I'm so sorry."

He sniffed and forced a smile, then thanked her. "How are you doing? Still in that same neighborhood? Grove Park, was it? Actually, come to think of it, there's construction going on over there, isn't there?"

It was Virginia's turn to force a smile. "Developers came in and bought us all out. I'm actually living in Breeze Village now."

"Breeze Village, imagine that! I heard just the other morning that Breeze Village is haunted. One of the guys in my Tuesday breakfast crew was telling us."

"The Halloween party incident?" Virginia asked, bagging the last of his items. "With the lights?"

Arnold cocked his head to the side and screwed up his face. "I don't think Phil said anything about that. Something about a psychic and how spirits were messing with her, moving things around."

Colleen? Virginia leaned in. "We do have a resident psychic. I hadn't heard of any haunting."

"A resident psychic, bah!" Arnold spat as he tucked his bags into the grocery cart. "I told Phil I'm not surprised. Messing around in the spirit realm, I figure you're bound to make some mistake and bring mayhem on yourself. Satanic witchery, that's what I think it is, this psychic mess."

"All right, Arnie." Virginia reached across the checkout counter and patted his arm. "It was really lovely seeing you."

She watched him leave, thinking he'd fit in well with the new psychic-hating resident she'd heard arguing with Ronald and Patricia the other night. He was hardly out the door before another familiar voice rang out behind her.

"I didn't know you were working today!" Marney was already unloading her groceries onto the conveyor belt— mostly snacks, as she gladly took most of her meals in the dining room.

"I just heard the strangest thing. Have you talked to Colleen recently?"

Marney shook her head.

"Well, my high school prom date just told me she's being haunted."

Marney stopped loading her groceries. "I'm going to need you to repeat that sentence. Your *prom date* was in here, and he had information about *Colleen?*"

Virginia shrugged. "When he mentioned a haunting at

Breeze Village, I figured he'd heard about the lights going out on Halloween, but he said spirits are messing with Colleen, moving things around."

"That's odd."

Virginia finished scanning and bagging Marney's groceries, but when she started to say goodbye, Marney lingered. She opened her mouth as if to say something, closed it again, started to leave, and then stopped herself again.

"What's going on?" Virginia's stomach churned. Marney didn't hold back, not from her, and the weight of whatever Marney couldn't say felt heavy.

"I just… Things have been going well with my crochet shop, right?" Marney looked up at Virginia anxiously, and Virginia nodded. The whole of Breeze Village had celebrated Marney for opening her online shop just a few months prior. "Well, there's this other shop. The owner sells their own crocheted goods, which is fine, but lately they've listed a lot of the same things as me. And I'm not talking about us both selling stuffed animals. They're copying my exact product descriptions and then under-cutting me on price."

Marney's face scrunched up in frustration as she talked, and Virginia instinctively walked around to the other side of the counter to hug her. "Did you report their store?"

Marney nodded into Virginia's shoulder and mumbled an affirmative. "Nothing happened. They're doing this for all my products, and I've reported them every time." She pulled back and straightened herself up, clearing her throat. "Anyway, since you have an undeniable ability to come across information, and since you've got to be feeling a bit of a void without an investigation, I thought I'd ask you to just… keep an ear out, please."

"Of course!" Virginia gave her friend another squeeze before stepping back behind the counter. She gave Marney the most reassuring smile she could muster, though, in reality, she had no idea how she could 'keep an ear out' about the mystery owner of an online store who may live on the other side of the world.

Before she made it out of the store, Marney turned and called out, "Do you want to come over for pizza tonight? Maybe around six?"

"I can't." Virginia hesitated, then continued. "I've got to go to Pilates."

Marney's eyebrows shot up to her hairline. "You've got to go to what? Virginia, you hate Pilates. We went to the YMCA one time, what, twenty years ago? And you've told me about fifty times since then that spending an hour of your life doing Pilates is one of your major regrets since it was so miserable and you'll never get that hour back."

Virginia opened her mouth, already on the defensive, but Marney gave her a discerning look that said *I'll see through whatever lie you try to tell me.* Instead, she ducked her head and mumbled, "Sam is a Pilates instructor." The rest of the sentence—*and Sam is the younger, hotter grandma who I'm afraid my kids and new grandkid will prefer to me*—went unspoken, but Marney nodded in understanding.

"I've heard we should all be doing Pilates as we age," she said. "My doctor was trying to sell me on it during my last appointment, saying it would help with balance and injury prevention. Maybe I'll join you."

She wouldn't—Marney had hated that hour at the YMCA as much as Virginia did—but Virginia loved her for saying it.

"Is this line open?" A young man loaded a gallon of milk and a box of dishwasher detergent onto the conveyor, and Marney waved and set off, leaving Virginia to make small talk with the next customer. As she scanned his items and rang him up, Virginia stole a glance at her watch, counting the minutes until she could go home to Breeze Village and find out what sort of haunting was afoot.

CHAPTER 6

*I*f Virginia had to describe Colleen's reaction to her question about the alleged haunting in one word, it would be *unhelpful*. If she could use more words, she'd add *shady*, *dodgy*, and even a little *peeved*.

She'd found Colleen at dinner, enjoying her pot roast and vegetables, and they'd struck up a nice conversation about the lovely fall weather—the green leaves were holding on strong for November, and the temperature still hovered above seventy, but Seaview collectively agreed to pretend in conversation—and how much they hoped Diana would make her delicious glittery punch for all Breeze Village events from now on.

When the conversation had a lull, Virginia said, "Oh, I ran into someone in the store earlier. He and you must have a mutual friend. Someone named Phil?"

Colleen chewed slowly before nodding. "Yes, I know Phil."

"Well, my friend said Phil had been talking about Breeze Village being haunted. I thought he meant the lights on Halloween, but he said that you specifically were being haunted."

Colleen's fork clattered to her plate. "Excuse me, I'm sorry." She took another bite, chewing quickly, and still had food in her mouth when she continued, "No, I don't know what he was talking about. Your friend must have it wrong."

Caught off guard, Virginia started to apologize, but Colleen stood up to leave. "I'm not being haunted," she said. "I'm fine, perfectly safe. And I wish people wouldn't gossip so much, especially when they don't know what they're talking about."

She was gone before Virginia could question her any further. Virginia finished her dinner alone, cheeks burning with embarrassment. She'd clearly struck a nerve. She just didn't understand why.

The next day, the Garden Review Society was gathering at Breeze Village to meet with the landscaper. He did the landscaping at both Breeze Village and Harbor Vale, and with blooms less prominent in November, Gemma had been excited to interview him and feature photos from some of his recent projects.

The Breeze Village crew gathered in the lobby. Virginia sported her usual flower-themed jewelry she liked to don for garden reviews, and Gemma arrived in the most hideously vibrant orange and green dress. Though the dress was atrocious, Gemma glowed in it.

When she spotted Virginia, she squealed. "How are you doing? I feel like I haven't seen you in ages."

Gemma pulled Virginia into a suffocating hug, her squeeze competing with her perfume to choke Virginia's last breath from her. "It's good to see you, too," she gasped when she was released. "You need to eat in the dining room more often."

Gemma occupied the independent living cottage next to Marney's, behind the main building, but she preferred to eat in her cottage and rarely spent time in the main building. Their interactions since Virginia moved in were primarily waving at one another through Gemma's kitchen window, always left open, when Virginia walked to and from Marney's cottage.

Patricia was the next to join them. This was her first garden review, but she'd expressed interest and Virginia had extended an invitation. Soon after, Jan and Dorothea arrived together from Harbor Vale, where Jan had moved after selling her house to the developers and where Dorothea frequently visited her. Jan's dyed-black hair was piled atop her head, swaying with her every step, and silver jewelry dripped from her wrists and neck. She was thin and tall, made taller by her hair, and dressed mostly in black faux leather.

Dorothea, by contrast, was short and stout, her white hair adding nothing to her height. Her pink blouse flowed nearly to her knees, with sequins forming a butterfly across the entire front, and her wrists dripped with even more jangly bracelets than Jan's.

"Welcome!" Gemma greeted Dorothea and Jan. The door opened behind them and Ellen walked in, flanked by two women who looked to be in their thirties. "And, Ellen, welcome. Who are your friends?"

Ellen gave a crisp nod, her lips pursed tautly. "This is Sophia." She gestured to her right. "And this is Mirna. I thought the club could use some young blood. At this rate, we're about to become a group of nothing but retirees in senior living facilities. I figured we could bring in some younger members, enjoy their fresh perspectives, and help ensure the longevity of this organization. After all, someone needs to keep an eye toward the future, making sure we don't just fade into obscurity."

Gemma's eyes were wide and she took a step back, obviously surprised by the attack. "Well, thank you, Ellen, for considering the future of this organization. As its president, and having spent so many years making it what it is, I'm grateful."

When the group had featured the Breeze Village gardens in the spring, Ellen had been up in arms. "When's the last time we featured a garden by someone under the age of sixty-five?" she'd demanded. This ambush with strangers shouldn't have been a surprise, and yet Virginia felt blindsided, and it was obvious Gemma and the others did, too.

"We're excited to be here," Mirna said, extending her hand for Gemma to shake.

"It's lovely to be included," Sophia agreed. "I was actually thinking, have we already talked to…" And she was off, spouting off ideas faster than Virginia's brain could process them. Gemma seemed to be trying to keep up, filling Sophia in on the gardens the club had featured in their magazine recently.

Patricia looked to Virginia to gauge her reaction, and Virginia looked to Jan and Dorothea. Jan raised her eyebrows and Dorothea shrugged, neither of them sure how to react to this unexpected conflict. "It's not usually like this," Virginia whispered to Patricia.

"Can you just stop for one minute?" Gemma suddenly yelled. "Just stop!" She was breathing fast and hard, her body shaking, and she raised one giant hand to wipe a tear from her eye. "This group, this magazine, is my baby. For decades, maybe before you were born, I've been working with the gardeners of this town and beyond to make it great. You're welcome here, and your ideas are welcome here, but this is my baby. I'm not going to let you take it away."

Mirna looked stunned, but Sophia brushed off the outburst. "Of course not! We're just sharing our ideas."

A tenuous peace resumed, but Virginia was hardly present. She was stuck on Gemma seeing the Garden Review Society as her baby. *Is it her baby now?* Virginia wondered.

When they were young, maybe younger than Sophia and Mirna were now, Virginia and Gemma and the rest of the neighborhood had been enjoying one of their tea parties, gossiping about a particularly ostentatious garden across town. A couple from out of state had moved into the large house and poured money into the exterior, and the result was a vibrant garden with the most beautiful flowers surrounding the most garish statues and bird baths Seaview had ever seen.

"We should start a club," Virginia had said. "A magazine. The local hardware store might sponsor us, and we could interview people like them, showcasing the noteworthy gardens of the area."

Gemma had loved the idea from the start. "We could

include tips, too, for the seasons. What to plant and when, or which nurseries have the best stock."

Virginia had run the club up until the last year or two, leaning more and more on Gemma until, at some point, Gemma started calling herself the president and no one fought her on it. But standing there and hearing people argue over its future, Virginia felt the loss for the first time.

* * *

VIRGINIA DUCKED out of the Garden Review Society meeting when her phone rang, mercifully giving her an excuse. She was surprised when, on the other end of the line, a woman introduced herself as a journalist, though not as surprised as she would have been before solving Ruth's murder. In the months since, and especially since Liam's arrest following the murders of Russ and Michelle in the summer, she'd done a handful of interviews for the local paper.

"I'm with the American Association of Retired Persons, the AARP," the woman said.

"I'm familiar with the organization…" Virginia walked farther down the hallway off the lobby, searching for some privacy.

"We're doing a piece on hobbies and passion in retirement. I'm reaching out to members who have been enrolled with us for some time to see whether you'd give a quote or short interview for the piece. Are you interested in being included?"

Virginia held onto the grab bar along the wall with the hand not clutching her phone. "I, err, sure."

"Wonderful! To start, can you confirm your name for me?"

"Virginia Harold Walker."

"Thank you very much, Ms. Walker. Now, do you live in your own home, a retirement community, continuing care center, assisted living facility, or skilled nursing facility?"

Virginia looked around, regretting taking the phone call in the first place. "I'm not sure. I live in Breeze Village, in Seaview."

There was a pause on the other end. Then, "I see. I'd say that falls under *continuing care*. Can you tell me a little about yourself?"

Virginia looked around again. "Well, I'm retired. Actually, I got a job as a grocery store cashier to get me out of the house a little. I was a housewife while my husband was alive, then I worked a handful of different jobs while my kids were growing up. I retired, then went back to work as a secretary in a doctor's office earlier this year. And I've had some success as an investigator. I solved five murders."

"Oh!" Virginia could practically hear the other woman trying to figure out the appropriate response. "Congratulations, I suppose. That is... a lot of murders."

"Well, the first three were connected, and then the last two were connected, so it was really just the two cases."

"All right. Well, the theme here is around hobbies and passions. What motivated you to go back to work in retirement?"

Virginia's pulse sped. *I was going to lose my house if I didn't come up with a bunch of money quickly. Oh, and by the way, I lost the house anyway, just to an evil developer instead of the bank.* Not exactly the answer she wanted to give. "I wanted to keep some of my independence. A developer bought my whole neighborhood, so I was thinking of either downsizing or moving into a place like this, like Breeze Village, and I wanted something constant during the change."

"I love that. Former secretary and now a cashier. And going back to work in retirement gave you more of a sense of independence and consistency through the many changes in a difficult stage of life."

Former secretary. Cashier. The woman's words were accurate, but hearing herself described in those terms made Virginia's chest ache. That wasn't who she was. And yet, in a way, it was. *Former.* So she'd solved a couple of cases. But only because if she didn't, she'd have been homeless or imprisoned. And how much of solving those cases was her own doing, and how much had she lucked into?

"Hello? Are you still there?" The AARP representative's voice startled Virginia, who had let the phone slip away from her ear as she went down the silent rabbit hole of judgment.

"I'm sorry, I'm going to have to go." She hung up the phone, slid it into her pocket, and gripped the grab bar with both hands. She breathed deeply, working to compose herself, then straightened up before returning to the lobby. The landscaper had arrived, and the Garden Review Society was heading outside to discuss his work.

Patricia was visibly relieved to have Virginia rejoin the group. "There you are! I thought you'd fully abandoned me with these crazies."

Virginia mustered a laugh, but as they followed the landscaper outside, Gemma and Sophia firing off questions in competition, she felt herself fade into the background. *Former* club president.

CHAPTER 7

Virginia had hardly begun the walk to the elevator to return to her room when she was accosted by Colleen.

"Virginia, I'm so glad I ran into you." Colleen's gaze was intense. She'd come from the hallway where Virginia had taken her phone call. Her room was on the third floor, a floor above Virginia's, and by the way Colleen had come hurrying out of the hallway to meet her, Virginia wondered if Colleen had run into her at all, or if she'd been lying in wait.

"Would you mind coming up to my room?" Colleen asked. Her eyes darted around the space. Virginia hadn't seen Colleen like this before, and though it worried her, she agreed to go up to Colleen's room.

The space was as Virginia remembered: warm, stuffy, and fragrant, with a sense that one had left Breeze Village entirely. Gauzy maroon curtains filtered the light through the windows, and the smoke from burning incense twirled in the beams of light that made it through. Crystals occupied the flat surfaces of the end tables and bookshelves, and dried herbs hung upside down, suspended from the ceiling by shimmering metallic floss.

"Those weren't here last time." Virginia pointed to the herbs.

"From the garden, over the summer," Colleen said. "Gemma helped me grow them. I'm hanging them to dry." She was walking quickly through the small space, weaving around the large pieces of furniture in the semi-darkness. She ducked into her bedroom, the door replaced by a curtain of beaded strands, then emerged, tossed a piece of paper down on the coffee table, and plopped herself down unceremoniously on the small leather loveseat.

"I would like to request your aid." As she said it, Colleen looked up at where Virginia stood, her eyes tired and afraid.

"What's going on?" Virginia took the seat next to Colleen on the loveseat, unconcerned with being able to get back up again as she sank into it. She took Colleen's hand in her own, then turned her attention to the paper Colleen had tossed down onto the coffee table.

When she saw it, her heart caught in her throat. "Is that—" she choked out. "Is that from—"

Colleen nodded. There, on the table before them, was a handwritten death threat.

You're next, you psychic scum.

You thought you could best me. You thought you could destroy me. No one can. Not Irene. Not Herman. Not you.

—A

The *A* was practically slashed into the paper, the pen

dragged across with such force it broke through. Virginia covered her mouth with her hand, her breathing shallow. Acid rose in her throat, and she realized her other hand was gripping Colleen's painfully hard.

"When did you get this?"

"Halloween night," Colleen confessed, looking down at the letter as if it would rise up and bite her.

Virginia looked at Colleen, who wouldn't take her eyes off the letter. "And the hauntings I asked you about?"

This got Colleen to pull her gaze from the letter, looking at Virginia and then down at the floor with contrition. "I'm sorry I ran off. I'm just so… just so scared! The spirits are trying to warn me. I'll commune with them, try to ask for guidance, but nothing changes, and then I'll wake up and my lamp is missing from the nightstand, moved into the bathroom in the night. I think they're trying to warn me that I'm in danger." She nodded toward the letter.

Virginia stood, effortfully pushing herself up off the loveseat, and began to pace. "So you got this letter four days ago. And the hauntings started at the same time?"

Colleen nodded.

"Have you taken it to the police?"

Colleen looked down at her feet again, and Virginia felt her panic rise further. Her hands practically shook as she reached for the letter, only for Colleen to yank it away before she could reach it. "You have to show the police!" Virginia said.

"How did that go for Herman Walsh?"

Virginia ran her hands through her hair.

"I've received no guidance from the spirits to suggest the police can help me in this situation," Colleen said.

"And the spirits have told you I can help, have they?"

"Well, no. There's actually been no guidance at all, really. But frankly, you have a better track record than the Seaview Police when it comes to taking cases seriously. I don't think they're going to give me the time of day when I tell them I'm being haunted."

"Colleen, you have a death threat from a killer who has already struck twice. Don't lead with the haunting."

Colleen pursed her lips but said nothing, so Virginia continued. "Irene and Herman? They weren't just stabbed to death. They..." She took a deep breath. "They also had the letter *A* carved into them. And at least in Herman's case, he got a note warning him he was a target."

The color drained from Colleen's face. All of her usual bravado was gone. She started to speak, but only a whimper came out.

"You have to show this to the police," Virginia repeated. "They can protect you."

"How do you know about the mutilations? Herman's letter?"

"Someone told me at work, and Dylan confirmed it."

"So the police knew about Herman? They knew about his letter before he was killed?" Virginia nodded, and Colleen furrowed her brow and gripped the couch on either side of her. "If they knew, and he still died, then why are you so sure they'll be able to protect me?"

Virginia sank back down onto the loveseat, the full weight of the situation crashing down around her. Colleen wasn't wrong; the police had known Herman was in danger and had been working to protect him, but it hadn't been enough. But it didn't change the fact that she was wholly unqualified to pursue a serial killer, and if her friend died because she wasn't able to protect her, she'd never forgive herself.

"Okay," she said at last, her voice quavering. "I'll investigate. I'll try to figure out who this monster is and bring them down. But only if you take this letter to the police."

Colleen remained silent, shuddering softly, her knuckles white where she still gripped the edge of the couch cushion. She nodded, and Virginia reached over and grabbed one of her hands to squeeze it. The corner of Colleen's mouth turned up an almost imperceptible amount, and her eyes seemed to soften a hair.

"Virginia," she said, "did whoever told you about how Herman and Irene had received letters like this before their deaths tell you how long before their deaths they received them?"

VIRGINIA'S RINGTONE broke the silence that had set in. Virginia hovered behind Colleen while Colleen wrote out a list of all the people she thought might want to kill her. Each time she wrote another name, Virginia thought it had to be the last—the list had grown to fill a page and spill over onto the back—but then Colleen would add another name to the list.

"It's Jack," Virginia said. "Do you mind if I take this?"

Colleen waved her off, continuing her list of potential

killers, and Virginia answered the phone. On the other end, Jack sounded casual and upbeat.

"Stephanie just put a lasagna in the oven and I thought I'd see if you wanted to join us for dinner."

Automatically, Virginia found herself looking for the unspoken reason for the invite. Years of cynicism, of avoiding her kids in order to avoid confronting her needs as she aged, left her skeptical. She kicked herself.

"I'd love to," she agreed. "I'll head over now. Thank you for thinking of me."

When she hung up the phone and turned around, Colleen was looking at her with wide, scared eyes. "You're leaving?"

A pang of guilt went through Virginia's chest, and she felt the urge to call Jack back and cancel. Instead, she nodded and said, "I'm going to go have dinner with Jack and Stephanie, but give me that list, and I'll start looking into it as soon as I get home."

Colleen handed over the sheet of paper, and Virginia marveled again at the length of the list. "You think all these people might want you dead?" she couldn't help but ask.

Colleen shrugged. "Not everyone I've encountered in life has been grateful for the encounter." With that, she stood and made her way to the door, opening it for Virginia. "I appreciate your help. And I hope that with you on the case, the spirits see that I need no further warning, that I'm taking this seriously, and let me have some peace at last."

The little ranch-style home that Jack and Stephanie had put so much effort into was exactly as Virginia remembered, except the garden she had planted while living there in the summer was entirely dead. The limp, lifeless plants caught her attention as she pulled up, a bottle of wine tucked under one arm and sparkling grape juice tucked under the other. It was the first time she'd been back since she'd spent several months living in their guest room between selling her house to the developers and moving into Breeze Village.

On the porch, she tried to maneuver the two bottles so she could ring the doorbell with one hand, but before she could figure it out, the door opened and Stephanie came bounding through, her arms out wide.

"Virginia! When Jack told me he invited you, I got so excited. Come in, come in. Let me take one of those. This looks amazing!" She was moving a mile a minute, and Virginia could hardly keep up as Stephanie took both bottles from her and headed into the house.

It was toasty inside. On the coffee table, Virginia saw a half dozen books on pregnancy, childbirth, and early childhood development. Her heart swelled for her son and daughter-in-law, at the magic and wonder ahead for them, and ached with how much she wanted to be included.

"The house looks great," Virginia commented, pouring herself a glass of wine. "And smells great, too."

The oven timer went off at that moment, sending Stephanie levitating into the air. She threw her hand over her chest and gripped the kitchen island with the other. "Goodness gracious!"

"Let me give you a hand getting that out of the oven," Virginia offered, and Stephanie accepted immediately and graciously.

"I'm like one of those wobble toys with this thing." She gestured to her pregnant belly with a laugh, then perched on one of the barstools at the island. "Jack should be back soon. He realized we were out of ice cream and decided he'd get ahead of the pregnancy cravings, so he ran to the store while dinner was cooking."

"I wish I'd known. I could have picked some up when I grabbed the wine on my way." It was a little thing, she knew, but it hurt that he didn't ask her to pick it up for them. She wanted them to see her as someone who could be helpful, someone they could rely on.

Stephanie waved her hand in the air. "I think he really just wanted a few minutes of alone time. Anyway, I haven't seen you in too long. How are things at Breeze Village? I heard you got a job down the street at the Piggly Wiggly."

As Virginia talked about her work, the parts she loved —talking with people all shift—and the parts she didn't care for—looking up the PLU codes for produce— Stephanie was engaged, asking questions with enthusiasm.

"This sounds like it's wonderful for you," she said. "I'm so glad you found something that gets you out of the house and gives you purpose."

Virginia smiled and nodded, though her stomach sank at Stephanie's assessment. It wasn't wrong. The best parts of having a part-time job in retirement were a continued sense of purpose and getting out of the house. It was a reason to get up and get dressed in the morning. But the idea that she was now someone for whom the rest of her life wasn't enough to give her purpose, to give her reasons to leave the house, made her cringe.

Jack's entrance saved Virginia from having to talk any more about work. He came in the door with ice cream in one hand and a bouquet of flowers in the other.

"My goodness, everyone comes bearing gifts today!" Stephanie took the flowers from Jack and busied herself getting them into a vase while he put the ice cream in the freezer and set the table.

"It's good to see you, Mom," he said, kissing Virginia's cheek. "Can I get you anything to drink? Another glass of wine?"

She shook her head. "Not unless you plan to drive me home." The sound of Jack's and Stephanie's laughter was enough to expel any remaining pain, and as they settled in to eat, Virginia felt light and easy.

"Do you want to see the nursery?" Stephanie asked

when they'd finished their meals and Jack had begun to clear the table.

Stephanie led the way down the hall toward the guest room where Virginia had lived. She opened the door, and the room was hardly recognizable. The guest bed had been replaced with a crib and changing table, and the walls were now a warmer color with one wall covered in floral wallpaper. As they stepped inside, Stephanie seemed to glow.

"Isn't it gorgeous?" she said. "I know we still have a couple months, but I didn't want to wait, and then my mom set me up with this interior designer friend of hers."

The words knocked Virginia off balance. "Sam?"

Stephanie nodded as if it weren't surprising in the least. "She called a little while ago, and we've reconnected." She put her hands on her belly and smiled.

Shaken, Virginia turned to leave the nursery, but as she entered the hall, something caught her eye in the master bedroom. "What's that?" she asked, stepping into the doorway for a closer look. Inside, the big window overlooking their backyard was broken and covered in plastic sheeting. "What happened?"

Her pulse sped. In an instant, she was back at the house on Findowrie Street, her best friend staring down the barrel of a gun because of Virginia's actions.

"Oh, just some neighborhood kids," Stephanie said, waving her off. "We just haven't gotten around to getting it fixed yet."

But Virginia couldn't stop thinking about it. "Let me make some calls," she said. "It's not safe, living with a broken window. Anyone could get in."

"Anyone could get in if they really wanted to, broken window or not," Jack said.

Virginia already had her phone in hand, texting Lawrence to ask if he knew anyone. Not two hours before, she had been asked to take on the investigation of a serial killer, but all she could see now was a note being slid under Jack's door, her kids in danger because of her once again.

CHAPTER 9

Virginia hardly slept that night. She'd left Jack's house feeling panicked and guilty, afraid for their safety and ashamed that she would consider doing something that might put them at risk again. Jack had hugged her goodbye and told her how proud he was of her for embracing this new chapter and how happy it made them to see her happy.

But when she took the elevator up to the third floor, prepared to tell Colleen that she was sorry, but she couldn't get involved and put herself or her kids in danger, she heard crying coming from Colleen's room. With her hand poised to knock, she paused and listened, then immediately retreated.

Colleen had come to her scared and in peril. Virginia thought back to when she'd first found Ruth dead and tried to tell the police her concerns. She knew firsthand how seriously—or not—they'd taken her. She was old and easy to dismiss. And Colleen was, too. *This is different,* she told herself. *Colleen has a death threat from a killer who the police are already looking for.* But she couldn't shake the sound of Colleen's cries, the feeling that she had an obligation to her friend.

Those thoughts kept her up during the night, surfacing as she tossed and turned, drifting in and out of sleep.

She didn't help you over the summer. You were in danger, being framed for murder, and she avoided you.

She's your friend. She needs you.

She needs the police.

The police couldn't save Herman.

If you investigate, you're putting your children at risk. Your granddaughter.

She asked you for help. She needs you.

And so the night passed. When the clock on her night-stand read 4:30, Virginia decided it was useless lying in bed any longer. She splashed water on her face, pulled on her clothes, and stared at the same page of her book for an hour while her brain continued its arguments for and against helping Colleen.

Eventually, she pulled out the list Colleen had given her and tallied the names. Even if she cut it down to just the names starting with *A*, there were almost a dozen names. Virginia found it hard to imagine a dozen people wanting Colleen dead. Curious, she opened a browser window on her phone and typed in the first *A* name on the list: Alessandra Keck.

The search results began with images. Eight little pictures of eight completely different women. She scrolled down past the images. The results included a nurse, a lawyer, a teacher, and a podcaster. Virginia clicked each one, wondering how she was supposed to know which one might have wanted to kill Colleen. None of them were anywhere close to Colleen's age, and none of them lived anywhere near Seaview, from what Virginia could tell.

Frustrated, she set down her phone and the list, folding the paper so the names wouldn't be staring back at her, and returned to her book until it was late enough to go down to breakfast.

There was a limited crowd in the dining room at the very beginning of mealtime. Most of the residents would wake and come down a little later, but a small group rose before the sun, and all seemed to watch the clock. Virginia was too slow, beaten to the elevator by two men with walkers trying to cut each other off. She took the stairs, and by the time she'd made it down, the two men had parked their walkers with the others in a row along the far wall and were talking animatedly at a table.

Breakfast helped to restore her spirits. She ate alone, and by the end of the meal she felt silly for even considering taking on the investigation. This was what she needed: a community, a job to fill some of her time and organized activities to fill the rest, a place to live where she was comfortable, safe, and happy. Her kids were proud of her, and she was proud of herself. It wasn't an easy transition, and here she was, about to risk it all playing at being a detective when lives were on the line.

A little bounce had found its way into her steps as Virginia returned to her room after breakfast, and when her phone chimed and reminded her of the hair appointment she had that afternoon, she was glad for the reason to head downtown.

Virginia had seen the same hairstylist for twenty years and had spent the two years before that searching after her previous stylist of thirty years retired. Mabel's face lit up when Virginia stepped into the salon, and she'd no sooner led Virginia over to her chair than she was peppering her with questions.

"How are the kids? And how's sweet Stephanie doing? I just can't get over the fact that you're about to finally be a grandma!" She gave Virginia's shoulders a little squeeze and got to work while Virginia filled her in.

When Virginia had a fresh set of curls and was tipping Mable on her way out, one of the women sitting under a dryer caught her eye. She looked familiar. She had a round face and small eyes and was reading a paper. Virginia stared a moment too long, and the woman looked up and caught her. Virginia immediately tucked her head and went to leave, but the woman lifted a hand and waved.

"Virginia, right?" she asked. Virginia nodded and walked over. "We met the other day by the elevators in Breeze Village. You helped me find the activity room."

The memory came back to Virginia and she tipped her head back in recognition. "I'm sorry, but I don't remember your name. You're...?"

"Cece. Actually, I'm excited to run into you. When we met, I didn't realize I was meeting a Breeze Village legend." The woman blushed and looked down, then peered back up at Virginia sheepishly. "Someone else was giving me a bit of a rundown on Breeze Village, the history and people I should know. They mentioned you and your heroics, and then I looked you up. I'm sorry if that's intrusive."

"No, no," Virginia assured her, though it did make her feel uneasy.

"I think it's really impressive, what you did. And you're best friends with Marney Richards, right? I met her the other day and think she's so great. Opening her own store in retirement—talk about accomplished. I just can't believe I moved into a retirement home and suddenly I'm surrounded by some of the most inspiring people I've ever met."

Virginia felt herself standing taller and pushing her shoulders back. "That's very kind of you to say."

"I mean every word. Her starting a business and your investigative work are really amazing achievements. I won't keep you, but maybe I'll see you back at home."

VIRGINIA LEFT THE SALON ABUZZ, practically floating above the sidewalk. She reached her car but didn't feel like going home. It used to be that she'd get her hair done and then meet up with the neighborhood ladies and enjoy a full afternoon out, gossiping and window shopping and getting a meal downtown. Now she had hours until Lawrence's bowling match and nothing on her schedule.

She pulled out her phone, thinking of who she could call. Gemma would accept without hesitation, but Virginia wasn't in the mood to be reminded of the Garden Review Society at the moment. Marney would come spend the day with her, but she'd recognize Virginia's loneliness and pity her. She scrolled through her contacts and landed on Kim Nguyen, her old neighbor from Grove Park.

She hadn't seen Kim since the neighborhood tea party where she'd learned Bellemeade had been buying the entire neighborhood, not just targeting her. Kim had been adamant she'd never move until Bellemeade came knocking. She'd also been the first person Virginia had called when she'd learned Marney was moving, a key member of the Grove Park gossip train, though there was always an air of competition between her and Virginia. Who would have the juiciest piece of gossip, and who knew first?

Virginia dialed Kim's number and was surprised when it didn't even ring through once before someone answered.

"Hello?" a male voice said.

"Oh, err, I must have the wrong number. I'm looking for Kim Nguyen."

"Nope," the man said simply, hanging up before Virginia could ask anything else.

She looked at her phone screen, shocked, then looked around to decide her next move. Finally, she dialed Jan's number.

"Virginia!" Jan yelled through the phone, and Virginia held it out a few inches from her ear. "To what do I owe the pleasure?"

"I'm downtown after getting my hair done, and I thought I'd see what you were up to today. I actually tried to call Kim, too, but a man answered. She must have changed her number."

"Kim Nguyen? She's actually here at Harbor Vale."

Virginia stopped, taken aback. "Kim Nguyen moved into a senior living facility? Are you sure we're talking about the same person?"

Jan laughed. "She actually had a nasty fall not too long ago and broke her hip. She's insistent she's not here forever, that she'll be back on her own at some point, but she's here for the moment. You should come visit!"

Virginia rounded the corner, completing a circle of the block. Her car was twenty feet away, and Breeze Village was sounding better than before. "I actually forgot about something going on back at Breeze Village this afternoon. Another time?"

Jan let her go, and Virginia returned to Breeze Village deflated. All of the buzz of being told she was impressive had worn off. Restlessness still coursed through her legs, though every idea she came up with for how to pass the hours before Lawrence's game sounded unappealing.

She looked around her room. She could turn on the TV, though she doubted she'd be able to pay attention. She could read, though the same could be said for that. Her eyes landed on Colleen's list, still sitting folded on the side table where she'd set it down that morning. Against her better judgment, she picked it up.

Her phone was an inefficient way to look for information, what with its small screen and tiny keyboard. She could hardly type a word without at least one mistake. In search of a better option, Virginia headed to the second-floor common space directly above the lobby.

The common spaces on the second and third floors each had a TV, a small selection of comfortable chairs, and a big desktop computer where residents could browse the internet or play games if they didn't have their own computers in their rooms. Virginia sat down in the well-worn chair and gave the mouse a jiggle to wake the machine. Then she opened up a search window and took a peek at her list.

Alessandra Keck was a lost cause, she decided. Instead, she typed in the next name she found that started with the letter *A*: Andrew Bransil. This turned up fewer results than the earlier search, and the results seemed primarily concentrated around one man, a restauranteur in New York City. According to the third result down, he'd passed away a year earlier after a massive stroke. She jotted down a note next to his name on the list. *NYC restauranteur. Dead.* If this was the right Andrew Bransil, he wasn't the killer.

She moved on to the next name, not sure what she was looking for. A competing psychic? She realized she had no idea what Colleen's life before Breeze Village had been like. She was scrolling through an obituary for an Adrian Harris when someone tapped her shoulder.

Virginia spun around and found a resident she recognized but had never spoken with standing over her. "It's my turn," the woman said, extending an arm and pointing to the sign on the side of the computer that said *GIVE EVERYONE A TURN. PLEASE LIMIT COMPUTER USAGE TO 30 MINUTES AT A TIME.*

Virginia quickly closed out of her browser and relinquished the computer to the other resident, who wasted no time in starting up a game of mahjong.

CHAPTER 10

Lawrence bowled for the Seaview Seagulls and had for decades. After his partner, Ben, had died, joining the bowling league was the first move back out into the world Lawrence had made. And the bowling league had brought him structure and friendship and a wardrobe of tacky tracksuits.

The early uniforms didn't even feature a seagull but a pelican. Apparently, the team had two captains, and one of them led an uprising to change the team name and mascot to the pelican, arguing that seagulls were mere annoyances on beach days, but pelicans were impressive animals worth naming a team after. The other captain didn't want to lose the alliteration of the Seaview Seagulls, so they compromised and kept the name but featured a pelican on their uniforms for ten years until the pelican-devoted captain left the team.

This year's uniform included sequins accenting the seagull. They glinted in the dim light of the bowling alley as each player took his shot, and Virginia thought it added a fun bit of whimsy.

"Pancake, leave it alone!" Marney sat next to Virginia, crocheting, with Pancake on a harness and leash down by her feet. The cat was entertaining himself with the yarn Marney was working to turn into a hamburger bun. "I saw a kid's toy kitchen at the store the other day, with lots of little toy foods, and I thought it might be a fun project. The little foods crochet up quickly, and whoever is stealing all my ideas doesn't have anything like this in their shop."

Virginia swooped down and picked up Pancake, placing him on her lap.

"How's the investigation going?" Marney asked.

"Investigation?" Virginia's mind went to Colleen's list.

"My competition? The thief stealing my product descriptions and undercutting me? My sales are down. It's really starting to get to me."

"Oh, I haven't heard anything." Marney tried to mask her disappointment, but Virginia saw through it. "I'll do some looking," she said.

Lawrence bowled a strike. His hands shot up into the air. After high-fiving his teammates, he made his way over to where Marney and Virginia each wrapped him in a hug. "If Samuel keeps up his streak, and if I manage another one of those, the Kensington Kestrels are toast." His joy made Virginia's heart swell. He was in his element.

When he'd returned to his team, Virginia turned to Marney. "Do you think we're impressive?"

Marney snorted. "What do you mean?"

"Like, inspiring."

"What's going on with you?"

Virginia ran her hand down Pancake's back and scratched behind his ears, trying to decide how to phrase it. "I just feel like I should be doing more. Like I'm letting myself down, my kids down—"

"You know your kids are proud of you. They *want* a quiet retirement for you. Everyone who knows you and loves you is impressed you've overcome your need to be entirely independent and allowed yourself to move into Breeze Village and build a life you enjoy there. And you do enjoy the life you've built there, right? You're happy?"

"I am," Virginia said, but though it was the truth, a gnawing in her stomach said it wasn't the whole truth. "I just feel like… I feel like I've lost so much. I'm a former everything. Just a retiree working in a grocery store."

"You're eighty years old. Do you think you're *supposed* to be doing more than playing cards and working part-time for however long you enjoy it? And Pilates-ing, I suppose. Right? You're Pilates-ing now?"

Virginia paused rubbing Pancake. He turned his head and nipped her hand; then, when he saw it didn't convince her to start up again, he hopped down and resumed playing with Marney's ball of yarn. Virginia hardly noticed, because the wheels in her mind were turning. Maybe nobody expected her to be more than she was, but that didn't mean she wasn't supposed to be more.

"Colleen showed me something. It just has me a bit conflicted." Virginia confessed everything. "She got a letter, Marney. Signed with the letter *A*—violently, I might add. It said she was next and referenced Irene and Herman. Colleen is certain the hauntings Arnie told me about are the spirits trying to warn her she's in danger and make sure she takes the threat seriously."

Marney had stopped crocheting and was looking at Virginia, eyebrows knotted together. "She needs to go to the police, not to you!"

Though it was exactly what Virginia herself had said, the words coming from Marney stung. "That's what I told her," she said.

Marney turned her face back to her half-completed crochet hamburger bun. "What makes you feel sure it's real?" Virginia didn't have a good answer for that. "And even if the letter is real, are you buying into the haunting idea?"

"Well—"

"Isn't there a new resident who just found out she's psychic? I heard a man ranting about the perils of psychics the other day. You think it's more likely a psychic in a retirement home is a serial killer's next target and is also being haunted by spirits than it is that a neighbor who hates psychics is playing tricks on her?"

Virginia considered this. "How would he even know to give her a fake letter? The letters the other victims got aren't public knowledge."

"And yet you heard about it at the Piggly Wiggly." Marney had a good point, and Virginia could hear the smirk as she spoke.

"Fine. But the timing doesn't make sense. Ed was up in arms over Colleen being a psychic the day after the Halloween party. But Colleen got the letter on Halloween. He didn't have any reason to want to scare her yet if he didn't know she was psychic."

Marney shrugged, unconvinced. "Maybe he knew earlier. I've heard him fussing about her being a psychic on two separate occasions, each with as much passion as if it was a new revelation." Virginia didn't have a response. "Let the cops investigate. It's what they do. But if it's any consolation, I don't think Colleen is really in danger. I think they'll look into it and find that it was a tasteless prank."

LAWRENCE'S TEAM won their bowling match, and Virginia and Marney went out with the team afterward for celebratory drinks and dessert at a martini and dessert bar just blocks from the bowling alley. Pancake got the side eye from the bartender until Marney slipped him a twenty. Then Pancake got a discreet saucer of milk and a pat on the head.

After a heavenly slice of flourless chocolate torte, Virginia ducked out early. Her excuse was a morning shift at the grocery store, but in reality, she was out of energy to fake a smile when her mind was elsewhere. *Do you think you're* supposed *to be doing more?* Virginia couldn't shake the fact that she did.

And she couldn't shake the question of whether she believed Colleen was truly in danger. The more she thought about it, the more it irked her. She couldn't see any connection between Colleen and the two victims the killer had already slain, but she also couldn't see any connection between those two victims aside from their gruesome deaths.

Virginia was distracted all through her shift until Ronald came in, trailed by Patricia and the new resident Virginia had run into at the beauty parlor. She'd already forgotten the woman's name again.

"It's you again!" The woman said, following Ronald into the checkout line and placing a bag of gummy orange slices on the belt. "I didn't know you worked here. A detective and a cashier—you're a woman of many talents."

Ronald saw Virginia blush and broke into a snaggle-toothed grin. "Cece, you'd be better off not to encourage her."

Cece.

Ronald placed a pork loin onto the belt, and Virginia raised her eyebrow. "Not eating in the dining room this week?"

"I just have a hankering, and Patricia was scanning through the deals and saw that it was on sale here. We're going over to the Publix next because they've got the better prices on string cheese, and they're having a sale on ice cream."

Cece looked from Ronald to Patricia and Virginia with gleaming eyes. "Isn't it great?" she asked, just glad to be included.

Each week, Patricia scanned the sales catalogs for all the local groceries, and she and Ronald made their rounds. Though it wasn't allowed, Ronald kept a crockpot in his room at Breeze Village. When the menu for the week wasn't to his taste, he cooked for himself. Haley and the rest of the staff turned a blind eye since he'd never made trouble, and when he needed more than his crockpot and microwave, Gemma was happy to let him use the kitchen in her cottage in exchange for a plate of whatever he was cooking.

When they left, the remainder of the shift passed slowly. Her mind raced, and she couldn't stay focused. She saw her friends at Breeze Village, a zoomed-out picture of the life she'd made for herself, a life she wasn't sure was enough. She saw Colleen, scared and alone, asking her for help. By the time she clocked out and climbed into her car, she didn't want to go home to Breeze Village. Instead, she made the half-hour drive to the beach, parked, and slipped off her shoes as she began the sandy walk down to where the waves lapped at the shore.

Though winters in the South were nothing compared to most of the country, the wind whipped across the beach, and Virginia found herself shivering and wrapping her jacket tight around herself. She took one step, then two, onto the wet sand and waited until the next wave came in, its remnants washing over her toes and making her yelp. She felt alive.

With the roar of the wind loud in her ears, her hair blowing in her face, and the water icy cold on her feet, the beach overwhelmed her senses. Everything else fell away. When the next wave came in, she took another step, the water coming up to her ankles. A bird shrieked in the distance, and she shrieked with it.

"Earl!" she yelled. "I don't know what to do!" The wind carried her cries off, the sound dying almost as quickly as the words fell from her mouth. Sobs racked her body and she shook, yelling out again. "I need you, Earl! It should have been you. It should have been you who stayed behind." December would mark forty years since Earl's cancer had won. Forty years of being a single mom, a widow. As she stood crying on the beach, bending over to brace her hands against her knees, Virginia missed him as if it had been days.

"The kids would love you," she cried. "You would have raised them right. They would talk to you. You'd be so much closer to them than I am. You'd be the one throwing Stephanie's baby shower." She let out another wail, howling now. The gale thrashed her hair against her face, the little blows stinging. "You were always the better of us. You were always the one who should have been allowed to stay."

Virginia's throat burned with her sobs. "I don't know what to do," she repeated. Hugging herself, she cried until her swollen eyes dried up. She cried that she didn't have the relationship with her children she wanted. She cried that she was a failure. She cried that she wanted to live a life Earl would have been proud of but that she felt she'd let him and everyone else down. As she finally lost steam, so too did the wind, and by the time her cries had subsided, the breeze had stilled completely.

"I'm going to make you proud," she said quietly, lifting her chin to the sky. Her hands balled into fists by her sides, and she spoke with conviction. "You always did what you believed in, and you made me proud every day. It's my turn to make you proud, Earl."

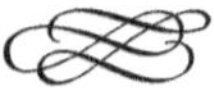

CHAPTER 11

"I'm going to need more information." Virginia set Colleen's list of potential suspects on the table where Colleen was finishing her breakfast and tapped it. Colleen looked up, surprised. Her eyes looked glazed over and dark bags rimmed them. Virginia softened her tone when she saw how worn down Colleen looked. "I've started looking into them, but there are a bunch of people with the same names. It would help me to know who they are and how you know them. And why you think they'd want you dead."

Colleen picked up her coffee and looked from the note to Virginia and back. "All right. Most of them are people I knew when I lived in New York. People I worked with, or for, or competed with."

"You lived in New York?"

Colleen nodded. "I climbed the corporate ladder for twenty years. I wore high heels. I hailed yellow cabs. I paid too much money for too little space. It was different then, of course. It's been two decades since I left New York, and I left the corporate world long before that."

"I'm having trouble picturing the psychic before me sitting in a corporate boardroom."

"Oh, I sat in many of those. I was in the consumer magazine industry. After I quit, I stayed in New York but pursued a life of entrepreneurship. And then I cashed in and moved south, chasing a man who didn't love me back."

Virginia frowned. "Herman Walsh, the second victim… wasn't he from New York?"

"That sounds familiar." Colleen sipped her coffee and stared off, eyes glazing over. After a minute, she turned back to Virginia. "I can't remember ever seeing him or hearing his name until the news about his murder."

Virginia didn't hide her disappointment. She'd just made what felt like her first connection in this whole mess, and Colleen dismissed it. "So how many of these names are from the—what was it?—the consumer magazine industry?"

Colleen pointed out roughly half the names, and Virginia labeled them *NYC Mag*. "And how many of the rest are from your entrepreneurial years in New York?"

"Almost all of them," Colleen answered.

"Were you a, err, magazine entrepreneur?"

At this, Colleen barked a laugh. Virginia flinched, surprised, but then a smile spread across her own face. "No, no," Colleen said, laughter still shaking her frame. "I had a handful of different businesses. I moved from one thing to the next whenever I felt called. For a while, I ran a restaurant. Our whole deal was that we'd serve a five-star meal in the back of a yellow cab. We catered to wealthy New Yorkers who were on the go, too busy for a restaurant, but who wanted a fine meal."

Virginia was stunned beyond words.

"It was a hit, but the Department of Health didn't love it. Anyway, I had a call about a freelance opportunity that turned into its own business. This one probably lasted the longest of any of my endeavors. I was a ghost hunter."

At this point, Virginia looked around to see if anyone was listening. Everyone else in the dining room was focused on their own breakfasts, so Virginia turned back to Colleen, though she lowered her voice. "A ghost hunter?"

Colleen nodded, amusement dancing on her face. "Maybe a ghost enticer is a better description. A couple of college kids wanted to make a film of them spending the night in a haunted house, and they wanted to capture the hauntings on camera. They called me since I was known in the New York City area as a psychic, mainly just for parties or corporate events. I think I'd done a reading for one of their mothers at a corporate Christmas party, and she'd been impressed. The kid called asking if I could actually commune with spirits. I told him I could, and we agreed that I'd commune with the spirits in and around the house upstate where they wanted to film. In exchange for passing along a few messages from the spirits, they'd participate in the theatrics."

"I don't... You used your psychic powers to help kids film ghost movies?"

"I did. I actually found myself traveling quite a bit. They told their friends, and word spread more than I expected. Every city has its favorite haunted buildings, and the people running the ghost tours had my number on speed dial."

Virginia's head spun. "And which of these enemies are from the ghost-hunting business?" she asked, tapping the list again. "I don't see how that would make you enemies in the first place."

"Well, not every message the spirits asked me to pass on was well-received, I can tell you that. And when I got popular with the ghost tours and was traveling a lot, I'd have to take some requests and turn down others. When some towns' ghost tours boomed, others went out of business, and at least one person blames me for their own business going under."

Colleen pointed out a handful of names, and Virginia marked them with the label *Ghosts*. "Which of these were from the taxi cab restaurant business?" Colleen showed her, and she marked those *Cab Restaurant*.

"There are still a few left," Virginia said.

Colleen nodded, the levity that had come from recounting her ghost-hunting life gone.

"The last job I had before fully retiring was a job I took working for someone else. I was tired of running my own business, and a friend of mine in New York was opening an ice cream parlor and needed a hand. It was part-time work, but it gave me some stability while I got back to doing readings at parties, and he gave me part ownership in the shop since I helped get it off the ground."

Virginia opened her mouth to ask Colleen how an ice cream shop had made her enemies, but Colleen held her hand up and kept talking.

"The shop was doing okay. Ezra enjoyed mixing up new flavors, and we had some of the most unique and interesting flavors of any shop in the city. One night while experimenting, we discovered I had a knack for naming the flavors and writing up little descriptions. You've got an index card's worth of space to sell someone on a flavor, and that turned out to be my specialty. So I took over doing it."

Colleen picked up her coffee cup and crossed the dining room to refill it, leaving Virginia alone at the table. When she returned, she held the cup in front of her chest with both hands. Virginia tried not to look impatient.

"The ice cream parlor was a success. We blew up, hugely popular. Not in the way that stores can now, with social media making people viral or whatnot, but we grew fast. Three ice cream parlors closed down in the wake of our success. And I was part owner, and getting older, and I'd visited Seaview when I was traveling for the ghost tours. I wanted out of New York, and it felt like the time to make it happen. I cashed in and left. Sold my stake and retired to Seaview."

"Was your friend upset that you left?"

"Not at first. He'd hired more employees, and with me gone, he owned it all. But not long after I left, the business took a downturn and never turned back up. He blamed me."

"So that would be..." Virginia looked at the list. "Ezra Pierson?"

Colleen nodded, wiping a tear from the corner of her eye, and then pointed to a few other names on the list.

"These were the owners of the other stores that closed down." Virginia marked them all.

"Anyway, that's my story. I retired here. It's been almost twenty years. I mean, I still worked. I did readings at festivals and parties, and I've had some long-term clients who come to me as well, but I don't need the money."

"There's one name left. Rosemary Snow. Who's she?"

Colleen scoffed. "She's the kind of person who gives us psychics a bad name. She's a fraud. Was, maybe. She could be dead, for all I know. But twelve years ago, I was working a festival and the organizers put my booth next to hers. It was a bad idea from the start, to put two people in the same business right next to each other. But that's what they did, and anyway, she brought it on herself.

"All day long, she disparaged me. She tried to convince everyone who walked by that I was a fraud. Mind you, I didn't try to directly compete with her. I sat quietly and only talked to people when they came up to me. But she made it her mission to ruin me, and finally, I snapped. I exposed her as the fraud she was, and she told me I would regret it and that she'd put an end to me."

"You think she's still upset after twelve years?"

Colleen shrugged. "I didn't want to leave someone who'd directly threatened me off the list of people who might want me dead, even if it was a long time ago."

Virginia nodded and picked up the list. She now knew who the people were, so at least she'd have a clue which person she was looking for if her internet search turned up multiple hits for the same name. The problem was, she didn't believe any of these people wanted to kill Colleen.

Virginia assured Colleen she'd go down the list and investigate, that Colleen would be safe, and not to worry. She hoped she projected more confidence than she felt.

"Oh, one last thing," she said as she stood to leave. "Can you tell me more about the hauntings you're experiencing?"

"It's just annoying," Colleen said, clearly frustrated. "Lights flickering, stuff not being where I left it, things like that. I haven't ever experienced anything like it, and I've spent my life interacting with spirits."

"Does it feel... err, is there an energy...? I'm not sure how this all works, but can your psychic powers give you any insight?"

When Russ had taken over Breeze Village from Michelle in the summer and brought Liam on board, Colleen had experienced such an energetic nightmare in their presence that she'd become closed off and took to numbing herself out any chance she got. Her visions had been so unpleasant in the presence of a murderer that she couldn't handle it. Virginia hoped that could help them now. Her hopes plummeted when Colleen shook her head.

"That's the weird thing. I can't get any sort of read. There's simply no energetic difference between now and before this all started."

"And the letter? It doesn't feel…?" Virginia wasn't sure what to ask.

"It doesn't feel like anything. It feels like a piece of paper."

"Do other special objects feel different?"

"I can usually detect something of the energy of the owner. But not with this."

Virginia caught herself frowning and instead flashed the most confident fake smile she could muster. Colleen's apologetic look let her know it didn't land. "Look," she said. "I'm on it. I'm committed to this investigation, which means it's only a matter of time before we catch the person who sent you that letter and bring them to justice."

* * *

VIRGINIA HEADED to the computer in the second-floor common area to resume her investigation. Enthusiasm turned to frustration the more she read over the list. *People don't hold onto grudges for thirty years and then decide to act on them via murder. It doesn't make sense.*

She'd rounded the corner to find the resident whose dedication to mahjong outshone anyone Virginia had met sitting at the computer when her phone chimed with an email. Pushing her glasses farther up the bridge of her nose, she stopped in the hallway and checked it.

From: Samantha Kelly <samiam@samtherealtorgenius.com>

Virginia's throat clenched, and she pulled the phone closer to her face. She tried to push down her panic with disdain, sneering at the email address Sam had given herself. It didn't work, and her stomach knotted as she turned her eyes to the body of the email.

Hiiiiii Virginia! Long time, no see! Hope you're well. Can you believe we're gonna be grandmas?? I am SO excited for our sweet Stephanie to experience the joys of motherhood and excited for us to wrap her in love at the baby shower.

I wanted to send an apology for not sending you an invitation sooner or including you in the planning process. That was an oversight. You know how we moms can be when we're focused on our kids. It's so easy to forget something important.

ANYway, can't wait to see you. I'm having the shower catered by Miss B's. Let me know if you have any allergies I should be aware of.

Love love love!! xxx Sam

Virginia looked up from her phone, dizzy as her eyes adjusted from the screen and re-focused on the area around her. Her down-the-hall neighbor was still playing mahjong, oblivious to the way the world seemed to shift under Virginia's feet. Leaning against the wall to steady herself, Virginia replied to Sam's email.

Looking forward to it. Stephanie prefers Luigi's to Miss B's. Says Miss B's is overrated.

xxx Virginia

Her fingers felt like foreign bodies as she copied Sam's

sign-off. As soon as Virginia hit send, she shoved the phone back into her pocket and pressed her back to the wall, leaning her head back and closing her eyes. Her face felt hot with embarrassment and anger. She wanted Sam to know that Virginia was as much of a mom to Stephanie as she was, but she knew if Stephanie or Jack saw the message, they'd be disappointed in her.

She looked over at the woman playing on the computer once more and thought of asking her to give Virginia a turn, but the idea of going down the list, searching name after name and coming up with nothing, made Virginia want to scream. Happy this time to let the woman keep playing, she turned and made her way to her room, the floor still feeling uneasy beneath her.

COFFEE further upset Virginia's already-upset stomach, and a lie-down was about as restful as a redeye flight. A cool shower brought a modicum of relief, and lunch—a pulled pork sandwich and a tall glass of sweet tea— restored Virginia to feeling merely tired instead of on the verge of death. When Ronald asked if she wanted to play cards, she found herself agreeing before she even realized it.

"You look like crap," he said, dealing out the first hand.

Patricia sniggered, pulling up a chair to join them. "Sorry," she said, "but it's true."

"Haven't been sleeping well," Virginia said, pulling her cards toward her across the table and peeking at them before setting them back facedown in front of her.

Virginia and Ronald played a heads-up game while Patricia took on her favorite role as observer. She peered at both players' cards and maintained a perfectly neutral face the entire time. Her photographic memory gave her an unfair advantage, according to Ronald, and she never minded not playing.

Virginia played poorly, and after three wins, Ronald flopped his cards down in front of him. "What's going on today? It's not even fun to beat you when you put up so little fight."

Virginia squirmed. "Like I said, I haven't been sleeping well." In reality, her mind had been on Colleen's list. Every one of those names was someone Colleen had known ages ago in a former life. Try as she might, Virginia couldn't buy into the idea that someone Colleen had wronged decades ago would come back and murder her for it now. She'd certainly known people in her thirties or forties whom she'd thought wronged her, and no matter how much she'd hated them then, for the life of her, she couldn't remember any of them now. She thought whoever was threatening Colleen now had to be someone who'd been in her life more recently.

Both Ronald and Patricia gave Virginia an *I don't believe you* look, and she sighed. "Fine, my mind is elsewhere." Ronald and Patricia looked at each other and smiled.

"Want to share where?" Ronald asked.

"What do you know about the resident who's all up in arms over Colleen being a psychic?"

"Ed? The guy's a jerk," Patricia said. "He's new. I met him because he came to the book club meeting just a couple of days after he moved in. He seemed nice, but then someone mentioned Colleen's powers, and he flipped out. They just said they wanted to ask Colleen for some insight before they asked someone they met at church out for a date, and Ed said they might as well ask the devil himself."

"Every time someone mentions Colleen, he goes off," Ronald said. "He's an okay guy if you just don't mention her. Or psychics in general. Or the weather."

"The weather?" Virginia asked.

"Weathermen are too much like psychics, trying to predict the future," Ronald said. Both Patricia and Virginia lost it.

"Anyway," Ronald went on, "he lives on the first floor next to Jimmy. I don't think he's Jimmy's favorite person. Apparently, Ed spends his time watching cop shows with the volume up too high, which doesn't go over great with Jimmy after three years of living here with neighbors like Quiet Mike and Edith."

Virginia played another miserable hand, then called it. "I promise I'll be a better opponent next time," she assured Ronald as she headed out. She started toward the elevator, but the hallway off the lobby caught her eye. Before heading back to her room, she might as well pay Jimmy a visit and see how he was faring with his new neighbor.

CHAPTER 13

"What do you want?" Jimmy Hudson was a tall man, bald, whose face was always screwed up in anger, but who was rarely actually angry. That was just his face. His barking voice didn't help his image, but Virginia hadn't heard of him saying a mean thing to anyone. That was just his voice.

Virginia poked her head into the room and saw Jimmy sitting in a worn recliner reminiscent of the ones three-quarters of the residents at Breeze Village spent most of their time in. Breeze Village furnished a bed, desk, and dresser in all the rooms, but residents brought the rest of their furniture, and almost everyone brought a recliner. Jimmy's was burgundy leather, with what looked like cat scratches up both sides.

"My name's Virginia, and I was hoping to talk to you for a minute," she said, stepping into the room.

"I don't date fellow residents anymore," Jimmy said, waving her away. "Too awkward."

"Oh, no, that's not why I'm here. Actually, I'm a private

investigator." Virginia felt herself straighten unconsciously as she said it.

"Did you find out who's been taking all the pudding cups out of the communal fridge?"

"That's Gemma," she said. "From the cottages out back."

"Gemma," he said quietly to himself. Then he looked up at Virginia and smiled. "All right, then. I appreciate you looking into it." He turned away from Virginia and picked a book up off his side table, cracking it open and settling in.

"That's not what I came to talk about," Virginia said. "I was hoping to talk with you about your neighbor, Ed."

Jimmy shut his book, his face flushing. "That bastard? What did he do? Are you going to arrest him?"

"What? No. Jimmy, I'm a resident here. I live upstairs? I'm friends with Ronald. I think you know him?"

Jimmy grunted. "Yeah, I know Ronald."

"I'm looking into Ed because of a connection with Colleen. Do you know her?"

"The psychic," Jimmy said. "She's wonderful. You know, I was at breakfast last week, and Colleen zoned out, having one of her visions or whatnot. When she came back around, she turned to me and Ed and asked what day it is, if it was the seventeenth. It wasn't the seventeenth, and Ed had a whole field day about how ridiculous psychics are, but then Colleen just said she had a feeling about the number seventeen. Ed went on and on, but I went down to the gas station and bought myself a lottery ticket, number seventeen. And would you guess what happened? I won a hundred bucks!"

"Do you know why Ed hates Colleen so much? Is it just that she's a psychic?"

"At first, I thought it was just because of his wife leaving him after a psychic told her to, but I've got it on good intelligence that Ed's actually an internet pirate. He watches those cop shows so loud, and I think he's recording them and putting them on the internet illegally. I think he's worried Colleen's going to find out because of her powers. Since you're an investigator, I have some ideas for how we can catch him. I was thinking that we could—"

Virginia cut him off. "Wait, back up. His wife left him because a psychic told her to?"

Jimmy nodded gravely. "I can hear him on the phone through the vents." He pointed to an air vent on the wall. "He still talks to his wife every night. They're still madly in love. But after fifty-seven years together, from what I could gather from his conversations, Marcia's psychic told her that she shouldn't be with him anymore. It sounds like he lived in an apartment on his own for a spell, then had a little fall, and he and Marcia decided he should move in here."

Virginia's heart ached in her chest. She tried to imagine the pain if Earl left her, and if he did it on the advice of a psychic. She wasn't sure she'd feel any differently than Ed did, though she hoped she wouldn't come out as bitter as he had. "That's awful," she said quietly, looking toward the vent in the wall as if she could see Ed crying on the other side.

At that moment, the TV in Ed's room turned on, the volume so loud it made Virginia jump. "I'd feel bad for the guy if he didn't make it so hard," Jimmy yelled over the noise. "And if he didn't take his grief out on everyone else."

Virginia thanked Jimmy for his time and started to leave.

"If you're going to take him down, will you let me know first? I want to be there to witness it."

Virginia smiled. "You've got it." She was halfway out the door when Jimmy called to her again.

"I know I said I don't date residents anymore, but if you're ever looking for a good time, you let me know. All right?"

* * *

VIRGINIA PRACTICALLY RAN to Marney's cottage. When she arrived and threw the door open without knocking, she was out of breath. "Marney?" she called. "It's me!"

Marney came out of the kitchenette, wiping flour from her hands onto a dark blue apron. "What's wrong?"

Virginia shut the door behind her, moving straight to the couch and lying back. "Nothing's wrong. Give me a minute to catch my breath. I hurried over here."

Impatient, Marney stood over Virginia with her hands on her hips. "Why'd you hurry if nothing's wrong? Virginia, if you're in trouble and you're not telling me, I swear to you—"

"I'm not in trouble." Virginia sat up, peering over Marney's shoulder into the small kitchen. "What are you cooking?"

"Chicken pot pie." Virginia felt herself salivating

immediately, lunch not even a distant memory yet. Marney's face remained stern. "You don't get any if you don't tell me what's going on."

Pancake emerged from Marney's bedroom to see what the hubbub was all about. He jumped up onto the couch, then up onto the back of the couch to bat at Virginia's curls. She scooped him up and put him on her lap.

"I just talked to Jimmy. Do you know him?"

Marney thought about it. "First floor… Edith's neighbor before she passed?" Virginia nodded. "I never met him, but she mentioned him in my crochet class a few times. Said he looks like he'd rip your head off but he's really a sweetheart."

"He's also Ed's neighbor, now that Ed moved into Edith's room."

"Ed… he's the one who hates psychics?"

"That's the one. And apparently, he's not such a great neighbor. Watches TV too loud, talks on the phone too loud, and is generally unpleasant."

"I'm failing to see what you had to rush over here to tell me about." Marney returned to the kitchen, looking over her shoulder at Virginia as she resumed working on her pie crust.

"I had to rush over here and tell you about the conversation because Ed's loud phone calls carry through the vents into Jimmy's room, and Jimmy had some insight into why Ed hates psychics so much."

Marney hesitated in the middle of rolling out her pie dough and turned to Virginia. Virginia continued, revealing what she'd learned about Ed's wife's decision and the psychic guidance that led her to leave her husband.

"She dumped him because of a psychic? After more than fifty years together?" Marney brought her hand to her mouth, leaving a trace of flour on her face, then crossed the kitchen to wash up and lean against the sink. "That's awful."

"That's why he's such a jerk about Colleen being a psychic."

"Obviously his behavior is inexcusable, but can you imagine? The poor man!"

Virginia's brow wrinkled and her lips turned down in a frown. "Don't get too sympathetic. You said yourself that you think he's haunting Colleen and faked a death threat. He wasn't at the Halloween party. Maybe that's because he was in Colleen's room planting a death threat!"

"I said his behavior toward Colleen was inexcusable," Marney snipped. "But while I can't excuse it, now I understand it."

Virginia remained on the couch, giving Pancake belly rubs while the cat luxuriated on her lap, and mentally tallied what she knew about Ed and Colleen. She knew from Patricia that Ed learned about Colleen's psychic abilities before Halloween, so he could be behind the letter. She knew he had a motive. She couldn't work out what he stood to gain through scaring Colleen, other than perhaps some enjoyment of seeing her suffer.

"I need to get into his room," Virginia said suddenly.

"No." Marney's reply was immediate and to the point.

"I need to get a sample of his handwriting to compare to the letter Colleen got. If it matches, he's our guy."

"Can't you just ask him to write something down for you?"

Virginia considered the possibility. "If he *did* write the letter and I ask him to write something down, he'll suspect that I'm onto him. And we both know subtlety isn't my strongest asset."

Marney giggled at the truth of it. Virginia was charming and could talk a person's ear off, but she got information because people told it to her plainly. She didn't weasel it out of them without their knowing.

"What would I even ask him to write down? 'Hey, Ed, I have two perfectly good hands, but could you please take a note for me?'" Virginia joked.

"I was thinking more along the lines of asking him for directions somewhere, but you're right. You'd end up making a scene."

"So I'll break into his room, find a sample of his handwriting, and then take it to the police."

Marney cocked her head to the side, thinking it through. Finally, she turned to Virginia and pointed a finger at her. "Fine, but not without me. You need someone to keep watch."

CHAPTER 14

With Marney otherwise occupied making a pot pie, which Virginia absolutely intended to sample later, their little breaking-and-entering expedition would have to wait. Before Virginia could get down about it, her phone chimed. Pilates started in ten minutes in Activity Room A. Virginia groaned and racked her brain for excuses but, finding none, plodded off to the main building.

When Virginia took an open seat next to Jane, who was maneuvering her oxygen tank and cable out of the way, Jane looked surprised to see her. "You're back," she said with a chuckle. "I have to say, I didn't expect to see you here again."

Diana entered the room before Virginia could respond, along with Carol from the YMCA. "Welcome, everyone!" Diana said with an enthusiastic smile. "I'm so happy to see so many smiling faces here. If you've taken this class before, you know Carol."

Carol, a perky young woman with a bouncing ponytail, waved to the class. "Hi, everyone! As always, everything I do up here can be modified. We'll do lots of chair-based moves today, but I think you'll leave feeling like you got in a nice workout."

Diana left and Carol started the class in a warm-up, reaching overhead. Half the class was focused and engaged, excited to be there, and half the class looked like they felt the way Virginia did about Pilates. They were there because their kids wanted them to be. Carol didn't care. Her enthusiasm seemed to know no bounds, and she circled the room, correcting people's forms and giving encouragement.

Kim wheeled Midge in during the warm-up. Haley's mom lived on the memory ward, and after the last Pilates class Virginia attended, Jane told her that Midge had taught Pilates for most of her life. Though she didn't always remember who or where she was, the familiar movements returned a vitality to her eyes, and for the half-hour, she was herself again.

"I heard you're back on the investigative train," Jane whispered while they extended their legs and drew circles in the air with their toes. "Something about Colleen?"

Virginia wasn't being overly secretive about the investigation, but she didn't want the whole town to know Colleen may be in a serial killer's sights. It would create unnecessary panic.

"It's nothing big," she said. "Colleen thinks she's being haunted. I'm looking into it." It wasn't a complete lie.

"She *thinks* she's being haunted?" Jane planted her feet on the floor and moved to the next exercise, twisting her chest to one side. Virginia followed suit, her range of motion considerably smaller. "If Colleen is rattled," Jane continued, "it must be serious."

She was right. Colleen wasn't one to go asking others for help. "You've been here as long as she has, right?" Jane nodded. "Do you know anything about any disagreements she's had with other residents? Anyone here who has an issue with her?"

"Well, there's Ed, of course."

Virginia let out a low laugh. "Anyone else?" To her disappointment, Jane shook her head.

"We're not the closest friends, so there could be things I don't know about, but I'm not aware of anyone here who has had issues with her."

They continued with their exercises, Virginia trying to put her focus on the movements and off of how much she hated Pilates. Her muscles protested at every turn. It felt like an eternity passed before Carol announced that class was over. All she wanted to do afterward was lie down and take a nap, but she had a meeting she'd scheduled after her walk on the beach. One she'd promised Earl's memory she wouldn't miss.

THAT EVENING, over the best chicken pot pie she'd ever had, Virginia told Marney what she'd been up to that day. "I'm not convinced Pilates is actually good for my health. Everything I've read says that feelings of happiness are healthy, along with managing stress. Since Pilates brings me more stress and less happiness, really I'm doing my health a disservice every time I go."

"Tell that one to your doctor at your next appointment. I'm sure it'll go over well."

"Very funny." Virginia chewed slowly, her stomach fluttering at what she had to say next. "After class, I went over to the community college. I talked with someone in the Admissions Office." Confusion crossed Marney's face, and Virginia went on. "I've been thinking about taking some classes. Just one—I'm not trying to load up with a full schedule or anything. But I've heard learning a foreign language is good for brain plasticity, and I've been thinking of taking up German."

"German?" Marney's face was a confused stare followed by a wash of realization. "Earl."

Virginia nodded. Earl had spoken fluent German. He'd sung her love songs in German when he walked up behind her in the kitchen, hugging her from behind while she cooked. She'd swat him away, saying, "You're going to make me burn our dinner!" but laughed the whole while. After her moment on the beach, in her promise to do Earl proud, she'd been struck by inspiration. She felt closer to him as she sat in the office of the Admissions counselor, and she couldn't wait to see the look on Jack's face when she told him. He'd be impressed, and she knew he'd go on about brain plasticity and the benefits of learning a second language.

"That's marvelous," Marney said. "I love the idea."

Virginia's cheeks flushed at the praise.

By the time they'd finished their meals and washed up, the little cottage felt charged with electric energy. Neither had spoken about their impending crime, but each knew it was on the forefront of the other's mind. Even Pancake seemed to pick up on the fact that something was afoot. He swirled between Marney's legs as she walked from the table to the sink, nearly tripping her, and wouldn't be shooed away.

"You can't come," Marney told him firmly when she and Virginia slipped their shoes back on to leave. Still not vocalizing where they were going, they busied themselves getting ready, running their hands over their clothes nervously. Marney checked her makeup in the mirror hanging in her entryway twice. When she made to check herself a third time, Virginia said, "All right, all right, you're the most put-together burglar Breeze Village has ever seen. Now, let's go catch a killer. Or prankster. We'll find out, I suppose. A jerk, for sure."

Marney laughed and reached for the doorknob. She'd half turned the knob when Pancake shot between them, shoving his nose into the crack and preparing to bolt. Virginia stooped and picked him up, but when Marney opened the door, he protested, wiggling until Virginia could barely hold him. At his remonstrance, Marney shut the door again and lifted his harness off the hook where she hung her car keys. And just like that, Pancake was ready to take on the title of cat burglar.

CHAPTER 15

Marney and Virginia, with Pancake content on his leash between them, stopped and knocked at Jimmy's door before their big moment. The door swung back and Jimmy towered over them, his face cross as it had been when Virginia had talked with him earlier. In his barking voice, he said, "The investigator is back."

Virginia offered a smile and gestured to Marney. "And I've brought my friend and sidekick, Marney." Marney offered Jimmy her hand and he took it, his hand enveloping hers completely.

"A pleasure," he said, though his visage contradicted the statement.

"Do you know if Ed's home?" Virginia asked. "We were hoping to ask him a few questions."

Jimmy stepped back into his room, and Marney and Virginia remained in the doorway, unsure whether to follow. He resumed his position in his recliner before turning to them and responding, "You just missed him. He left about ten minutes ago."

Virginia tried to hide her pleased expression. "Do you know how long he'll be gone?"

"Beats me." Jimmy shrugged, picked up the television remote, and turned his attention to the screen. Virginia and Marney looked at each other and retreated back to the hallway.

"Thanks, Jimmy," Virginia called behind her, pulling the door shut. When it clicked shut, she whispered to Marney, "Perfect."

Virginia walked the few steps down the hall to Ed's door, leaving Marney and Pancake to follow behind her, then stopped confidently in front of the door. With a deep breath in, she grabbed the handle and turned. Locked.

She tried it again to no avail, then turned to Marney in a panic. Marney stepped forward and offered Virginia the end of Pancake's leash. "Let me try."

"It's locked," Virginia whispered, but before she'd even gotten the words out, Marney was reaching into her purse, bending over the lock, and jiggling a pin in the hole. "What are you doing?" Virginia hissed.

Marney shushed her and continued wiggling the pin. In a matter of seconds, the lock clicked, and Marney gestured to the door handle. "Try it now." The handle turned, and the door swung open with ease, revealing a dark room.

Virginia marveled at her friend's hidden talent. "Why do you know how to do that?"

"A woman needs hobbies in retirement," Marney said.

"The internet can teach you how to do almost anything. Now, come on!"

The three entered, Pancake tugging at his leash, excited to explore a new room with new smells, Marney and Virginia hanging back. Virginia shut the door behind them and felt on the wall for the light switch. They each squinted as the light blinded them for a moment, then looked around and surveyed the room in front of them.

Ed's room was sparsely furnished. His was the smallest floor plan Breeze Village offered, a studio style instead of a suite. A low bed occupied one corner, the pillows up against the bare wall where a headboard belonged. The sheets and blankets hung messily off the mattress. Beside the bed was a nightstand that held a single book and a small lamp, and a child-sized dresser stood on the other side of the nightstand. There was a door to the bathroom, a tiny counter with a microwave and mini fridge, and on the opposite wall, a low bookshelf supported a small television. The requisite recliner faced the television, and a TV tray served as a side table. There were no papers strewn about, no obvious pieces of evidence lying in plain sight.

"Where's all his stuff?" Marney breathed, spinning to take in the room.

"Well, he's got one book over there and a spare pair of shoes by the door. What more does one need, really?"

Marney dropped Pancake's leash, and the cat went straight for the recliner, hopping up and making himself at home. Virginia moved to the nightstand and pulled open the drawer. Inside, she found a glasses case and a sleep mask but no diary or other writings. Marney examined the bookshelf supporting the TV. Its shelves sported a handful of knick-knacks but no books or other items.

"This isn't exactly looking promising," Virginia said.

At that moment, the unmistakable sound of a key in the lock startled Virginia and Marney out of their search. They locked eyes, terror freezing them in place, and the door swung open to reveal Ed standing there. At first, Ed didn't seem to notice anything amiss. He extracted his key from the lock, stepped inside, and reached his hand over to flip the light switch. Then he seemed to notice that the room was already lit.

The color drained from his face, and he looked up and saw Marney and Virginia, frozen where they had been looking through his things. Pancake walked over, dragging his leash behind him, and planted himself in front of Ed, looking up at him expectantly and waiting to be pet. The fear in Ed's eyes morphed to rage.

"What the hell are you doing here?" he demanded.

Virginia started, her jaw opening and closing as she attempted to construct a response.

"Out!" he yelled. "Both of you, get out right now!" Ed thrust his arm out in a gesture toward the door.

"I want to apologize," Marney said, the words tumbling out of her mouth hurriedly, like Marney was afraid to be saying them. Virginia's head snapped around, and she looked at Marney, confused. Ed's face echoed her confusion.

"I heard about your wife. I think it's really sad and really unfair, and I wanted to say I'm sorry for what you're going through," Marney said, more confidently now.

Ed's rage softened slightly, the gears in his head turning. He looked from Marney to Virginia and back. "That doesn't explain why you two are in my apartment."

Unable to come up with a reasonable explanation, Virginia's instinct was to leave as quickly as possible. She couldn't talk her way out of the situation, so the next best thing would be to physically remove herself from it.

"I'm terribly sorry," she said, starting toward the door. "We'll be going now and not giving you any more trouble."

She made it within feet of the door when Ed stepped to the side, blocking the exit. "No," he said. Virginia's breath caught in her throat. "Before you leave, I want to know why you two were here." The booming anger had vanished from Ed's voice. He spoke now with a chill precision.

A tingle crept up Virginia's spine as she looked from Ed to the doorway and back. There was no way she could get around him. She was trapped.

Virginia's eyes darted to where Marney stood by the television. "We were in your apartment because we wanted to find a sample of your handwriting," Marney said simply. Virginia gave her a pleading look. What was she doing?

"And why is that?" Ed asked, his voice razor-thin and threatening. He took a step farther inside the room. All Virginia could see was him with the same dangerous expression on his face, sliding a note under Colleen's door.

"Because a resident in this community has been threatened, in writing, and we have reason to believe you might be the threatening party," Marney said. She maintained eye contact with Ed while she spoke, chin up high while Virginia trembled. Pancake, oblivious to the situation, made figure-eights around Ed's legs, rubbing against the hem of his pants.

Marney's explanation seemed to fluster Ed, and belligerence crept into his voice when he responded. "I haven't threatened anyone. Not even you two burglars. Whose connection, by the way, to this whole threat investigation, I still don't understand."

"I'm a private investigator." Virginia found her voice, taking inspiration from Marney's confident stance.

Ed barked a contemptuous laugh. "You? A private investigator? You know, I've heard the stories about you. You were banned from Breeze Village premises, isn't that right? And then a suspect in two murders just a few months later."

"For which she was completely cleared," Marney sniped, defending her friend.

Ed stood silently, considering Marney and Virginia. Then he looked to Marney. "So someone has been threatened, and you two think I did it. The only person here I have a problem with is Colleen. I take it she's the one under attack?"

Marney looked to Virginia for guidance, but she'd been doing fine on her own so far, so Virginia just shrugged. "That's right," Marney said.

"Well, I didn't."

"You'll forgive us for not just taking your word for it,"

Virginia said. "Given how often and with what enthusiasm you've shared your disdain for her."

"Will I now?" Ed responded.

"We're terribly sorry for this mistake," Marney said. "Now that you have our explanation, we'd like to be on our way, and we promise never to trouble you again."

Yearning tugged at Virginia. She wanted to defy Marney, to tell Ed they wouldn't leave until he turned over a handwriting sample. But she didn't. Virginia looked to her friend, saw confidence where she felt none herself, and did what she rarely had the wherewithal to do: she reined herself in. She gave Ed a tight smile and a nod, then followed Marney out the door when he stepped aside to let them pass. Marney scooped Pancake up into her arms and gave Ed a final apology before he called them a choice word and slammed the door shut behind them.

"I can't believe we failed," Virginia said miserably. They began their walk down the hall, their steps heavy with disappointment. With each step, disappointment soured further, turning first to frustration and then anger. She turned to Marney and lashed out.

"You were supposed to keep watch. When you said you'd come with me, you said that someone had to keep watch. Then we wouldn't have been caught like that."

Marney looked stunned. "We only made it inside because of me. I'm supposed to be your golden key and then stand off to the side and let you have all the fun?"

"It would be a lot more fun," Virginia snapped, "if a lookout made sure we didn't wind up trapped in a room with a potential killer."

"Fine." Marney took a few steps ahead of Virginia and then turned to face her. "Next time, I'll keep watch. But if I was keeping watch, we wouldn't have these." The breath caught in Virginia's throat as Marney pulled up her cardigan to reveal a bundle of letters tucked into the waistband of her pants.

CHAPTER 16

Virginia's eyes were so focused on the letters Marney had stowed in her waistband that they didn't notice the man standing in the entrance to the hallway, and she plowed right into him. "I'm so sorry," she said, eyes wide and bracing for his reaction.

The man opened his mouth to respond, taking a gasping breath as if preparing to yell, but then his eyes fell on Marney, and his jaw snapped shut. Instead of yelling, he mumbled his own apology and shuffled along down the hallway.

"What was that about?" Virginia asked Marney as the two traversed the courtyard to her cottage.

Marney shrugged it off, shifting Pancake's leash from one hand to the other. "Martin's scared of me." The hint of a devilish grin shone on her face, and at the mention of his name, Virginia remembered seeing him at the Halloween party.

"He's the one with the thing for Nurse Kim? Who needed a lesson in keeping his hands to himself?"

"The very same."

Marney turned the key in the lock and Pancake ran inside ahead of the two of them. He paused long enough for Marney to remove his harness before hurrying to his food bowl and then retiring for a nap under Marney's bed.

Virginia tried not to look too expectant. It was all she could do not to hurry her friend along. When Marney finally pulled the letters out and set them on the dining table, Virginia reminded herself to breathe and move at a normal pace. She wanted to just start grabbing in a frenzy. Answers were right there in front of her, and she couldn't stand to waste a second.

Virginia and Marney each grabbed a letter, carefully unfolding them. Virginia's eyes scanned down her own, too excited to make sense of what she was seeing.

"This one was written by his wife," Marney said, disappointed. She set the letter to the side and picked up another.

"Mine, too," Virginia realized. It was a love letter, tender and tragic, from the wife who felt she had to stay away on the advice of a psychic but missed her husband, her partner in life, dearly. She set the letter aside and picked up another but could tell before it was even fully opened that it, too, was from his wife.

Next to her, Marney set aside the second, third, and fourth letters she picked up. Their pile was dwindling quickly and with it, Virginia's hope of proving Ed's involvement in Colleen's case.

"Hey," Marney said, barely more than a whisper. "This one's different." She slid the letter over so Virginia could see it, and they both leaned over and studied it. The handwriting was different, and as they scanned down the letter, Virginia's eyes sought the sign-off. She had to know if it was Ed's writing or just another letter he'd received from someone else. Marney, thinking similarly, flipped the paper. Their eyes landed on the letter's close.

All my love,

Ed

Virginia released the breath she had been holding. Here it was, the handwriting sample they'd gone looking for. She scanned back up the letter, triumph thrumming under her skin. It was a response to his wife, begging her not to send more letters. He poured his pained heart out on that page and then, it seemed, couldn't bring himself to send it.

As she read the letter, the triumph and glee drained from Virginia's body like air from the inflatable Halloween decorations on the lawn across the street, leaving her ghastly and deflated. Ed's handwriting was entirely unfamiliar to her. Ed didn't write Colleen's death threat.

* * *

TWO DAYS after their fateful break-in, Virginia and Marney were summoned to Hashim's office. They met in the lobby before knocking on the door, hands clasped in one another's as they waited to be invited inside.

"Come in," Hashim said. He gestured to two chairs facing his desk. One was an antique wooden chair with leather upholstery on the arms and seat. The other was one Virginia recognized from the dining room. It seemed Hashim rarely had more than one visitor at a time.

Marney took the dining chair, so Virginia took the other. The leather was smooth on her arms, and the seat depth was perfect, cradling the backs of her knees just right. She made a mental note to see if Hashim would sell it to her when she wasn't in trouble.

"Virginia," Hashim demanded, and her head snapped up. She'd been so enraptured that she hadn't heard what he had been saying. She looked over at Marney and saw her friend wide-eyed and worried.

"As I was saying," Hashim continued, "Ed Owens has come to me asking to be transferred to Harbor Vale. Since both Breeze Village and Harbor Vale are under my ownership, transfers are relatively simple, and he got lucky that there was a room available. Today is his last day at Breeze Village."

Virginia looked to Marney and back to Hashim, guilt pooling in her gut.

"My understanding is that Ed's desire to move comes from feeling unsafe here." Hashim's eyes bored into Virginia's. "Ed wouldn't come right out and say that you two broke into his room. If he had, you'd both be gone right now. But he said enough that I'm giving you a warning: one misstep and you're gone. Do you understand me?"

Virginia and Marney nodded like bobbleheads, and Hashim waved his hand, dismissing them.

As soon as they were back in the lobby with a closed door separating them from Hashim, Marney and Virginia turned to one another. They stepped forward and rested their foreheads against the other, faces inches apart. They trembled, fear and relief intertwining like the fingers they laced together, and they squeezed each other's hands in silence until they could find words.

"Ed didn't rat us out," Virginia finally choked out.

"I mean, he kind of did," Marney said, a laugh escaping around the tears that welled up. She pulled back and wiped the corners of her eyes. "But you're right. He could have gotten us kicked out, and he didn't."

"Not a killer and not vindictive enough to send us packing," Virginia marveled.

The gratitude the two felt toward Ed was short-lived. No sooner had he packed his bags and hauled his recliner off to Harbor Vale than Jan gave Virginia a call to let her know of the gossip about her spreading around Ed's new home.

"What is he saying?" Virginia wanted to know.

"Just that he had to relocate because Breeze Village wasn't a safe space. He's mostly on it about how the resident psychic is certifiable, but he's also talking about how she sicced her private investigator and her sidekick on him."

Virginia laid back on her bed, still holding the phone to her ear. Great. Enough of the senior population of Seaview knew about her that they'd recognize her as Colleen's investigator.

"The guy seems like a real jerk, though," Jan assured her. "I don't think anyone is taking him seriously."

A whiff of pity hung on Jan's tone, and Virginia felt heat color her cheeks. "Jan, I've got to go," she said.

With no other leads and two hours before her next

shift at work, Virginia decided to go down and have lunch, hoping to take her mind off her situation. She slipped her feet out of her slippers and into her sneakers, ran her fingers through her hair in the mirror, and then pulled open the door. Her hand flew to her chest and she let out an expletive, jumping back and nearly tripping over her coffee table.

"Colleen!" The psychic stood in her doorway, brows set hard and malice rolling off of her. She wore a gauzy maroon robe over black clothes, and her eyes blazed, half-obscured by untamed hair.

"Is now a bad time?" The words were razor-sharp, and Virginia took another step back, not confident that Colleen couldn't slice her up from afar with just her voice. "I'm kidding," Colleen said, stepping into the room and shutting Virginia's door behind her. "I know it's not." She gestured to her head as if to say her psychic abilities informed her of the convenience of the timing.

"Come in." Virginia's invitation was weak, and Colleen seemed to toss it aside as she planted herself on Virginia's glider chair and looked up at her.

"How's the investigation going?" Colleen asked.

Virginia, unsure how to respond, stuttered but failed to construct a phrase. She busied herself picking items up and moving them around, avoiding looking at the psychic.

"I understand you've cleared a suspect. I'd offer you congratulations, but I never thought Ed was a suspect. In fact, I handed you a list of several dozen suspects. Instead of investigating those, you went rogue. Now I'm still facing the vexing barrage of hauntings from the spirit realm, I'm no closer to knowing who is after me on this plane of the living, and gossip about me has spread to the halls of Harbor Vale."

Virginia's chest ached, and she waited for Colleen to continue, but the silence stretched on. "I'm sorry," she finally choked out.

"Good." Colleen nodded and stood, seemingly satisfied. "So you'll stick to the list, then?"

Virginia agreed, and Colleen was gone in a flash of maroon gauze.

CHAPTER 17

The crash of the waves and the bite of the cold water on Virginia's toes softened her pain in the way only another unpleasant sensation could. Her belly, throat, and chest were full of guilt and frustration and disappointment, but the soles of her feet cried out for her entire attention, and the rest of her loosened. She could pick up her feet at any moment. The freedom to leave gave her the will to stay. She sucked air through her teeth and shuffled out one step deeper so the previously untouched skin of her ankles felt the ocean's chill.

Her meditation was interrupted by the ping of her phone in her pocket, and she instinctively pulled it out and checked it without a thought. No sooner had her eyes scanned the notification than she wanted to chuck her phone into the water. But on a practical level, she needed it to remind her of her work shifts, medication schedule, friends' birthdays, and the few remaining bills that weren't on auto-pay. If she destroyed her phone, she'd have to get one of her kids to help her set up a new one, and the thought alone was enough to bring her to slide it gently back into her pocket. She took two more steps out into the water, the hem of her capri pants submerged now, then emerged and walked shivering to her car.

Three rounds of poker and a generous addition of dark liquor to her tea did little to take her mind off the nagging notification. When she'd done all else she could to avoid it—showered, dressed for bed, stared at the same page in her open book for twenty minutes—she finally brought her phone to her and opened it up.

From: Samantha Kelly <samiam@samtherealtorgenius.com>

Thank you SO MUCH for the info. I knew my Steffy had a refined palate. I should have guessed the town's most popular restaurant wouldn't be her thing. Luigi's it is! Any insight you can offer into her favorite dish??

Also, I wanted to check in with you about what you're planning to wear. I just want to make sure we don't clash in the photos. I'm torn between two dresses—when you get a chance, can you send me a photo of yours? It'll help me pick. Here are the two I'm torn between.

Two links stood between the rest of the email and the sign-off.

Thanks again! See you soon!! xxx Sam

Virginia clicked the first link. Her eyes nearly bugged out of her head at the price tag. It was a $700 dress, blush with a billowy pleated skirt and lacy three-quarter sleeves. It was lovely, but it sent Virginia's idea of wearing her usual capri pants and a nice but casual top up in smoke. She clicked the second link. The price was similar to the first, but the dress was bright magenta, knee-length, and form-fitting.

Virginia shoved the phone away and slid beneath the blankets. Replies to the email drafted themselves in her mind as she tossed, each one worse than the previous.

* * *

"WELL, you'll need to get the upper hand back somehow, that's for sure."

Virginia was in Gemma's cottage, standing in the kitchen where a massive pot of gumbo simmered on the stove, the smell and sound of slow bubbling stock making Virginia's mouth water. She and Gemma each had a glass of sweet tea in one hand, and Gemma had Virginia's phone in her other hand.

"I assume you weren't planning to buy a $700 dress for this occasion?" Gemma asked.

"That would be a 'no.'"

Gemma nodded, stared off into space in contemplation for a moment, then turned back to Virginia. "All right. We need a picture of you with Stephanie. One where you're dressed nice. Maybe from a night out, a fancy dinner?" Her face lit up and she said, "Oh, even better: one of her gallery showings. Do you have a picture from one of those?"

Virginia thought about it. She probably did, but she wasn't sure.

"There's no way you're going to wear anything like what Sam is talking about here. But instead of her making you feel bad for not having that kind of cash—or, let's be real, that kind of body—you're going to make her feel bad for not being the mother she wishes she was. You send a picture of you with Stephanie and say, 'I was thinking of wearing something more casual, like this outfit I wore to Stephanie's art show last year.'"

It was mean. It was petty. It was exactly what Virginia had hoped for when she went to Gemma for help. "You're an evil genius," she said. Gemma threw her head back in a deep belly laugh and handed the phone back to Virginia.

"Happy to help." She gestured to Virginia's glass and asked, "Need a refill?"

Virginia accepted, then moved from the small kitchen into the living room, planting herself on the velvet sofa. "I have another area where you might be able to help me."

Gemma raised an eyebrow and came to sit knee-to-knee with Virginia.

"You and Colleen are close," she started cautiously, gauging her friend's reaction to the subject. Gemma's face gave no clue as to her willingness to talk about Colleen, so Virginia continued. "Do you know how she's been doing lately?"

"Well, she's mad at you, for starters." Gemma's voice was teasing, but it still made Virginia's stomach ache to hear. "She's been a little on edge, maybe, but nothing crazy."

"Do you know of anyone at Breeze Village she's had a fight or disagreement with in the last few years? Has she mentioned anything like that?"

"Well, I've only lived here a few months. You know that."

"I mean, has she told you any stories of having a row with anyone in her time at Breeze Village? Besides Ed."

Gemma leaned back into the couch and laced her fingers behind her head. "You know about Colleen's little agreement with Genie, of course. Matt and Genie stole prescription medication from residents here so Matt could sell it on the street. And Matt gave Genie marijuana to sell to residents. Colleen was Genie's distributor, and for the most part, being the bearer of something that could help with chronic pain won her over to people here. At least, as far as I'm aware. That all came to an end in the spring with Genie's untimely death, of course."

Virginia nodded, eager for Gemma to continue.

"From what I've heard, there was one resident who didn't like that drugs were making the rounds in Breeze Village. I don't know his name, but he went to Michelle to try and get Colleen kicked out for dealing."

"He was unsuccessful, obviously," Virginia said, trying to speed Gemma along.

"Colleen hid the drugs, and Michelle took her side over the other resident. He died mad about it."

And there it was. Her next suspect was dead. Virginia fought to keep a neutral face and not display her disappointment. "Did anyone else at Breeze Village feel the same way as that resident?"

Gemma gave a grunt. "I'm sure they did. But I don't know of anyone specifically."

"And you're not still…?"

"No, ma'am. After Genie died, Colleen and I grew some just for ourselves. She was having awful visions, just a real terrible time of things with Russ and Liam around.

It threw her entire energy off. But we pulled the plants up a while back."

Virginia drained the rest of her tea and stood, thanking her friend. Gemma stood and wrapped her in a hug. "Let me know how the email goes over with Sam." Another barking laugh escaped her at the thought alone, and Virginia let out a nervous giggle.

She was closing the door to Gemma's cottage when motion in her periphery caught her eye. It was Marney waving her down from her own porch.

"I was just coming to find you!" she yelled. "I have news!"

CHAPTER 18

$\mathcal{M}$arney's "news" was that she'd received a pleading call from Lawrence asking her to bring Virginia to the farmers market to stage a chance meeting with his new beau. "You should have heard him," Marney said. "He was hiding in the bathroom, practically begging us to come. We're supposed to be at the beekeeper's booth at eleven to 'accidentally' run into them."

Virginia's heart swelled. Lawrence had been looking for love for months, but this was the first time he'd wanted them to meet someone he was dating. The two wasted no time heading across town to the only year-round farmers market in the area.

"Did he tell you anything more about this man of his?" Virginia asked, pulling her car into a narrow spot in the field the market used for a parking lot.

"He said they've been on four dates and that he just stayed overnight for the first time, and now Lawrence is panicking and wants us to meet him."

"Lawrence? Panicking?"

The ground beneath them was muddy and rutted, torn patches of grass laying lopsided along the soggy tire tracks. It squelched beneath them as they got out of the car and made their way to the market.

"I also wanted to let you know I found Ed's wife on Facebook, and I sent her a friend request," Marney declared.

Virginia stopped in her tracks. "You *what?*"

"I friended her. And she accepted. She's seriously into tarot cards, crystals, and fancy candles. She goes to a psychic weekly for readings. Her name is Lucinda—the psychic, not the wife—and she's a sham, according to all the online reviews."

"I'm still hung up on the fact that you sought out this woman online." Virginia hurried the few steps to catch up with Marney, nearly slipping on the mud.

"I felt bad about breaking into Ed's room and even worse about stealing his love letters. I want to try and fix things for him."

"What do you mean, 'fix things?'"

"Get them back together." Marney clutched her tote bag to her chest, and Pancake popped his head out, surprising Virginia.

"You brought the cat?" she asked.

"He wanted to come," Marney said simply, as if it were normal practice to bring one's cat to the market in a tote bag. "Anyway, Ed's wife is loyal to this sham psychic, and Lucinda's advice is the only reason she and Ed are split up. If I can convince Tina—that's Ed's wife—that Lucinda isn't a real psychic, maybe she'll let Ed move back in. Then I'll feel less guilty about the whole *burglary* thing."

The farmers market was bustling. The streets were blocked off on three sides of the field being used as a parking lot, and booths took up the full width of the street. In the summer, the market extended another block.

"How are you going to convince Tina that Lucinda's a fake?"

"I was hoping you could help with that."

"Me?" Virginia reeled.

"You help Colleen by figuring out who's pranking her—"

"Or who is legitimately trying to kill her."

Marney nodded, acquiescing. "Then, as a thanks, Colleen talks with Tina and convinces her not to trust Lucinda."

Virginia recalled Colleen's story of discrediting another psychic at a festival. She knew it was possible.

She picked out a stalk of Brussels sprouts, a favorite of Ronald's, and some plums for herself. Marney picked up a pomegranate. "I hardly know how to eat these," she said, sliding her change into her pocket, "but Dylan loves them."

Virginia started to ask after Dylan, curious whether she'd let slip any news on the investigations into Herman's or Irene's murders. Before she could open her mouth to ask, Marney let out a squeal and took off at a jog. Lawrence and a man, presumably his new beau, stood a handful of yards away, picking up jars of honey at the beekeeper's booth, and Marney flung herself at them, wrapping Lawrence in an embrace.

"What a surprise!" she cried. *Convincing,* Virginia thought.

When Marney's feet were back on the ground, Lawrence straightened his jacket and introduced them to the scruffy man beside him. "This is Douglass," he said. Not *my boyfriend* or *my friend* or *my anything*. Leaving it open to interpretation.

"You can call me Glass." The man extended his hand and Virginia shook it. His grip was limp, and Virginia resisted the urge to wipe her hand on her pants when he released it. *What kind of name is Glass?* She looked over to Marney, trying to make eye contact, but Marney evaded her and shook Glass's hand instead.

Pancake stuck his head out of her tote bag and Glass stepped back, surprised. He reached out to pet him, but the cat let out an uncharacteristic hiss and ducked back down into the bag. Glass grimaced, and Marney hugged the bag to herself protectively.

"So, Glass, are you from the area?" Virginia asked.

Glass shook his head. He had long, thinning hair, hanging in greasy curls down to his chin, and he wore dark, baggy clothes with visible wrinkles. Everything Lawrence was—neat, pristine, attentive toward his appearance—this man was the opposite. "I'm from Atlanta. Well, south of Atlanta. You know Blacksville?" Virginia and Marney both shook their heads, and Glass waved them off. "No matter. Anyway, I met Lawrence online and thought I'd come down for a few days to spend some time with him, see if I liked him as much in person as I did over the phone. I'm staying at the Hampton Inn on Waterford."

Now Marney met Virginia's glance, her face as shocked as Virginia felt. Then Glass went on. "Lawrence mentioned me staying with him next time, maybe while I look for a place in Seaview, so hopefully, I'll be seeing more of you two in the near future."

While Virginia's brain worked to compute what he'd just said, Marney sputtered, "You're moving in together?"

"It was just an idea," Lawrence cut in, "and it wouldn't be permanent."

"My landlord is terrible, and I've been looking to get out of there for a while," Glass said. "I don't have anything tying me to the Atlanta area, and at our age, is there any point in taking things slow?"

Neither Virginia nor Marney could conjure a response, so Lawrence stepped up. "We don't want to keep you, but let's set something up to get together soon. Maybe you can come over for dinner?"

Marney, ever quick to pull herself together, graciously agreed on both of their behalves, then practically tugged Virginia down the street until they were out of earshot.

"No," Virginia declared. "I don't like it."

"A hiss! Pancake hissed at him!" Marney seemed in disbelief at the idea.

"Moving in together? After four dates? Has Lawrence lost his damn mind?"

Marney went quiet. "It's really hard, putting yourself out there again for the first time after decades of being alone. And when that first relationship ends badly... Let's not say anything to Lawrence yet."

Virginia remembered the way Marney had lit up over Byron in the spring, and how much it hurt her when Virginia thought he could have been a killer. Marney understood more than Virginia could about what it would feel like if they told Lawrence he was mad for moving too fast with this new man. So Virginia agreed.

"Yet," she stipulated. "But I still don't like it."

Marney shook her head. "Neither do I. I'm not saying we can't look into the guy. I'm just saying we keep it to ourselves for a bit."

They headed for the car, Marney reaching down into her bag to stroke Pancake.

"Glass," Virginia muttered, and they both dissolved into a fit of laughter.

CHAPTER 19

When they returned to Breeze Village, Virginia spied her hallmate, the mahjong champion, welcoming family to visit her. Ms. Mahjong, as Virginia had taken to calling her, was grinning from ear to ear, little ones who had to have been her great-grand-children toddling underfoot while their parents tried to wrangle them for photos. As the last of the visitors signed in at the front desk and donned visitor's badges, Virginia had an idea. She brought her book down to read in the dining room, waiting until the lobby emptied out before approaching the desk.

"Hello, Anita," she said brightly. Anita had started working the front desk shortly before Virginia moved in, and she was warmth and welcome wrapped up in a no-nonsense package. She remembered the names of residents and visitors alike, greeting everyone with a smile and a hello in a Southern accent that made Virginia's heart glow. But if someone tried to sneak past her without signing the logbook, Anita wouldn't have it.

"Virginia," Anita said, returning the greeting. "How can I help you?"

"Do you have the visitor logs from Halloween?"

When Virginia had told Colleen she'd stick to the list, she'd meant it, but the conviction wore off shortly after Colleen left her room, and she was once again unconvinced that anyone from Colleen's distant past had it in for her now. She still wanted answers—who was the resident who'd tried to have Colleen evicted, and did anyone who was still alive at Breeze Village feel the same?—but while keeping alert for signs of potential foes within the community, she thought she should know who from outside had been within their walls when Colleen received her threat.

"I do," Anita said. Her right eyebrow shot up as if in a dare. *And? You want me to give them to you?*

"Would it be possible for me to see them?"

"Considering you show no sign of vision impairment, I would guess that, yes, that would be possible. But given that I am not at liberty to share them with you, I'd say it's unlikely you'll be in a position to do so." Anita's eyes gleamed, proud of her quip, and Virginia, though disappointed, couldn't help but grin.

Virginia reached into her bag and pulled out a slip of paper, then slid it across the desk toward Anita. "How about now?"

Anita looked down at the paper. It was a coupon from Piggly Wiggly—the employees got two each month, a major discount or free item—for a free basket of fried chicken tenders from the deli. Anita's deep brown eyes looked from the coupon to Virginia and back again. Then she straightened up, planted her hand over the coupon on the desk, and discreetly slid it toward herself while saying, "I apologize, but it's improper. I can't share the logs with you."

As she spoke, Anita flipped the pages of the log back, back, back, until the date across the top read October 31. She turned, busying herself with her computer, and Virginia looked around before bringing her face toward the book and studying the lines of names and signatures. She scanned frantically down the page, waiting for something to jump out at her, but she didn't recognize any of the names, and before she knew it, Anita was turning back around.

"How'd this get turned to the wrong page?" she asked innocently. She flipped the pages back and looked at Virginia. "Anything else?"

"Would... Would it be possible for me to take a picture of that page?"

Anita's eyebrows raised again as if to say *I don't know, would it?* Virginia reached into her bag and pulled out the second coupon for the month. A free half-gallon of ice cream. She slid it across the desk, and Anita muttered, "Huh, it's really breezy in here today," as she flipped the logbook back to Halloween.

Virginia pulled out her phone, glanced around to see whether anyone was coming, then hastily snapped a picture of the logbook. No sooner had the camera clicked than Anita snatched the book away, returned it to the proper page, and waved Virginia off.

Stepping into the elevator, Virginia looked down at the photo on her phone screen. She had a list of everyone who had come into Breeze Village on the day in question. Now she just needed to know which of them had it out for Colleen.

* * *

COLLEEN'S DOOR flew open before Virginia could knock. She would never get used to Colleen's predictive abilities.

"Come in," her voice beckoned from inside.

Before entering, Virginia took a breath to remind herself of her goals: see whether Colleen recognized any of the names on the visitor log or if she picked up on any strange energy from any of the names. After Gemma's reminder of how Russ's and Liam's energies completely threw Colleen off in the summer, Virginia also wanted to ask whether she felt anything new now.

Virginia moved into the room, phone ready to show Colleen the photo, when Colleen slapped a newspaper down on the coffee table and looked up at Virginia.

"What's this?" Virginia asked. Colleen, in answer, pointed to a letter to the editor. In the dim space, Virginia had to pick up the paper and hold it close to her face to read it. Her stomach dropped when she did. It was a letter from Ed, warning the good people of Seaview of the dangers of psychics. It called out Colleen by name, highlighting that she'd hired a wanna-be investigator to break into his room, then mentioned how the investigator and her sidekick had internet stalked his wife.

"Oh, no," Virginia murmured. She set the paper back on the table and looked sheepishly up at Colleen. "Colleen, I am so sorry."

"You were coming here in relation to your investigation." It wasn't a question, but Virginia nodded in answer anyway. "When we last spoke, you promised me to stick to the list of suspects I gave you."

Without a question or even an accusation, Virginia couldn't defend herself. Colleen just spoke facts, and Virginia sat in the shame of having lied and gone behind Colleen's back.

"My reputation is sullied. The spirits have only increased their efforts to warn me of danger since you began trying to help me. I need you to stop investigating altogether. I shouldn't have asked you in the first place."

The words felt like a slap to the face. "Are you sure?" Virginia didn't know whether it was her own pride or concern for Colleen's safety that made her want to continue the inquest.

"Positive," Colleen said.

"Look, Colleen, the article is bad, I agree, and I already apologized for looking into Ed. But this has got to be slander or libel or something illegal. We can talk to an attorney and go after him for damaging your reputation. My son can help us find someone."

Colleen shook her head, resolute in her decision. "I'm confident in the spirits' protection. The police are looking into the letter I received, but they don't seem convinced I'm in serious danger. I overreacted when I asked you to help me, and I am asking you now to stop trying to help."

Virginia couldn't argue any further. She swallowed the lump in her throat, nodded, and returned to her room, where she stared at the picture on her phone. She cross-checked the list of visitors against Colleen's list of suspects—no matches—before setting both aside and pulling the pillow over her head.

CHAPTER 20

All through work the next day, Virginia's mind was consumed by the thought of how to apologize to Colleen and win back her favor. She wanted to keep her safe—she told herself that was the top priority—but she also wanted to fix what she'd bungled with Ed and soothe the nagging guilt that had taken up residence in her gut. When all her brain power could only come up with one viable idea, she found herself knocking on Marney's cottage door with Colleen's original list in hand.

"What are you doing this evening?" she asked, holding the list aloft. Marney ushered her inside and poured them both tea.

"So these are all the people Colleen thinks might want her dead?" Marney asked, surveying the list. Virginia nodded. "But you don't think the killer is someone on this list?" Virginia cocked her head to the side, sucking her bottom lip in between her teeth.

"I just think they're all a bit too removed. I mean, who

wakes up one day and decides to murder someone they worked with thirty years ago?"

"Do you have any more ideas?" Marney wanted to know.

Virginia pulled out her phone and opened up the picture she'd taken of the visitor log. "These are all the people who visited Breeze Village on Halloween. Whoever slid the note under Colleen's door either lives here or is on this list."

Marney leaned in to read the names. "Or our violent criminal eschews more rules than just 'Don't kill people,' and didn't sign in at the desk."

Virginia gave Marney a hard look. "I've got little enough to go on without opening the possibilities up completely."

With a soft apology, Marney dragged two fingers across the screen to zoom in on the photo. "That's Diana's mom. She came to visit her daughter at work." She pointed to another name. "And that's, oh, what's his name? Lives on the third floor and only wears orange shirts? Anyway, that's his granddaughter." Marney identified a few other names, the list of unidentified visitors dwindling, and they turned their attention back to Colleen's list.

"I just feel bad," Virginia said. "And Colleen seems so sure whoever is behind this is on this list."

"You started with the *A* names, I assume?" Marney asked. "Because of the, erm, the mutilations?"

Virginia nodded. "There are only two left I haven't checked, but I didn't definitively rule out most of the others I looked into."

"I wonder if the *A* stands for something besides the killer's initial," Marney speculated.

The two worked their way down the list, crossing off the names of people who had died since Colleen knew them. For the ones still living, if they lived more than four hours from Seaview, they noted them as unlikely suspects, only to be revisited later if the rest of the list lacked anyone more promising. For the few who seemed to be located nearby, Virginia turned them over to Marney to find them on social media and see if she could glean anything there. "See if they posted anything from Halloween or the dates of the other two murders," Virginia told her. "If they have an alibi."

They were losing steam when Virginia ran a search for Jenson Haider. Recently relocated to Charleston, South Carolina, he was an attorney. Colleen had noted him as one of the people associated with her taxi cab restaurant business. Near the bottom of the first page of search results, Virginia found an article recounting how his law firm had represented a client suing Colleen in connection to the business and lost.

The client sued for damages and lost wages after he spilled his dinner on his Armani suit, turned up late to an important meeting, and was let go thanks to his tardiness and unprofessional appearance. The man blamed it all on the reckless driving of the cab operator. Colleen represented herself—a foolish decision, by all accounts—and won. It was Mr. Haider's first loss in court. And now, as of this summer, he lived only two hours from Seaview.

"Check this guy out," she said, showing Marney the article. As she scanned down it, she nodded appraisingly.

"We've got to give this guy a call," Marney said.

"Call him?" Virginia hadn't reached out to any of the suspects yet. She'd asked Marney to find them on social media, but that was it.

"Everyone else we've looked into is either dead, lives far away, or lives nearby but has for years. This guy only moved down South a couple of months ago. It seems more likely that someone with a grudge moved nearby and finally has their chance to get revenge than someone with a grudge has lived nearby for years and just finally snapped."

Virginia still wasn't sure, and Marney conceded, "It's probably better just to pass this along to the police. They'll be in a better position to call up and interview potential suspects, anyway." The hint that she couldn't do it and a spot of liquid courage were all it took for Virginia to dial the numbers of Haider's Charleston law firm. Marney gave her a thumbs-up while she listened to the ringback tone.

Finally, "You've reached the offices of Brody, Spinner, and Pine, attorneys at law. How may I help you?" The voice on the other end was female. She sounded young and quick, speaking with precision.

"Hello, I'm looking for Mr. Jenson Haider."

"Of course, give me one moment. Who should I tell him is calling?"

"Erm, Virginia Walker," she said. She grimaced at Marney, who gave her another thumbs-up, then waited with bated breath to see whether Haider would take the call.

A moment later, she heard low voices on the other end

of the line, and then, "Hello, this is Jenson Haider speaking." Virginia perked up, thrilled that he answered but suddenly at a loss for words. "Hello?" he repeated when she said nothing.

Marney nudged her, and Virginia responded, "Hi, erm, hello, Mr. Haider. My name is Virginia Walker. I was hoping to ask you a quick question." She regretted not coming up with a story, a plan, ahead of time.

"Is this about Irene?" Mr. Haider sounded weary on the other end, as if this was his third time that day receiving the same question.

"Irene?" Virginia asked, puzzled. Her brain whirred, working to put the puzzle pieces together until they finally fit. "Irene Pushton? Murdered in Seaview?"

"You didn't tell me what news outlet you're from, Ms. Walker, but my answers aren't changing. Yes, Irene was a partner at my New York law firm. Yes, we had a romantic relationship that ended badly shortly after we relocated to Charleston and shortly before she relocated to Seaview. No, I didn't kill her. I was at work at the time of the murder, and several secretaries and paralegals can confirm that alibi. Now, I must be—"

Virginia cut him off before he could hang up. "Wait! I wasn't calling about Irene. I'm sorry."

"You weren't?" She couldn't tell if Haider sounded relieved or disappointed.

"I was calling about Colleen, um..." With a sinking feeling, she realized she didn't know Colleen's last name. "A woman named Colleen who ran a restaurant in the taxi cabs of New York in the early aughts."

The line was quiet as Virginia assumed Mr. Haider's

own brain whirred, putting the puzzle pieces together. "I'm afraid I don't understand," he said finally.

"You and Colleen went to trial in 2003. You were representing an investment banker who was recently let go after a bad experience in Ms., err, Colleen's restaurant. She represented herself and won."

"I'm sorry, I don't remember." His answer was swift and told her that he absolutely did remember.

"Where were you on Halloween?" she asked.

Mr. Haider sputtered, then asked, "What is this about?"

"Colleen has been threatened recently. I'm investigating people she thinks may want to hurt her."

"I don't remember Colleen. As you said yourself, that was a long time ago. And I don't appreciate being called up and questioned. On Halloween, I was hanging art in my new apartment. I hired someone to help me with the larger works, and if the police request it, I can probably find his name and number to vouch for me. As for you," he spat, "I'd appreciate it if you didn't contact me again."

The line abruptly went dead, and Virginia set the phone down. She felt heavy and guilty, but when she looked up at Marney, her friend was grinning broadly.

"That was a success!" she said. Virginia gave her a questioning look and she went on. "We know Irene was a partner at the law firm that sued Colleen and lost. We know she was cheating on her husband with Mr. Haider. These are *clues*, Virginia. You can't get hung up on the fact that someone didn't like you calling and asking questions. You're an investigator, remember? No one likes being questioned by investigators, but everyone likes when you crack the case wide open. Well, everyone except the killer, I suppose."

Virginia narrowed her eyes at Marney. "When did you get so supportive of my investigative career?"

"When it became clear it was something you were going to do whether I supported it or not."

CHAPTER 21

Virginia showed up to work tired the next morning. The opening shift was always slow. You had the people who waited outside and rushed in to buy milk or bread or the cupcakes their child neglected to mention they needed to bring to school until the night before, and then it was empty until mid-morning.

After her phone call with Mr. Haider the night before, she and Marney had continued down the list. As exciting as it was to find a connection between Colleen and another of the murder victims, and even though Haider was the most promising suspect they'd found yet, he had an alibi, so their search continued.

After a few duds, they enlisted Pancake's help. They plopped him on the table and said, "Who's next?" and he put his paw on a name. They played like this for a bit, but everyone Pancake chose was dead, so after a bit, they decided to call it. Still, Virginia lay in bed awake most of the night, thinking of Haider's alibis, dependent on the word of people in subordinate positions to himself. She thought of the connection between Irene and Colleen, then went down the Google rabbit hole searching for connections between either of them and Herman Walsh, the other victim.

Her hunt was unsuccessful, though it took most of the night, and through her slow opening shift Virginia was groggy, only half-present. When her lunch break came around, she spent it in her car, napping. She returned to work more alert and ready for the last few hours of her shift, but when she walked into the store, she could feel the tension. Several cashiers and managers were gathered around one of the registers, and one of her co-workers, a young woman taking a year off between high school and college, was in tears, her head in her hands.

"What's going on?" Virginia asked, stepping forward and putting her hand on the girl's back.

When her response was indecipherable, another of their coworkers pulled Virginia aside and said the girl had just found out she'd been conned out of a hundred bucks on her last shift. A scammer had come through her line when things were busy, buying just a bottle of dish soap. He paid with a $100 bill and pulled a trick on her, so she unwittingly gave him back the $100 bill along with $97 in change from buying the soap.

"It's on camera," she wailed. "I can't believe I did that!"

The coworker said their manager had called her into his office and showed her the security footage where she could be clearly seen handing him back his bill and then counting out his change.

"Are the police going to catch the guy?" Virginia asked her manager before returning to her register.

"For a hundred bucks?" The manager laughed and shook his head. "No. The police aren't going to go after this guy at all. We're printing out his photo to paste up at all the registers, but it's not great. I don't have high hopes we'll identify him."

Virginia looked over to where the girl was inconsolable. "I can investigate," she said, looking back to her manager. "I'm a private investigator."

She'd hardly uttered the words before her manager was shaking his head. "That won't be necessary. I don't want us to kick off a whole investigation and scare off regular, law-abiding customers. It's a hundred bucks, barely a drop in the bucket."

When Virginia returned to her register, flipping her light on to signal that she was back from her break and open for customers, she saw the manager go over and console the girl. Then the girl headed outside to collect carts in the parking lot.

"She can't be on the register for a month," one of her coworkers said when they had a break in the flow of customers through their lines. "Carts and bag duty only. Poor thing."

When Virginia went to leave the store two hours later, she passed the girl on her way out. The girl waved Virginia down, jogging the few steps to close the distance between them. "Virginia, right?"

Virginia nodded and looked down at the girl's name tag. *Eliza.* Their shifts often overlapped, but they'd rarely spoken. Still, Eliza knew Virginia's name, and Virginia felt a short stab of guilt that she hadn't remembered Eliza's.

"I heard you offer to look for the guy who scammed

me." Eliza's voice wavered toward the end, and she sniffled before going on. "I just wanted to say thanks."

Her swollen eyes and blotchy red face stayed with Virginia throughout dinner and cards with Ronald and Patricia. She retold the story to them, and Ronald got more riled up than she expected.

"I just can't believe there are folks out there that would do that. Just takin' advantage of people at their jobs like that. It's awful!"

"The worst part," Virginia said, "is that the guy is just on the loose to keep scamming people. The manager said police won't care for that amount of money."

Patricia shook her head. "What about you? Are you going to try to hunt the guy down?"

Virginia was caught off guard and her poker face betrayed her. Ronald cleaned up, scooping her quarters toward himself, and dealt out the next hand. "My manager told me not to," Virginia said. "He doesn't want to scare off regular customers."

"Virginia Walker, listening to authority figures," Ronald marveled. "Some thought we'd never see the day!"

THE HARSH RING of Virginia's phone roused her from a deep sleep. Startled, she shot up, disoriented in the dark. She didn't remember turning her ringer up so loud. A glance at her bedside clock told her it was eleven, sending her into a panic that she'd overslept and was missing Stephanie's baby shower. She answered the phone, throwing her legs over the side of the bed.

"Jack," she breathed into the receiver. "I'm up. I'm awake. I'm so sorry. I'll be there in fifteen minutes."

"Hello?" A voice that was definitively not her son sounded perplexed on the other end of the line. "Is this Virginia Walker?"

"Yes." She tried to slide her feet into slippers, but they weren't there. She flipped on the light and squinted into the brightness, blinking until her eyes adjusted and she spied her slippers across the room. *Weird.*

"This is Dan Armstead, Eliza's father. I apologize for calling so late. It sounds like I may have woken you."

So late? Virginia looked back at the clock, then out the window into the darkness. The moon was shining brightly overhead, casting a silvery glow over the trees, their branches more visible as they began to shed their leaves. It was still evening, she realized.

Relief cascaded over her with such force that she felt momentarily dizzy. She wasn't going to miss the baby shower. It was still evening.

"Hello?" The man on the other end sounded impatient, his voice dragging Virginia the rest of the way into the present.

"Sorry," she said breathily. "What's this about?"

"Our daughter told her mother and me about what happened at work. She feels horrible, absolutely violated, and I think it's unconscionable that someone could do this and get away with it." Virginia's brain struggled to keep up as he spoke. "Eliza said you're an investigator and that you offered to go after the con artist. Her mother and I wanted to call you and ask you about your rates so we could take you up on it."

"Oh, I…" Virginia didn't know how to respond. She'd never charged for her investigative services before. In fact, she'd had to fight to be allowed to investigate in the first place.

"We were thinking five hundred dollars plus whatever fees you incur over the course of your investigation."

Virginia's eyes sprung open, and she held back a laugh. Was he joking? The man had only stolen a hundred bucks, and not even from Eliza personally, and her parents were offering Virginia five times that to investigate?

"If that's too little, we're willing to negotiate," Dan said.

"No, that's… that's my rate exactly," Virginia coughed out.

"Fantastic. Can you have a report in a week?"

Virginia agreed, eager to end the unexpected phone call. As soon as she set the phone down, she wondered if it had been a dream. In case it wasn't, she grabbed a notepad from her end table and wrote *DISH SOAP SCAMMER—REPORT, ONE WEEK*. She'd need to figure out what sort of report investigators usually wrote up, she decided, since all her investigative work so far had culminated in dramatic arrests without requiring a report.

Underneath, she added the other investigations on her plate.

COLLEEN—IRENE LAW FIRM?

MARNEY CROCHET COMPETITOR

DOUGLASS

The list immediately overwhelmed her, so she flipped the pad over and crossed the room to pour herself a glass of juice from her mini fridge. She opened the door and was surprised to find a slice of cake inside. A single slice, sitting on a small dessert plate.

Baffled, she shut the fridge door and started to return to bed. As she crossed the room, the lights flickered three times. Her confusion began to feel a bit like fear, and with a quick check that her alarm was set, she pulled the covers over her head. Everyone knew ghosts couldn't get you under the covers.

CHAPTER 22

Virginia sat in her car in the Breeze Village parking lot for ten minutes working up the nerve to turn the key in the ignition and drive to Jack's and Stephanie's house for the baby shower. It was a breezy day, chilly enough to really feel like November. After a few minutes, Cece emerged from Breeze Village and hurried to her own car, her arms full of bubble mailers. Her SUV was parked next to Virginia's, and when she spied Virginia in the car, she jumped, startled, and dropped her packages.

"I'm sorry to scare you," Virginia said, stepping out of her car to help pick up the dropped parcels. "What's all this?"

"Oh, gifts for the grandkids," Cece said. "Are you okay? What were you doing, sitting in your car?"

Virginia made an excuse, muttering about listening to a program on the radio, and was relieved when Cece didn't question it.

When she was alone again, she surveyed herself in the

tiny mirror on the back of the sun visor. Her hair was set in perfect rows of curls. Her lipstick and blush made her look lively. She felt uncharacteristically put together and hoped it made her look every bit the character she was trying to put on.

She was relieved to find she felt like a whole person after the previous night's interruption. When she woke, she thought she'd dreamed the entire thing, but a glance at her notepad confirmed she'd written a list, whether the phone call was imagined or not, and when she pulled open her mini fridge there was, indeed, a slice of cake inside. She'd donned the outfit she'd worn to Stephanie's first solo gallery showing a few years before. It was a navy set: loose pants with rhinestones around the hem and a long matching jacket. She wore it over a white linen tunic top and added bright, colorful jewelry.

She'd halfway convinced herself to turn around just as she was pulling up. In her mind, all she could see was disappointment in the eyes of her children. Stephanie would be over-the-moon thrilled to have Sam there. Why did Virginia need to be there at all?

Just as the torrent of negative self-talk nearly compelled her to turn the car around and make a bee-line back to Breeze Village, she heard a muffled squeal through the rolled-up car windows. "Virginia!" And there was Stephanie, barefoot and running across the front lawn to greet her.

"You look amazing," Virginia said. It was true. Her daughter-in-law was glowing. "Where are your shoes?"

Stephanie wrapped her arms around Virginia before she'd even extracted herself from her car. "They're inside," she laughed, "but I just couldn't wait to see you. Both my moms in one place! It's a dream come true!"

Virginia's throat constricted. She hoped her smile looked genuine. She followed Stephanie inside to where a small crowd was gathered. Jack greeted her at the door with a hug and a kiss on the cheek, then offered her juice and champagne. Lucy followed on his heels, a champagne flute in one hand and a baby bottle in the other. "Rum punch," she said when Virginia raised a questioning eyebrow.

Pink and white streamers hung from the doorways, and a balloon arch framed a chair in the living room beside a table overflowing with gifts. Virginia was taking in the scene, slowly making her way to the kitchen and promised champagne, when she heard a voice she thought she'd never hear again in her lifetime.

"Grandma!" Across the room, emerging from the hallway, Sam beamed and pointed a finger at Virginia as if to say *I'm coming for you.*

Virginia winced, not expecting the first person to call her "Grandma" to be someone she regarded with such distaste.

"It's good to see you," she lied, accepting Sam's embrace. "The decorations look wonderful." That was true. Every aspect of the décor was tasteful, enough to transform the space without being over-the-top.

Virginia guided them toward the kitchen as Sam gushed over her friend from the gym who helped her plan the decorations. She graciously accepted a champagne flute from Sam, but the moment she held it up to offer a cheers, Sam spied another friend and brought her over.

"Virginia, this is my friend Heather. Heather's a surgeon. She knew me back when I was at my worst. She helped care for Stephanie on a few occasions."

The woman's plump lips formed a smile, but the rest of her face remained unmoving. It was as devoid of emotion as it was of wrinkles and fine lines. "It's been one of my great joys in life to see Samantha remake herself and now to see her become a grandmother! Oh, I am just thrilled." She didn't look thrilled. She looked bored.

"Virginia is Jack's mother, of course."

"Is it as exciting when you have other grandkids?" Heather asked. Her voice lilted up at the end though her face displayed no curiosity.

"I don't have any other grandchildren," Virginia said. Heat colored her cheeks and she found herself looking down at her shoes, clunky clogs compared to Heather's Louboutins.

Heather raised a hand to her chest in a theatrical gesture of embarrassment. "I'm so sorry. I just assumed..."

"It's all right." Virginia shifted uncomfortably from one foot to the other.

Sam cleared her throat. "Virginia is quite the mother. She'll be an excellent grandmother. I'm jealous of how close she lives! She's in Breeze Village."

"How lovely," Heather said.

"I can't imagine how nice it must be to be able to pop in whenever you want," Sam opined.

Her cheeks prickled with sweat as Virginia took a long sip of champagne and cleared her throat. "Well, I can't just stop in whenever. Jack and Stephanie have busy lives." Sam and Heather nodded, unconvinced. "And I've got quite a lot going on myself. I work down at the Piggly Wiggly a few days a week. I've taken up Pilates." Her words didn't even convince herself. Reaching for something that would catch their attention, she said, "I'm also a private investigator. I'm looking into the murders of Irene Pushton and Herman Walsh."

Heather and Sam did raise their eyebrows at this last remark, but instead of asking Virginia questions or going on about how impressive she was, how they had no idea she was working on something so important, they exchanged wary glances at each other and then made a production of waving at someone else across the room. "Please excuse us," Sam said, and then they were gone.

CHAPTER 23

Marney and Lawrence were united in their advice to forget Sam and Heather, to apologize to Colleen, and to share what she'd learned with the police before letting go of the investigation.

"It's wearing you down," Marney said, her eyes soft and sad as she took in Virginia's haggard appearance over their lunch together.

"Sam and Heather are irrelevant, and you certainly don't need to be solving crime to be worthy of love and celebration," Lawrence added. "But I agree with Marney. You don't seem happy anymore. You seem tired."

Virginia stuffed another french fry in her mouth and chewed slowly. The only words she could think of were "yes, but," and she didn't have anything convincing to follow up the "but." *Yes, but I'll be embarrassed to give up. Yes, but I don't want to be a failure. Yes, but Colleen is still in danger, and I don't trust the police to keep her safe.*

"How's Glass?" she asked instead. It was Lawrence's turn to squirm a little.

"He's good. We're good. He's coming down again for the Harvest Festival."

Seaview held a Harvest Festival every November. It was part farmers market, part craft festival, part fair. Vendors sold heavy, greasy foods; a Ferris wheel and a smattering of other rides attracted children and teens; local home cooks competed for best chili and best baked goods, and local gardeners competed to grow the largest vegetables. It was one of the town's biggest events, and Virginia had forgotten it until Lawrence's mention. When she lived in Grove Park, she'd see them setting up days ahead of time, but she hadn't had any reason to drive by there this year.

"Are you going to have a booth?" she asked Marney. Her friend nodded and offered a sad smile.

"I sure am. My online sales have been abysmal since Crochet Dreams started stealing my product photos and selling the same things for less. It's just so disheartening."

Virginia's chest tightened. She had no idea who was behind the shop undercutting Marney. And she had no idea how to find out. It was yet another investigative arena where she was in over her head and entirely unhelpful.

"Everyone does their Christmas shopping at the Harvest Fest," Lawrence said. "I'm sure you'll clean up. When people lay eyes on a Marney Richards original, they'll never buy from some cheap competitor again."

When they parted, all three seemed to be forcing faked happiness. Marney pretended to be bolstered by their friends' assurances around her store. Lawrence pretended to be at ease about bringing Glass around again. And

Virginia pretended to be ready to let go of her investigation. But a current of unease ran underneath the surface as they said their goodbyes.

For Virginia's part, she tried to take her friends' advice to heart. She couldn't refute that she'd bungled things for Colleen and was no longer welcome investigating. But she didn't want to just cut and run and hope time smoothed things over between them.

Over a cup of spiked tea, when her anxiety had kept her up well past her bedtime, Virginia decided to prepare her first investigative report. She recalled Eliza's dad asking for a report on the man who'd scammed their daughter at work, and she thought that if she was going to abandon Colleen's investigation, the least she could do was to put together a report of everything she'd learned. She hoped the report, along with a heartfelt apology for the damage she'd done, would be enough to win Colleen over.

She spent the two evenings before the festival working on the report, torn between feeling like a solid investigator as the document grew and feeling like a quitter and a failure for giving up on the investigation. "This is for Colleen," she reminded herself every time she wanted to quit.

On the morning of the festival, Virginia woke with a stomach ache. She and Lawrence had agreed to go early with Marney to help her set up. She downed a cup of coffee despite knowing it was the last thing her nervous stomach needed, then made her way to Marney's cottage to help her load up her car.

Marney's booth was about as far from Colleen's as it

could be, and Virginia was grateful as they set up. When the band started playing, officially opening the festival to the public, Marney made three sales within the first song. To see relief on Marney's face inspired a degree of confidence in Virginia.

"It'll be fine," Lawrence said, nudging her side and winking when he caught Virginia staring off toward Colleen's booth. "She asked you to step back. You're offering her information she doesn't have. She's going to appreciate it."

Virginia wasn't so sure. Colleen's entire list of suspects hinged on the idea that people might be willing to kill over a grudge they'd been holding onto for decades. What did that say about Colleen's views of grudges and forgiveness?

Her heart beat wildly as she weaved her way through the growing crowd, a third rhythm in her ears along with her footsteps and the band's music. The chaos felt disorienting, and she focused on her breathing, trying to stretch each breath in and out to four counts. She shifted the pages of her report from one hand to the other, trying to avoid permanently marking the pages by gripping them too tightly in nervous, sweaty hands. They flapped in the breeze, which strengthened as the morning wore on.

With the sounds of her steps, her pulse, the wind, and the band's frenetic jig swirling together in her ears, and her focus on slowing her shallow, quick breaths, Virginia walked right past Colleen's booth without realizing. It was only when she saw the roadblocks marking the end of the festival that she realized her mistake and turned around, spotting the psychic's table nearby.

Colleen was set up inside a deep purple tent, fabric loosely draped over the tent frame to form an enclosure. Tassled ties pulled back the fabric on the fourth side, and a table with a crystal ball was visible through the entrance. Virginia could just make out Colleen sitting behind the table, shuffling a deck of cards. A scarf was wrapped around her head, and she swayed back and forth before shouting, "Enter!" and welcoming the first person from a rapidly-forming line into the tent. For a woman who scorned the perception of psychics as con artists and grifters, she was whole-heartedly playing up the theatrics for her patrons.

The first person in line stepped into the tent, and Colleen stood to release the tie-backs and let the curtain fall closed, sealing off the booth from view while she performed her reading. Virginia moved toward the line, which was already five people deep.

Behind her, she heard a shuffle and a man shouted, "Hey!" She turned to see the man wiping at his newly-soaked sweater with his hands, another man holding an empty cup and apologizing profusely. She turned to look back to where she was walking but tripped over the thick cables running from the bandstand to the speakers. In an instant, she went sprawling, the pages of her report flying through the air, and landed atop a cloaked figure who was waiting in line to see Colleen.

"I'm sorry," she said at the same time the person beneath her yelled, "Argh!"

She pushed herself up onto her knees, then to her feet, but when she made to offer the other person her hand and help them up, the figure was already on their feet and running away. Confused, Virginia watched as their dark cloak floated behind them until they had passed the road-block and turned the corner out of sight.

"Is that yours?" Another woman standing in line pointed to where an object glinted on the ground, just where she and the figure had been moments before. Virginia knelt to see what it was, then recoiled in shock when she saw the sharp edge of a knife gleaming back at her.

CHAPTER 24

"You literally stopped a killer." Marney was finishing crocheting a pair of moose-shaped slippers while Virginia chopped vegetables for Dylan's favorite soup. She had been working overtime since Virginia's encounter at the Harvest Festival, and Marney wanted to bring her something nutritious to sustain her but was booked with orders after her booth at the festival.

"Accidentally," Virginia added.

After Virginia's accident in front of Colleen's booth, police collected the knife and found dried blood between the blade and the hilt. When they tested samples against DNA from Irene Pushton and Herman Walsh, they came back as conclusive matches. The knife left by the mysterious cloaked figure at the festival was the knife that killed both Herman and Irene. It was no longer speculation: Seaview had a serial killer on the loose.

Virginia couldn't cling to Marney's theory that the

letter Colleen received was a hoax anymore, either. Whoever was hiding under that cloak had gone to the festival to kill Colleen. And they would probably have succeeded if not for immaculate timing and poor cable management.

"Still," Marney insisted. "You prevented a murder. You saved Colleen's life." Virginia glanced over to see her friend looking at her earnestly and felt tears prickle her eyes. She turned back to the cutting board in front of her, swallowing down the emotion.

"I just wish I'd stopped them," she said softly.

In the nights since the festival, pride and relief had been tempered with regret. She'd lucked into accidentally committing what would probably be the most heroic act of her life, and yet the threat was still at large. The fingerprints on the knife didn't match any of the fingerprints in the databases the police had access to. They were no closer to catching the killer. Colleen was still alive but no safer than she'd been before.

Marney set her work down and came to stand beside Virginia. "I went to see Tina yesterday," she said.

"Who?"

"Ed's wife." Marney spoke with an intentionally casual tone that set off Virginia's alarm bells. Before Virginia could object, however, Marney plowed on. "She, by the way, loved Pancake. Absolutely adored him! And Pancake took right to her. Not like Glass. Anyway, I went to see her at her home, and it's all very clear, exactly like I thought. She's a woman still madly in love with her husband after decades of partnership, led astray by a quack psychic whose primary concern is money, not the truth, and certainly not the wellbeing of her clients."

Virginia resumed chopping vegetables, waiting for Marney to continue. The rhythmic sounds of the knife thunking on the wooden cutting board soothed her.

"Tina is open to talking with another psychic," Marney said. "She doesn't feel that Lucinda has ever led her astray, but the distance with Ed is rough on her, and I think part of her hopes that it could be a mistake."

"You want me to try to convince Colleen to talk with Tina." Dread pooled in Virginia's stomach. Colleen and Virginia hadn't spoken since the festival. Virginia had given her the report, but though the report had been intended to close out her involvement in the investigation, she felt that she couldn't very well step away now when the threat was more real than ever. Colleen hadn't said anything in response, and Virginia didn't even know whether Colleen was grateful for Virginia stopping the killer, or upset that Virginia hadn't actually caught them. She wasn't eager to go to Colleen asking for a favor.

"I do," Marney said with a nod. "But first, I have to convince Tina to talk with Colleen."

Virginia turned to Marney quizzically. "I thought you said Tina was ready to talk with another psychic."

"She is, but she's also heard Ed's ravings against Colleen specifically. She's hesitant to bring her into the mix, but obviously, I don't have a host of other psychics I can turn to."

Virginia didn't respond. A lump in her throat threatened to turn her into a sobbing mess if she tried to speak, so she reached over to grab a stalk of celery and continued chopping.

Marney stepped closer, placing her hand on Virginia's back. "I'm sorry. I shouldn't have brought this up yet. You've been through a lot recently."

Virginia shook her head. "No, it's fine," she insisted. "I'll talk to her."

She could feel Marney brighten beside her, sense her standing just a touch taller. When she looked over, Marney was beaming. "Thank you." She practically skipped across the room to return to her crochet, and her joy melted some of the dread Virginia was feeling. Enough that Virginia could manage a smile herself.

RONALD COULD ALWAYS SENSE when Virginia was distracted. He could tell when she needed a friend and a distraction in their games of cards and when she needed a victory. But he never dialed himself back to let her win. He just dialed back the jokes a bit when she was feeling low.

On this afternoon, he was on a roll. Virginia thought she must look even worse than she felt because he'd hardly boasted at all. "Do I look like I'll fall apart if you poke fun at me?" she asked.

Ronald looked up from where he was shuffling the cards and appraised her before answering. "You don't look like you've got a lot of room for people to say mean things, even in jest. You look like you've been hearing enough of that in your own head."

It was the last thing she expected him to say, and she nearly burst into tears on the spot.

"Which is crazy, by the way," he continued. "You being mean to yourself. You stopped a killer and saved someone's life. You deserve congratulations."

He dealt out the next hand and Virginia peered at her cards. "By accident. I stopped a killer *by accident,* and I saved someone's life *for now.* I didn't catch them. They're still out there."

Ronald set his own cards down and looked at Virginia intently until she returned his gaze. "You have a gift, Virginia, for being in the right place at the right time. You have a natural instinct. You always find yourself where you need to be when you need to be there, even if you have to get it wrong a few times on the way, and you really ought to let yourself enjoy this moment of victory. Sure, there's still danger out there. But you *saved someone's life.* Not everyone gets to do that."

Virginia couldn't speak, but Ronald didn't hold out for a response. He resumed playing, now with a few more barbs when he beat her. After two more rounds he said, "Jimmy asked me to thank you, by the way. He's quite enjoying Ed's absence. I'm not sure the folks at Harbor Vale would have such positive things to say." He shook with laughter, and Virginia glared at him.

"I'm so glad he's enjoying the aftermath of my poor decision-making."

Ronald grinned broadly, exposing his gums, teeth occupying only about half the spaces where teeth normally went. But he did it so unselfconsciously that

Virginia thought it was one of the most beautiful smiles she'd seen.

"I just think maybe you miss some of the bright sides of your mistakes."

"I'm so glad my buffoonery has such silver linings," Virginia said acerbically.

Ronald cleared his throat. "In all seriousness, I think you don't give yourself enough credit. And I think if you keep investigating, it's only a matter of time before you crack the case wide open."

Virginia squirmed in her seat under the praise. "You think so?" Her voice sounded tiny and childish in her ears, but instead of mocking her, Ronald nodded gravely. Before she knew what she was doing, she pulled out her phone and showed him the picture of the visitor log from Halloween.

"What's this?" he asked.

"Someone was in Colleen's room on Halloween. This is the list of everyone who signed in at the front desk that day. Do you recognize any of the names?"

Like Marney, Ronald recognized a few of the names, and Virginia made a note of them. "If you haven't already, you should talk with her neighbor. Harriet doesn't get out much. Maybe she heard something."

In the same breath, Ronald revealed his hand and let out a whoop at defeating Virginia yet again.

When she finally emerged from the elevator and reached the door to her room, Virginia couldn't put a name to her emotions. There were too many: pride, regret, gratitude, shame, and fear. But when she pushed open the door and laid eyes on the slip of paper waiting for her on the carpet, only the latter remained. Familiar handwriting glared up at her.

A DETOUR? WHAT FUN. THE PSYCHIC WILL HAVE TO WAIT.

YOU'RE NEXT.

—A

CHAPTER 25

The last time Virginia had set foot in her daughter's home had been during the height of summer, spending a week at Lucy's to give Jack and Stephanie some time alone while they housed her. She'd had nowhere to go, having sold her house to the developers without an open room at Breeze Village.

Where Jack and Stephanie had bought a house in a nice neighborhood, decorated for the holidays, and lived out their version of Virginia's own life, Lucy had been living in an apartment for the better part of two decades. When she'd had a housewarming, Virginia had expressed confusion; it wasn't a house, after all, but a two-bedroom apartment with no yard and no place for children to run and play. Jack had given her an exasperated look and told her she didn't "get it." She kept waiting for Lucy to move, to say she was finally settling down and buying a house, but that day never came, and eventually, she stopped waiting.

Now she was here because she knew she couldn't keep the threat to herself, but Lucy was the only one she thought might not entirely flip out at the news. Marney was traumatized enough from Virginia's past escapades putting her in danger. Jack and Stephanie were bringing a new life into the world and didn't need something else to worry over. But levelheaded Lucy could tell her what to do.

"Mom?" Virginia hadn't warned Lucy that she was coming over. If she had, Lucy would have known something was up. She'd have worried and called Jack, and Virginia's plan to keep things quiet would have been foiled. "What are you doing here?"

Virginia gestured to ask permission to come inside, and Lucy stepped back to allow her in. "I wanted to come see you," she said. Lucy's brow furrowed, challenging Virginia's lie, but she stepped into the small kitchen and began to pour two glasses of sweet tea. Ever the Southern hostess, she'd call Virginia on her lies after making her at home.

"It's not that I'm not happy to see you," Lucy said cautiously, "but it's a little out of the ordinary for you to just pop by like this. Is everything okay?"

The two settled onto the couch, a pristine white sofa Virginia was petrified to disturb. She sat up straight, holding her tea out in front of her to avoid any chance of a spill. Lucy leaned back casually, looking more comfortable lounging in her pencil skirt and blazer than Virginia ever felt, even in pajamas. She was effortlessly chic, and Virginia wondered for a moment how she had produced a daughter so unlike herself, so put-together in ways Virginia never was.

"You heard about my accident at the Harvest Festival?" Her stomach was fluttering, and she sipped from her tea, draining the glass before she realized it.

Standing to refill her mother's glass, Lucy nodded. "You tripped into the person who killed those two people. The police have the murder weapon because of you." Virginia thought she detected a hint of pride in Lucy's voice, and it steeled her for what she had to say next.

"Well, that person was there to kill Colleen, and now they're after me." She pulled the folded letter from her bag and offered it to Lucy.

Lucy's eyes tightened as she read it. "You've shown this to the police?" she asked, jaw set.

"I'm going to the station from here. I wanted to talk to you first."

"You haven't gone to the police yet?" Lucy set her own glass down and walked back to the kitchen, this time pulling a bottle of something stronger from the freezer and taking a swig. "Mom, I don't understand. We're not... We're not that close. Why did you come here first?"

The words were a punch in the gut, wrenching the air from her lungs. "I..." was all she could manage in response.

"If you haven't gone to the police, I assume you haven't told Jack." Lucy had her phone in her hand, pacing as she launched into action mode. She so resembled her brother.

"Wait," Virginia said. "I came to you first because I needed to tell someone and I didn't want to worry them.

With the pregnancy, I just… I don't want to put more on their plates. But I needed to talk to someone. I needed to make sure I wasn't overreacting. I needed someone to know."

When Lucy looked at her mother, Virginia thought she saw heartbreak in her eyes. "Of course, I'm here for you," she said. "But you can't keep this from them."

"I don't want them to worry," Virginia repeated.

"If your life is in danger, of course they'll worry. Anyone who loves you will worry. But that doesn't mean it's fair to keep that information from them. When did you get this?"

"Yesterday." Acid rose up and stung Virginia's throat at the memory of seeing the note waiting for her on the carpet of her room. "It was in my room when I got back."

Lucy perked up. "Where in your room?"

"On the floor. I opened the door and it was sitting on the floor."

Lucy released a breath and sat back down on the couch. "So someone could have slid it under your door? They weren't necessarily in your room?"

Virginia nodded. She hadn't considered how the killer had left the note. Hadn't even thought that maybe they could have been in her room.

"Still," Lucy continued, "the fact that they can access Breeze Village with no issues is a concern. Are you sure you want to stay there?"

"Yes," Virginia said without a moment's consideration. Breeze Village was her home. A home she'd never anticipated for herself. A home she'd resisted for a long time.

But she'd already lost one home against her will to people she was too powerless to fight. She wasn't about to lose another.

Lucy gave a sharp nod, her face calculating. "We'll go by Jack's. He'll want to know as soon as possible. I'll go with you, and then one of us will take you to the police station." Virginia opened her mouth to protest, but Lucy put her hand up. "Jack will agree with me. You shouldn't be alone right now. And if you'd rather call Marney or Lawrence, they'll agree with me, too. You know they will."

Lucy was right, but it didn't make Virginia feel any less small on the ride to Jack's. It also did nothing to ease the guilt she felt when Jack's and Stephanie's eyes contracted in fear, their faces betraying the efforts they were making not to look as afraid as they felt.

"We'll go to the police, of course," Jack said, his reaction so like his sister's. He looked at Lucy. "Can you take Mom, and I'll stay with Stephanie?"

He was working out ways to keep them both safe, and Virginia's heart ached for the situation she'd put them in. Though it was an accident, and though her accident had saved Colleen's life, at least for the time being, she couldn't quell the regret that she'd landed her own family in danger.

As if reading her mind, Stephanie came over and placed her hand on Virginia's shoulder. "It's not your fault," she said softly, though her own voice shook as she spoke. "And it'll all be okay."

"It's not your fault," Jack echoed. "But the sooner we get this into the hands of the police, the better."

Lucy nodded and grabbed her purse, then turned to face Virginia. "Let's go."

* * *

VIRGINIA'S limited experience with law enforcement left her dreading this encounter. She was prepared to be brushed aside, ready for them to tell her the letter was likely a hoax but that they'd look into it. She expected them to advise her to lock her doors and windows and take the usual precautions. Instead, the first officer they encountered called Dylan over immediately, and the two of them pored over the letter with ashen expressions.

"You received this when?" Dylan asked, beckoning two more officers over in the same breath.

The officers took the letter, and Dylan and the first officer asked Virginia questions about where she'd been, what time she'd found the letter, if she'd noticed anyone suspicious around. Virginia and Lucy waited while Dylan spoke with a handful of detectives on her team, and when Dylan finally dismissed them, it was with the promise that they'd be talking with Hashim about posting officers for surveillance around the premises.

"Are you sure that's necessary?" Virginia asked, though the idea made her feel reassured.

"The budget is limited," Dylan admitted, "but given that we have reason to believe the author of this letter has murdered two people, we're taking this very seriously."

An unmarked police car followed them back to Lucy's apartment, where Virginia dropped her daughter off, and then back to Breeze Village. Virginia had called Marney and asked her to invite Lawrence over, so the two were waiting for her in Marney's cottage when she arrived.

"What's going on?" Marney asked.

Virginia looked from one friend to the other, exhausted from the day and unable to beat around the bush any more. "The killer who's been after Colleen? Apparently, I'm their new target."

With Hashim's approval, officers took shifts watching Breeze Village. Marney made excuses to spend time with Virginia, and both Jack and Lucy took to texting her multiple times a day to check in. Dylan asked her to stop working at Piggly Wiggly and spend as little time alone as possible, but she refused. The killer was quickly taking her freedom and independence from her, robbing her home of any feeling of safety and security, but her job was one thing she wouldn't let them take. So instead, she drove to work and back pretending not to see the unmarked cop car tailing her the whole way.

On the second evening after breaking the news to her loved ones, she sent Marney back to her cottage, saying she needed alone time, and found herself pacing her room like a tiger in a cage. It wasn't that there was something in particular she wanted to do, but knowing that if she left she'd be followed, that she couldn't do anything truly alone, made her restless. She knew Dylan had her best detectives on the case, looking for whoever it was that was after her, but every time she sat down, she felt wrong, like she should be doing more to figure it out herself. It was her life in danger now. It didn't feel right to leave the figuring things out to other people.

Remembering Ronald's tip, Virginia took the elevator up to the third floor and knocked on Colleen's neighbor's door. The doorways were around fifteen feet apart, close enough that she thought it possible that the neighbor heard someone in the hallway, but unlikely given the average hearing abilities of the residents of Breeze Village. Her concern was amplified by the lack of response to her knock.

Virginia knocked again, louder this time, and heard shuffling from inside the room. Moments later, the door opened to reveal a woman in a turquoise lounge set clutching a walker with one hand and the doorknob in the other.

"You're not Haley," she said, sounding disappointed. "Or Kim." She turned away from the door, leaving it wide open as she shuffled with her walker to the recliner she'd positioned so like the other residents. "Sometimes Haley's busy or on vacation and Kim comes to help me. Sometimes it's someone else, but Haley knows she's my favorite, so she usually comes."

"I'm not Haley," Virginia confirmed, not sure whether she should have come. "My name is Virginia."

"I'm not going to remember that," the woman said matter-of-factly.

"That's fine. May I come in?" When Colleen's neighbor nodded, Virginia stepped inside and shut the door behind her. "I'm friends with Colleen. What's your name?" She hoped the woman wasn't close enough with her neighbor to know she wouldn't consider Virginia a friend at the moment.

"Harriet," the woman answered. "Who's Colleen?"

Virginia stammered her response. "She's, erm, she's your neighbor." She pointed to the wall, indicating Colleen's room on the other side. "Someone came to see her on Halloween, but Colleen wasn't there, and I wondered if you might have seen or heard anything since you live next door."

"Colleen," Harriet repeated softly. "Colleen... That name doesn't sound familiar."

Virginia winced and regretted coming here at all.

"Colleen," Harriet said again. She looked up at Virginia, eyes brimming with tears, and started to apologize for not remembering. Before Virginia could reassure her, could apologize herself for calling unannounced and asking questions, a familiar voice drifted through the space.

"This isn't right." Colleen's voice, dampened and echoing but unmistakably hers, rang through the air. "I can't."

Virginia looked around for the source of the sound, and Harriet smiled. "That's my ghost," she said. "She keeps me company."

"No, you don't understand. I—I'm working on it." Colleen's disembodied voice rang out again, and this time, Virginia pinpointed the source: the vent in the wall. Her eyes went wide and she crossed the room to get as close to it as possible. She'd occasionally heard her neighbor's television if the volume was up high, but never like this. She spun around to face Harriet.

"You hear her a lot?" she asked.

"My ghost friend? Oh, yes." Harriet didn't elaborate, and Virginia turned back to the vent. Could Harriet have heard the visitor on Halloween?

"I said I'm working on it," Colleen said. "But I can't send you any more right now."

Virginia held her breath, waiting for any more information, but none came. Colleen must have ended the conversation. Virginia hurried to the door and poked her head out to see if anyone left Colleen's room. When no one did, she figured Colleen had been on the phone.

Turning back to Harriet, Virginia asked, "Do you ever hear other voices with your ghost?"

"No, just her."

"And how often do you hear her?" Virginia worked to keep her voice steady. It was agony waiting for Harriet to ponder the question and slowly get out a reply.

"Well, I'm not sure." At seeing Virginia's face fall, her eyes began to water.

"That's fine," Virginia assured her. "It's okay. Thank you for sharing your ghost with me. I feel honored."

Harriet seemed to hearten at Virginia's words, and Virginia bid her goodbye before practically running to Marney's cottage.

* * *

"SOMEONE WANTS MONEY FROM COLLEEN!" Virginia wheezed, doubling over in Marney's entryway with her hands on her knees. "Or maybe not money," she said, considering. "But Colleen has been sending someone something, and they want more of it. She doesn't have any more, but she's working on it."

Marney stepped out of her bathroom, seemingly unsurprised to see her best friend gasping for air after letting herself in. "What are you talking about? And do you want sweet tea or something stronger?"

Virginia pretended to consider before requesting the spiked beverage, then settled on the couch to recount her visit to Colleen's neighbor.

"And you're sure it was Colleen you heard?" Marney asked when Virginia finished her story.

"Positive," Virginia replied. "Harriet couldn't tell me how often she hears Colleen, and I didn't ask her if she could remember hearing other conversations where someone seemed to want something from her. Harriet seemed a little... well, she thinks Colleen's voice is a ghost friend who keeps her company."

Marney raised an eyebrow. "How kind of the ghost."

The wheels turning in her brain, Virginia began to think out loud. "So someone wants something from Colleen. My first thought was money, but we don't actually know that. Colleen did use to sell drugs to the residents here..."

"I thought that all fell apart after Genie died?" Marney asked.

"Maybe someone is blackmailing her?" Virginia asked. "As far as I know, Colleen has money. At least she did, from her stint in the ice cream business."

"Ice cream business?" Marney asked, but Virginia waved off the question.

"So either she's lying or she's already given them all her money."

"Or she spends a lot more on crystals and decks of cards than you'd think."

Virginia stood and started to pace back and forth. "We know Colleen has a crazy past. Some time in the corporate world, then entrepreneurial success, which included shutting down competitors. Small-time drug dealing to retirees with chronic pain. We know someone wants her dead."

"And we know someone wants something from her, and she's kept that bit to herself," Marney finished. She looked at Virginia, the new target in this killer's sights. Her voice took on a new edge. "You tried to help her and now you're in danger, and she's keeping things to herself."

Virginia paced a few more times, stopping when she noticed the laundry basket full of yarn and half-finished crochet pieces. It was tucked into the corner by the sliding-glass back door, illuminated in part by the shaft of moonlight peeking through the curtains. On top was what looked to be a gingerbread house.

"What's this?" she asked, picking up the little house and turning it over in her hands. Four colors of yarn dangled from an unfinished edge.

"It's part of a Christmas village. The ceramic ones are gorgeous, but I thought it would be fun to make a crocheted version. I made a little train and a handful of buildings." She pulled pieces from the basket, and Virginia gasped at the intricacy.

"These are incredible," she breathed.

Marney took the pieces back from her. "The day after I listed them on my shop, that competitor stole my pictures and listed them on their own shop. Of course, they listed them for a lower price, and I haven't had a single order."

Marney pulled open the closet door and tucked the Christmas village components in among the shelves full of finished works. "I reported the shop, but I don't know what else to do. Every time I think of something new and clever, they just steal the idea and undercut me."

"There's no way they're actually able to deliver," Virginia said. "You designed these patterns yourself, right?" Marney nodded. "So the thief will try to replicate them and fail. When it becomes clear that the thief can't produce the items listed, the customers will come back to your shop."

Marney opened her mouth to reply, but the shrill ring of her phone cut her off. She picked it up, announced that it was Lawrence, and answered it. "Sure, we'll be there," she said after a moment. When she hung up the phone, she turned to Virginia and said, "I hope you didn't have plans for tomorrow. We're having dinner with Lawrence and Glass."

CHAPTER 27

Turning from Marney's cottage toward the main building, Virginia saw lights on in Gemma's cottage. If Colleen shared her secrets with anyone, it would be Gemma. She knocked on the door, going through the questions in her mind. *Does Colleen owe someone money? Is someone blackmailing her? What hasn't she been forthcoming about?*

"Go away."

Virginia reeled at the sound of Gemma's voice through the door, then knocked again. "It's me," she called. "Virginia."

"I know." Gemma's response was immediate. "I said, 'Go away.'"

"I don't understand." Virginia wracked her brain for reasons Gemma might have to be upset with her but couldn't come up with any. She was one of the few people Virginia was pretty sure she hadn't wronged, at least not recently.

The door unlatched and Gemma pulled it back an

inch, just wide enough for Virginia to see her deep brown eyes and the arch of her drawn-on brow raised in a challenge. "You mean you *didn't* tell Jimmy I stole all the pudding cups from the first-floor fridge?"

Virginia winced. "I did, but—" The door shut in her face.

"I knew it!" Gemma yelled from the other side.

"I was trying to get information on Ed. Jimmy didn't believe I was a private investigator. He asked if I'd investigate who was stealing the pudding." She sighed and lowered her voice. "I shouldn't have said anything. I'm sorry."

Gemma pulled the door open and Virginia jumped, startled. "No, you shouldn't have," Gemma said coldly. Then her face broke into a conspiratorial smile. "I took Jimmy on a second-floor heist a few nights ago. We feasted on tapioca, and now he wants to plan another pudding theft date for next week."

Gemma stepped back and gestured for Virginia to come in. Virginia's legs moved, carrying her inside while her brain worked to process Gemma's words. "Date?" she finally choked out.

"He fancies me," Gemma said, wiggling her eyebrows.

Virginia thought back to her first meeting with Jimmy. "He specifically told me he doesn't date residents."

"I suppose he's made an exception." Gemma shrugged. "If the pudding is this good…" Her voice trailed off and she laughed suggestively.

Virginia chuckled, blood rushing to her cheeks. When she'd found a seat on Gemma's velvet sofa, Gemma joined her, her face serious.

"Are you still trying to figure out who's after Colleen?" Gemma asked.

Virginia nodded, trying to decide whether to tell Gemma that she was the killer's new target. Marney was the only one at Breeze Village who knew besides Hashim. Residents assumed the police presence was because the killer was still focused on Colleen.

"Good," Gemma said. "I'm worried about her." Virginia encouraged her to go on. "When Russ and Liam were here, she was withdrawn and always high. Their energy really messed with her, and the visions were awful, apparently. Anything to get out of her own head was welcome. But this... this is different. She's closed off, jumpy." Gemma took a breath and looked like she was trying to decide whether to reveal something or not. "I saw a picture in her wallet once. A kid."

"Who?" Virginia hardly got the question out before Gemma responded.

"I didn't ask. A month or so before that, she and I were at the park downtown. The yoga class was on, and the last time I was there, I'd heard one of the girls telling another one how she'd taken a DNA test and discovered her dad wasn't who she thought he was. Forty years old, and this bombshell was dropped on her. I told Colleen this, just gossiping, you know. Anyway, Colleen said, 'Sometimes secrets should stay secret,' and changed the subject."

"You don't think...?" The picture in Colleen's wallet. 'Secrets should stay secret.' Did Colleen have a secret child? Maybe a secret child trying to cash in on decades of hurt and abandonment now that he'd discovered who his mother was?

Virginia didn't finish the question, and Gemma seemed eager to move on. "I just want you to have all the information. I want you to figure this out. You, Dylan, the rest of the cops. I want that person behind bars."

On her way out, Virginia waved to the officer posted up at the back door to Breeze Village. When she stepped out of the elevator and reached her door, she was surprised to find another officer sitting directly outside. She recognized him but couldn't remember his name. "Officer…?"

"McNeil," he said, standing and offering his hand for her to shake.

"I didn't realize there would be officers inside by my door." From what she could recall, the budget was limited, and it was a stretch just to have the perimeter covered.

"The killer got in once to slide a note under your door," Officer McNeil said. "We don't want to take any chances." When Virginia didn't respond, he sighed and said, "There won't always be an officer here. I'm volunteering. A handful of us have volunteered to rotate so your room will have coverage overnight as much as possible, but be aware it won't be constant coverage. Just… be careful, okay?"

The emotion in his voice made something catch in her throat, and Virginia nodded as she unlocked her door and stepped inside. Officers were volunteering to guard her door. They wanted her safe. And in the eyes of law enforcement, she was clearly in danger.

WHEN VIRGINIA EMERGED from her room the next morning to find the hallway outside her door empty, she felt a pang of relief and a jolt of fear. The empty hallway felt like normalcy, but the emotion in Officer McNeil's voice the night before had stayed with her, and she found herself looking both ways before crossing to the elevator lobby as if the killer were lurking in the shadows, ready to pounce on her in the hall.

After breakfast, with a chocolate muffin in hand, Virginia knocked on Harriet's door. She had to figure out who Colleen had been talking to. If Colleen had a child, she'd certainly kept that to herself. But whether it was her child or not, someone clearly felt Colleen owed them, and it was a clearer, more immediate motive for murder than any of the people from Colleen's past had.

Harriet seemed surprised to see Virginia at her door but invited her in graciously. "What's your name?" she asked, reclaiming her seat in the recliner.

"I'm Virginia."

"Virginia," Harriet repeated. "That's a lovely name. It's nice to meet you."

Virginia winced before offering Harriet the muffin. "They had chocolate muffins at breakfast this morning. They're my favorite. I thought I'd see if you wanted one."

Harriet cocked her head to the side, confused. "You're not the usual nurse who brings my breakfast. Are you new?"

"Oh, no, I'm not a nurse." Heat rose in Virginia's cheeks, and she wished she hadn't come. "I was just coming to chat. I'm a friend."

"You brought me breakfast."

"I thought you might like chocolate muffins like I do. I'm not a nurse," Virginia repeated. "We met before. You told me about your ghost friend who keeps you company."

As soon as the words were out of Virginia's mouth, she wanted to take them back. She wanted to apologize to Harriet for using her in this investigation. She wanted to leave and never come back and let Harriet go on enjoying the company of her ghost friend, who was really her endangered neighbor. But more than any of those things, she wanted to save that neighbor and herself from someone who had already taken two lives. And though part of her hated herself for it, she had to cross some lines to do that.

"My ghost friend." A smile crossed Harriet's face. Her eyes didn't seem to be focused on anything in particular. "She's nice. I like her."

Virginia nodded. "Your ghost friend is really nice. I came to see you before, and you told me about her. She was talking with someone else. Does your ghost friend always talk with other people?"

"I only have one ghost friend."

"Right, but does she say anyone else's name when she talks?"

Virginia had knelt down in front of the recliner to bring her face level with Harriet's and was practically begging her to remember, begging for a scrap of information that might help her piece together who was trying to kill her. Harriet's brows knit together, the very picture of concentration, and she opened her mouth to respond.

Virginia held her breath, her heart pounding in her ears as she waited.

"Virginia." Virginia jumped at the sound of her name coming from behind her. She whirled around to find Kim standing in the doorway, a tray of food in hand. "What are you doing here?"

Virginia stood the rest of the way up, steadying herself on the side table while she waited for a wave of dizziness to pass. Kim's eyes bore down on her, condemnation written across her face.

"I'm just here visiting with Harriet," Virginia said, though she was already moving toward the door.

"I've got Harriet's breakfast with me. I think it's probably best if you let her enjoy it in peace."

Virginia nodded vehemently, halfway to the door, then turned in the doorway to wave goodbye. To her surprise, Harriet's eyes were fixed on her, a clarity in them Virginia hadn't seen before.

"Adam," Harriet said. "She talks to Adam."

"Adam," Virginia whispered. Someone who wanted something from Colleen, and their name started with an A.

"Come see me again," Harriet said, and then Kim closed the door behind Virginia, and she was alone in the hallway with a shred of information and hope that made her want to shout and whoop and pump her fist in the air.

CHAPTER 28

Hope does funny things to people. For Virginia, it seemed to make her forget she was eighty with mediocre balance and convinced her that standing on a chair to inspect the register in her ceiling was an entirely reasonable idea. She'd heard the sounds of an overly loud television through the walls before but never voices through the vents like in Harriet's room. The vents were positioned differently in her room than Harriet's, but she wondered if she brought her ear up to it if she might have better luck. Instead, she just heard the whoosh of warm air being pumped into her room and felt her eyes begin to itch and swell at being brought into such proximity to the rarely-dusted vents.

"What on Earth are you doing?" Marney's voice startled Virginia. She hadn't noticed a knock at the door or heard it open. Virginia wobbled on the chair beneath her, reaching up to touch the ceiling for stability, then scrambled down onto the stable floor to greet Marney.

"I was inspecting the register," she said cheerfully. "All good up there."

"I'd press you for more information, but you wouldn't tell me even if I did, so instead, I'll just remind you that we have a dinner date with Lawrence and Glass so let's get a move on."

Lawrence's beachside condo was Lawrence incarnate. The building was new and modern with polished concrete floors. One wall was entirely glass, with a view of the ocean just a few blocks away, and the others were painted bright white. The appliances were stainless steel, the cabinets were sharp and white, and the whole place seemed like it belonged more in New York City than in Seaview.

And then Lawrence furnished it. An area rug unfurled with color beneath a dark charcoal couch, and two caramel leather armchairs sat on the other side of an intricate wooden coffee table. Black and white photographs hung alongside vibrant modern art and small antiques in an eclectic gallery wall above the side table he'd inherited from his mother. A model airplane hung from the ceiling in one corner, an homage to his late partner, Ben.

Light and airy met dark and heavy, with pops of color snaking through it all, every bit of it pristine. And every bit of it Lawrence.

To Virginia's surprise, when the door opened it was Glass standing there to usher them inside, with Lawrence visible in the background setting the table. The smell of roast beef made Virginia's mouth water.

"Can I take your jackets?" Virginia turned back to

Glass. His arms were outstretched to Marney and Virginia, and Virginia followed Marney's lead in slipping off her sweater and handing it to him.

"It smells amazing in here," Marney said.

"Doesn't it?" Glass looked appreciatively at Lawrence. "He amazes me in so many ways."

Virginia schooled her face into neutrality. Lawrence liked cooking, she reminded herself. It makes sense that he'd be the one cooking tonight. Still, she felt a wave of unease at Glass's presence in Lawrence's home while Lawrence was still the one doing all the work to host them.

Neither Lawrence nor Marney brought up the investigation or Virginia's status as the killer's next target in front of Glass, something Virginia appreciated though she couldn't quite put a finger on why. There wasn't any specific reason she didn't want him to know about it, but it felt too personal to share with him.

"Are you still planning to move to Seaview?" Marney asked between bites of food. "When we met you at the farmers market, you mentioned staying with Lawrence while you looked for a place of your own."

Glass took his time chewing, then sipped his wine and cleared his throat. "I am. No luck yet, but I'm still looking."

Virginia stole a glance at Lawrence, but his face didn't give away how he felt about the situation. "How long is your visit?" she asked. This time, Lawrence looked at Glass along with Virginia and Marney as if he, too, were curious to know the answer.

"I'm heading back to Blacksville next week," Glass said.

"I've got a few things to take care of there, and then hope-fully, I'll be back down here another week or so after that. And if things go well, the next trip down after that might be a more permanent move."

Marney coughed. Virginia hoped her face conveyed pleasant surprise and not concerned bafflement. "If you find a place and sign a lease?" she clarified.

"Mm-hmm." Glass shrugged, his confirmation noncommittal.

Lawrence seemed unconcerned, and neither Virginia nor Marney pushed it any further. When Virginia asked about the business he had to take care of back in Blacksville, Glass gave another non-answer. Virginia wasn't sure if she'd ever felt so awkward next to her two best friends, not sure which direction to take the conversation.

Marney made an excuse for her and Virginia to return to Breeze Village almost as soon as the table was cleared. It had been a long day, she said, and she had two orders she needed to finish crocheting for the next day.

"I'll walk you out." If Lawrence was put out by their early departure, he didn't show it. Instead, he walked with Virginia and Marney in contented silence down to Virginia's car.

When they reached her silver Honda, Lawrence made to open the doors for them but stopped short. "So," he said, turning back to face them. "Tell me honestly what you think?"

"Of Glass?" Virginia asked, buying herself time to put nicely that she didn't trust him as far as she could throw him.

Lawrence nodded.

"You seem happy," Marney said. "He makes you happy." Her voice sounded almost sad, though she smiled as she said it. Marney would know how it felt to find someone who makes you happy after a long, long time. And how much it hurts when someone dear to you doesn't trust that person.

"I am. But that doesn't answer my question. I already know what *I* think of Douglass. I want to know what you two think."

Marney looked at Virginia, her face begging Virginia to say something and for the love of God to say it tactfully.

Virginia cleared her throat. "I have concerns."

"Concerns?"

"The man hardly gives a straight answer to anything. He won't talk about his life back home. You barely know him, and now he's staying with you while he looks for a house, although to me, it seems like he's not all that concerned with finding a home of his own. He seems more than content to just stay with you as long as you let him."

When she finished, Virginia couldn't look at Lawrence's face. Instead, she looked down at her own feet while she shifted her weight nervously between them. After a long silence, she looked up to see that Lawrence didn't look upset or even hurt. In fact, his lips were pulled up into a small smile.

"Thank you for your honesty. Marney, I assume you feel similarly?" Marney nodded, and Lawrence smiled. "You're both perceptive. Glass doesn't have a crappy landlord in Blacksville making him eager to move. He doesn't have a landlord there at all. Or a place of his own. He's been couch-surfing at friends' and family members' homes for a while now. We met online, as you know. He told me everything from the start. He's not secretly plotting to stay with me indefinitely while lying to me about looking for other accommodations. He and I are openly communicating about the possibility of him living with me."

Virginia's mouth hung open. "And you're just... okay with it?"

"What, okay with a man whose company I enjoy living in my home? A man who was honest with me from the start? Yes. I am okay with that."

Virginia didn't like it, but she couldn't disagree with anything he'd said.

"Why is he going back to Blacksville next week, then?" Marney asked. "And why lie to us at dinner?"

"Appearances, mostly," Lawrence said with a wave of his hand. "He does have some sentimental belongings to collect from a friend, but he doesn't want people to think he's using me for a place to live or to gossip about us moving too fast."

Both were entirely fair concerns, Virginia thought, but she didn't say so. She stayed quiet while Marney told Lawrence how happy she was for him, and then Lawrence opened the car doors for them and sent them off with a kiss on the cheek.

In the privacy of her car, Virginia turned to Marney. "You still don't like this, do you?"

"Oh, no. Absolutely not."

CHAPTER 29

$\mathcal{V}$irginia had hardly laid her head on her pillow when the shrill ring of her cell phone made her heart stop. Throwing her hand to her chest, she donned her glasses, saw an unfamiliar number on the screen of her phone, and answered it.

"Hello?" Her voice betrayed her exhaustion, and there was a pause on the other end of the line.

"Is this a bad time?"

"Who is this?"

Another pause. "This is Dan Armstead. Eliza's father?" The caller waited for Virginia to indicate she remembered him. She jogged her memory, trying to recall why his name sounded so familiar. Her stomach sank. She knew this person wanted something from her, but she couldn't remember what.

"Err, yes, I remember you," she said.

"I was calling for a status update on the investigation. When we spoke before, you said you'd have a report within a week. It's been almost two."

A lightbulb went off in Virginia's head. The dish soap scammer. She thunked her hand to her forehead, closing her eyes and trying to think up an excuse. Nothing came to her.

"Sorry," she said. "I've been busy."

"I understand." The tone of the man's voice said that he did not understand. That further explanation was required. "Have you given up, then?"

"No!" Virginia said, the response flying from her tongue before she had time to consider it. She wasn't giving up, right? Her instinct was that giving up was never the right choice, but this man seemed to be giving her an out with minimal disapproval, and she hadn't made any progress. She'd forgotten about the incident completely in the aftermath of the festival. Maybe she should take him up on the chance to move it off her plate.

Before she could change her mind, however, the man sighed with relief. "Good. So, no report yet; that's fine. But can you let me know what you've got so far? How close are we?"

"How close?"

"To catching this guy." The man's voice carried an urgency that Virginia's tired brain resisted. She was putting all her effort into keeping up with the conversation.

"Well, I haven't actually, err, done anything yet."

The other end of the line went quiet long enough that Virginia started to ask if he was still there, but then the man said, "Nothing? You haven't asked around at other grocery stores to see if they've had similar incidents and maybe got a better look at the guy? You haven't checked with any of your, I don't know, underworld contacts or whatever it is investigators use to see if anyone's heard of some guy scamming an innocent girl at work?"

Virginia wished she was taking notes. While she didn't have underworld contacts to feel out, the idea to ask around at other grocery stores was a good one, and she hadn't even come close to thinking of it.

"When do you think you'll have an update for me?"

"How about in another week?" With no experience as an investigator-for-hire, Virginia wasn't sure how this would be received, but the man grunted his approval. Without another word, the line went dead.

Virginia pulled open the tiny drawer on her small desk and retrieved a notepad and pen. *ASK OTHER GROCERY STO*—. A frantic knock at the door interrupted her note. A glance out the peephole showed a distraught Marney clutching a wriggling Pancake in her arms.

"What's wrong?" Virginia ushered Marney inside, Pancake eagerly leaping free from her arms and making himself at home on Virginia's recliner. "What happened?"

"My cottage." Marney burst into sobs and choked out the rest. "Someone broke in."

Virginia went weak at the knees. She clung to the wall for support while Marney clung to her, the two a wobbling mass of fear and disbelief.

"When?" Virginia forced the word out, though she knew the answer.

"When we were at Lawrence's."

"Police?"

Marney just nodded that she'd already involved them. She took to Virginia's recliner, scooching Pancake out of the way to make room. The cat didn't protest, scurrying off to sniff another corner of the room. Virginia heated up her electric kettle—technically not allowed, like Ronald's crockpot, but the staff turned a blind eye—and made them two cups of tea. She'd nearly drained hers when Marney finally sniffed, wiped her eyes, and cleared her throat.

"When we got back from Lawrence's and I went to unlock my door, it was already unlocked. I thought it was odd but figured I must have had a senior moment and just forgotten to lock it. Then I noticed things were out of place. A crochet work in progress on my chair instead of the side table where I usually leave them, patterns rearranged, the closet doors all hanging wide open. The last straw was that there was a pen on my kitchen counter that I've never seen before. It was pink and had a hair salon's name on it. I might get confused and forget where I left something or leave the door unlocked, but when I saw that pen, I knew for sure someone else had been in my cottage.

"I called Dylan right away, of course. She radioed for the officers around the perimeter to leave their posts and get to my cottage before she could get here. I feel a little bad taking your security away from you, Virginia, but I have to say that one of those officers was extremely muscular and I felt very much safer in his presence."

A guffaw ripped from Virginia's throat, her belly shaking with laughter. Only Marney could show up at her apartment in tears following one of the most traumatic acts of violation a person could experience and then make her laugh.

"Dylan came running. Literally sprinting across the lawn. She beat the rest of her team by a full seven minutes. I don't even want to know what speeds she was doing on the road. Then you and I both have had enough run-ins with crime in the last year to know what comes next. I gave my statement about five times more than I felt necessary, they assessed the scene and determined it was clear, and Dylan had to be practically dragged from my cottage, hysterical that I might be in danger. And now here I am."

Her voice quavered at the end. Though Marney was putting on a brave face, Virginia knew her better than that. Marney was terrified, and by the next morning, she'd be pulling into herself, a trembling bundle of nerves anxious beneath an intentionally calm exterior. Virginia didn't want to let that happen.

She leaned over the back of the recliner and wrapped her arms around Marney's shoulders. "Stay here tonight," she said. "Like we used to." Like when Marney and Dylan were new to Seaview and the memory of her abusive ex-husband got to be too much. Marney would turn up on Virginia's doorstep to ask for a sleepover, her trembling hand clutching Dylan's. Like when Earl died and Virginia was sleeping alone for the first time in practically her entire adult life and she'd wake up surprised by the empty bed beside her every night. She'd call Marney, and Marney would bring Dylan over without a second thought.

The two eased onto Virginia's bed, the creaking of joints and bumping of bodies as they navigated the small space making way for the peace only the closeness of someone who knows you completely and still loves you can bring.

"It could have been a ghost," Virginia whispered. "A ghost burglar instead of a human burglar."

Virginia felt Marney shake her head in the darkness. "There's no such thing as ghosts. If any trace of Dean could remain on this earth after his death, that's one degree of unfairness too far. Life isn't fair, we both know that, but ghosts… once people die, they're gone, and that's one truth I'll cling to until I myself am a not-ghost entirely gone from this world."

Virginia didn't believe in ghosts either, except for maybe the one that left cake in her fridge, but if a person had broken into Marney's cottage, the only thing she could think of was the danger she was in. Virginia was supposed to be the target, but their villain didn't seem interested in playing by the rules.

"There wasn't a letter though, right?" When Marney shook her head again, Virginia could have cried with relief. They might be breaking into Marney's cottage, but the killer wasn't making her a target.

The bed creaked when Pancake leapt up, then settled himself in between Marney's and Virginia's heads. Like Dylan and Lucy had been all those times, he seemed eager for the sleepover and blissfully unaware of the motivation.

arney was up and gathering Pancake in her arms to leave when Virginia wiped the sleep from her eyes. "I need to get back to my cottage. I want to make sure everything's all right. No more burglars, you know. And Pancake is eager for his breakfast." She was pulling back like Virginia expected.

"Want me to walk you there?" Virginia offered.

Marney shook her head. When Virginia put on her glasses, she could see the strained look on Marney's face, the way she kept glancing up toward the ceiling. She was holding in tears.

"Hey, hey," Virginia said softly. "It's okay. We'll figure this out. Dylan's on it, and has she ever not figured something out?"

Marney gave Virginia a wry look. "Isn't the whole premise of your investigative spiel the shortcomings of my daughter in her profession?"

"Not *her* shortcomings. The shortcomings of the police as an institution, particularly when it comes to crimes that involve the elderly or me personally. Besides, her motivation is a little different in this case. It's personal to her."

Virginia's thoughts wandered to Ruth's death, the first case she'd investigated. It had looked like an old lady had just accidentally taken too much of her regular medication. Virginia didn't usually think about the blasé attitude of the police she encountered right after Ruth's death. She tried to think only of the feeling of victory at the airport when Matt and Christine were arrested, not of the way her own death could so easily be dismissed. *Things happen. She was old. It's tragic. Let's have fried chicken at the memorial.*

Despite Marney's insistence that she was fine to return to her cottage alone, Virginia moved to slide on her shoes and accompany her downstairs. "I need to go down to breakfast," she said defensively when Marney repeated that she didn't need supervision. "I'm just going to the dining room, same as always." Never mind that she'd be watching through the glass doors to the courtyard as Marney walked the path to her cottage, holding her breath until Marney was safely inside.

"Do you see my other shoe?" With one sneaker on, Virginia hobbled across the room in search of its match.

"I see a slipper," Marney said, holding it up. Virginia took it, figuring she could wear slippers to breakfast and no one was likely to care, except maybe Wanda, though she criticized everyone's outfits no matter how put-together they looked.

"Do you see the other slipper?" Virginia asked. One foot was clad in a slipper, the other a sneaker, and no matter how hard she looked, she couldn't find the match to either. At first, she figured she'd misplaced them, but when her search turned up one sandal and one clog, a single shoe from each pair she owned, her pulse slowed, and she felt her face go pale. Someone had been here. She thought of the cake, the flickering lights, and the hauntings Colleen was experiencing. Then of the burglar in Marney's cottage the night before. Who, or what, was toying with them?

Marney started to head out, reminding Virginia that she didn't need an escort, and Virginia decided she had no choice but to go down in mismatched shoes. Locking the door behind her, she nodded to the officer in the hall.

"What time did you get here?" she asked him.

The officer took a sip from a Styrofoam cup of coffee and considered the question. "Around six. I'll be here until ten. Then I've got to head to work. Another officer should be here in the evening, but for most of the day, it'll just be the perimeter."

So the burglar or ghost or whomever it was who took her shoes came and went before six. Otherwise, the officer would have spotted them. Virginia had worn both sneakers to Lawrence's house for dinner, so the shoes went missing sometime between getting home from dinner and six in the morning. Whatever person or ghost was messing with her, they'd been in her room while she and Marney were sleeping, unaware of another presence in the space.

She thanked him and stepped into the elevator with Marney. If Marney picked up on Virginia's concern, she didn't let on. There was enough on her mind already. She didn't need another reason to feel vulnerable and unprotected in what should have been a safe place.

When Marney was safely tucked away inside her cottage, Virginia poured herself a cup of coffee and set off to find Kim or Haley. Breakfast would have to wait.

"Kim!" she called, flagging down the nurse. "Got a moment?"

"Everything okay?"

Virginia wasn't sure exactly how to respond. "Yes, everything's fine. I just wanted to let you know… I think there's a prankster running around Breeze Village." She pointed down at her shoes. "Someone capitalizing on the Halloween scare and pulling tricks on people. I've got only one shoe from each pair as of this morning, when I had full pairs last night."

Kim frowned. "I'll let Haley know. We'll brief the rest of the staff and keep an eye out, and we'll remind everyone to lock their doors."

What Virginia didn't say was that her door *was* locked. When a friend shows up in tears because her home was just broken into, locking the door is step two after step one of pulling that friend into a hug. Whoever was stealing shoes wasn't deterred by a locked door.

Over pancakes, she considered the possibilities. The way Virginia saw it, the shoe thief may or may not be Marney's burglar, and also may or may not be the mysterious cake depositor, who may or may not be haunting Colleen. She decided to subscribe to Marney's position that ghosts weren't real and, therefore, she was dealing with someone who could sneak around and pick locks, not something that could walk through locked doors. But what she couldn't work out was whether this was the killer toying with them—someone already responsible for two murders terrorizing their prey before pouncing—or someone else entirely. And if it wasn't the killer, what were they after?

She was deep in this thought when Colleen plunked herself down in the next seat and said a curt, "Good morning."

Virginia jumped, startled as much by the fact that Colleen had joined her voluntarily as she was by her sudden presence. Virginia and Colleen had hardly spoken since the Harvest Fest. They weren't on the best of terms before the festival—Virginia had hoped her report detailing the information she'd found about the suspects on Colleen's list would help make up for the damage she'd accidentally driven Ed to do to Colleen's reputation—but in the aftermath, they'd mostly avoided each other.

"I never thanked you for saving my life."

Virginia responded with a smile, though Colleen still hadn't actually thanked her.

"I gave the police a copy of your report. I wanted to make sure they had all the information for the investigation. I heard… I heard you got a note, too."

Virginia wondered who told Colleen. The officers posted outside Virginia's door were a good hint to anyone who noticed that Virginia was in danger, but Marney was the only one at Breeze Village who knew about the threatening letter.

"Oh?" she asked, hoping to tease out more information.

"One of the officers let it slip when I was interviewed

for what felt like the fortieth time. I just wish I had more information that could help."

And what about Adam, Virginia wanted to ask. The person on the other end of the phone demanding something Colleen couldn't—or wouldn't—give him, whose initial was carved into Irene's and Herman's bodies. Had Colleen told the police about him? Because she'd sure kept it to herself when she came to Virginia asking for help early on.

Before she had a chance to say something she'd regret, Gemma came by and tapped Colleen on the shoulder.

"I haven't seen you in a while," she said.

Colleen stood to hug Gemma, Gemma's body entirely enveloping Colleen's wispy form. "Excuse me for one minute?"

Virginia nodded, and Colleen and Gemma stepped to the side to chat. Virginia watched them for a moment, trying to see if she could make out what they were talking about. As far as she could tell, they were either discussing a giant spider dancing ballet or a phenomenal crème brûlée. A buzz snapped her out of eavesdropping, ripples forming in her cup of coffee as the table vibrated. Colleen had received a text, Virginia realized. Colleen's phone was sitting there on the table, inches from Virginia's hand.

Seemingly without her taking any action at all, those inches turned to millimeters turned to no space at all. Colleen's phone was in Virginia's hands. Then it was lit up, the home screen right there for Virginia to take in. For someone who had secrets to hide, Colleen didn't take the measures Virginia would expect to lock down her phone.

Virginia thought for a moment. She should set the

phone down. She shouldn't have picked it up in the first place. But now here it was, in her hand, and Colleen and Gemma were thoroughly engrossed in their conversation.

She opened the call log and glanced down the list. Most were incoming calls from numbers Colleen hadn't saved in her phone. There were no repeat calls from the same one, though, so Virginia figured those were likely the spam calls Jack had coached her to ignore. But interspersed with those spam calls were a series of calls, both incoming and outgoing, with an Adam Grainger.

Adam.

Once again, Virginia's fingers moved without her brain giving them approval. They clicked on his name and the screen changed. She hadn't meant to call him, only to look at his contact information, and yet she was calling him. Panicking at the realization, she hung up before Adam could answer and then tossed the phone back down on the table, sloshing her coffee in the process. Colleen and Gemma glanced her way at the commotion and she smiled sheepishly, mopping at the spill. If Colleen suspected anything, she didn't let on. She simply turned back to Gemma and resumed their conversation about either dancing arachnids or decadent desserts or some third thing Virginia hadn't puzzled out.

What if Colleen sees the outgoing call in the call log? Virginia picked the phone back up, trying to work out if she could delete the call from the history. Her brain was working in overdrive. She felt like a squash ball bouncing from one wall to the next in a tiny room. One moment, she felt the urgent need to erase the call history. The next, she had the idea to write down Adam's number so she could call him later from the privacy of her room. She scrawled it on a sticky note and slid the pad deep down into her purse. But if she called him from an unknown number, he'd ignore it just like she did when she didn't recognize a number. Whereas if she called him from Colleen's phone, he'd answer. But what would she say to him? What information could she get from him before he realized something was off and hung up? And if he was the killer, she didn't want him to know she was onto him.

While her brain ricocheted from one idea to the next, not lingering on a single one long enough to tease out the consequences, Colleen and Gemma finished their conversation. Virginia had palmed Colleen's phone, thinking she'd steal it and use it to call Adam from her room after breakfast, when Colleen turned and rejoined her at the table.

"I think that's mine." She pointed to the device in Virginia's hand.

"Oh, is it?" Virginia shoved the phone back toward Colleen. "I'm so sorry. I thought it was mine."

Virginia couldn't get away fast enough. All she could think about was her need to get upstairs. To see what she could find out about Adam Grainger. The Mahjong Queen was nowhere to be seen, so instead of squinting at the small screen of her phone, Virginia signed onto Facebook on the communal computer.

She looked behind her before typing Adam's name into the search bar. A half dozen Adam Graingers showed up on the screen. She realized she had little idea what she was looking for. If Adam was a secret child of Colleen's, he could be anywhere from thirty to sixty years old. The

Adams on the screen lived everywhere from North Dakota to Louisiana. None of them were located in Seaview or New York. She clicked through each of their profiles, but none of them had any information linking them to Colleen.

Logging off, she reviewed what she did know. Adam wanted something from Colleen and she wasn't giving it to him fast enough. Colleen had been cagey about secret children in conversations with Gemma. Adam's name began with an A, the letter the killer had carved into their victims. But Virginia didn't know what link this Adam could have to Irene or Herman, and if he was Colleen's estranged child and was blackmailing her for money, Virginia didn't know what motive he'd have to kill her.

An orange bottle of Ajax detergent made its way down the conveyor toward Virginia. She stopped in her tracks, a packet of tuna held aloft above the scanner, staring it down.

"Everything okay?" The customer's voice brought her back to the moment, and she looked up, scrutinizing his face.

"Yes, everything's fine." She looked back at the customer between each item she scanned. The screen grab from the security footage was useless. She couldn't tell if this was the person who had come through Eliza's lane and pulled his con. This man certainly didn't look like a scammer. He looked in his mid-thirties, with light scruff on his face, wearing a cable-knit sweater. He looked like the kind of man who carried a toddler through a farmers market on a Saturday morning. Virginia pictured car seats in the back of his SUV and wallet photos of his children tucked behind his credit cards. Of course, you never really knew. That was the trouble.

The man paid with a card and was on his way, none the wiser that he'd been under investigation in Virginia's mind for the previous three minutes.

Between customers, Virginia reflexively pulled her phone from her pocket and stared at Adam Grainger's number. She'd programmed him in as a contact. Now the number was just there, accessible, waiting for Virginia to decide the time was right to make another bad decision. After a particularly snotty woman collected her bags and huffed away from Virginia's checkout line, she pulled her phone from her pocket once more, ready to take action.

> Do any of you know an Adam Grainger?

She fired the text off to the Garden Review Society group chat. The conversation was rarely used. Gemma had created it to try to coordinate meeting dates and locations, but most of the group found the text chain confusing, and instead, Gemma just unilaterally decided on the meeting details, called everyone on the phone, and that was that.

DOROTHEA

> Is this about an investigation question

> I want an update oh how do I go back oh oh no

> Sorry I'm using text to speech I thought I did a? But it didn't oh what the heck now there's a? Oh goodness gracious

> I want an update Virginia

Virginia giggled as the texts came through, one after another. Not that she understood speech-to-text any more than Dorothea did. She just knew not to use it, or she'd look as ridiculous as Dorothea.

JAN

I want an update too!

How about breakfast at Bo's Biscuits next Thursday?

My nephew Jackson has cancer everybody so please pray for him.

ELLEN

This text chain should be used for Garden Review Society business only.

DOROTHEA

Clarissa from the Methodist clerk says she knows a Hugh Grainger and he lives on School Street

Church not clerk damn it this thing doesn't understand me

JAN

Garden Review business only, Dorothea!

"Are you open?" A woman was unloading a mountain of groceries onto the conveyor belt and gave Virginia a tight look of disapproval. Virginia apologized and pocketed her phone before scanning the items, but her mind was on Hugh Grainger. Did Adam have a brother?

VIRGINIA DROVE her Civic up and down the length of School Street, heart thumping faster with every passing moment. Finally, she pulled to a stop at the curb in front of a low, brick, ranch-style home with a large oak tree in the front yard. A ring of hedges surrounded the tree, all neatly trimmed, and a paved walkway led from the curb to the front door.

A woman with a toddler on her hip answered the door almost immediately after Virginia rang the doorbell. "Hey, Liz—" The woman greeted her cheerfully, then staggered back a step. Her face fell and she took a moment to recover. "I'm sorry, I was expecting someone else."

"I'm sorry, I suppose I was expecting someone else, too. I'm looking for Hugh Grainger."

"Wrong house," the woman said cheerfully. "This is 1472. I keep telling Sean we need to hang our house numbers back up. We took them down when we painted the trim and then never put them back."

"My mistake. Could you tell me which house is his?"

The woman narrowed her eyes a hair and hesitated. Virginia thought she saw her pull the child closer to her body. At eighty, she wasn't used to being seen as a threat and didn't expect that reaction.

"Can I ask why you're looking for him?"

This, Virginia realized immediately, was a question she should have expected. She kicked herself for not coming up with some sort of story. Her brain failed to come up with a single reasonable response. Instead, her mouth opened slightly and a low sound, entirely unintelligible, slipped out.

"I'm sorry?" The woman took another half-step back

and angled her son away from Virginia. If her concern before was well-concealed, she was no longer trying to hide it.

"I, erm, I said I'm with the *Seaview Gazette*." It was the most recent reason anyone had come knocking at Virginia's door. By the look on the woman's face, this was the wrong lie to choose.

"Why does the *Seaview Gazette* want to talk with Hugh? And why don't you know what house number he lives at? That seems like something a reporter would know before going to interview him."

Virginia started to stammer a response but the woman cut her off. "I'm sorry. I can't help you." The door slammed shut, and Virginia stood for a moment, processing what had happened before she could adjust her plan. While she was standing there, a woman around the same age as the homeowner she'd just spoken to came up the path.

"Can I help you?" The woman seemed surprised to see an elderly lady standing on the porch of her friend's house. Virginia hadn't noticed her come up.

"No, no, I'm fine." Virginia hurried back to her car, where she watched the newcomer be embraced in the doorway and then shuffled inside. The homeowner poked her head out the door and frowned, evidently displeased to see Virginia still sitting in her car out front. Virginia started the car and drove off, not needing to add a police encounter to the day in case the woman decided to call them.

A few blocks down, Virginia parked her car for a second time. This time, she was prepared. She'd say she was with the *Seaview Gazette,* and they were interviewing random members of the town to see how they felt about the latest local ordinance that had just gone into effect, raising the minimum fine for speeding.

None of that was necessary. The person behind the door of house number two didn't think twice about revealing Hugh's address to a stranger.

"I'm looking for Hugh Grainger" was all Virginia had a chance to get out before the woman, stooped over with a cane and likely older than Virginia, pointed down the street and said, "Four houses down on the other side of the road." She shut the door before Virginia even had a chance to thank her for the information.

Virginia drove the short distance down the street. She could have walked, but it was an opportunity to sit in the safe and familiar space of her car and also afforded her the chance for a quick getaway if one was needed. Instead of pretending to be with the *Seaview Gazette,* Virginia's plan with Hugh was to mention both Adam's and Colleen's names as soon as possible. She'd see whether he reacted and go from there.

Hugh's house was almost an exact copy of the first home she'd knocked on. Brick front, an oak tree in the yard, and neatly trimmed hedges all around. A low-slung sports car was parked in the driveway. Virginia suspected Hugh wasn't a fan of the new ordinance.

When a man pulled open the door, Virginia couldn't help but gasp. He had to be pushing seven feet tall.

"Hugh?" The name slipped from Virginia's mouth before she could stop it.

"That's me." The man's voice was low and gravelly, and

Virginia found herself transfixed. "Can I help you?" he asked when Virginia said nothing.

Virginia snapped out of her trance. "I'm actually looking for Adam Grainger. I'm a friend of Colleen's." She couldn't have torn her eyes from the man's chiseled face if she'd wanted to. Her heart sank when there was no flash of recognition in his eyes.

"I'm sorry," he said. "Different Grainger. I don't know them."

Virginia didn't make any move to leave. When she had played the scene out in her mind, Hugh denied knowing Colleen and Adam, but she could tell he was lying. She'd pressed him, and he'd caved, revealing that Adam was his half-brother, Colleen's son, and had recently discovered he was included in her will despite being abandoned by her as a child. Hugh had tried to talk him down, but Adam was convinced revenge was deserved and was going after Colleen. In this fantasy, Hugh also revealed Adam's connections to Irene and Herman.

In actuality, Hugh didn't seem to be lying, and Virginia felt the house of cards she'd built up in her mind tumbling down. "Are you sure?" she asked stupidly.

"Pretty sure." Hugh laughed a little at the question. He wasn't acting cagey or trying to shoo her off his doorstep. "Anything else I can help you with?"

Virginia returned to her car crestfallen. Sitting in the driver's seat, she looked down at her phone and Adam's contact information. Later, she decided. When she was back home at Breeze Village, she'd give him a call. She'd make a plan, and she'd find out who Adam was and what he wanted with Colleen.

CHAPTER 32

Virginia's finger hovered above the call button. Adam's name glowed on the screen. This was it. Every time she thought she had a plan, she either immediately forgot it or decided it wasn't going to work, but she didn't want to waste any more time. An officer was giving up dinner with his family to volunteer his time to post up outside her door and keep her safe. And Colleen was keeping Adam a secret when he had more motive than anyone on her list of suspects to want her dead. It was time to get some answers.

Rap rap rap!

Virginia's phone fell to the floor and skittered under her chair. Her hand flew to her heart as her head swiveled toward the door.

"It's me!" Marney's voice carried through the wood. "Open up!"

Blood racing, Virginia leapt up and pulled the door open. "What's wrong? What happened?"

Marney took a step back, her foot connecting with the seated officer's ankle.

"Ow!" He yelped in pain. Marney yelped in surprise and took another step back, this time entirely losing her balance and tumbling to the floor.

"Marney!" Virginia rushed to her friend and extended a hand to help her up. "Are you okay?"

Marney wiggled her wrists and bent her elbows in and out, assessing. She flexed and pointed her feet, then bent her knees. Finally, she circled her hips, testing the range of motion. "No worse for wear," she declared. Virginia released a breath. "What are you doing, flying to the door like a madwoman? I swear you tried to give me a heart attack. Instead, Officer Murphy here is going to have a swollen ankle, and I'll have a bruised rump."

"Your knock startled me! I thought something bad had happened."

Marney waved her off as if the idea were preposterous, as if she hadn't come knocking less than twenty-four hours prior to say someone had broken into her cottage. "I'm fine. I have news."

Marney plowed ahead into Virginia's room with Virginia at her heels. After a brief apology to the officer outside, she shut the door behind them and turned to Marney. "This had better be good."

"Tina is ready to talk with Colleen."

Virginia looked at Marney with confusion. "Tina?"

"Ed's wife," Marney clarified. "She's open to talking with Colleen to see whether she gives a more accurate reading than Lucinda. And if she does, then Tina will take

Ed back. Then he can forgive Colleen for enlisting you to investigate her would-be killer and making him feel unsafe at home, and we can work on convincing him to publish an apology in the paper to restore Colleen's reputation."

"Whoa, let's take this one step at a time." Virginia's head spun as she worked to digest Marney's plan.

"So you'll talk with Colleen?" Marney asked. "You'll convince her to do a reading for Tina?"

Virginia bit her lip, not sure how to respond. "I can try," she offered. "Colleen and I haven't talked much since, well, you know."

"But you saved her life. She should be bending over backward to do you a favor." Marney's brows knit together in frustration.

"For now. I saved her life *for now*. And before the whole accidental life-saving bit, I gave her plenty to be upset over."

"But this is our chance to fix all that! To get Ed back together with his wife and get him to tell everyone he was wrong about Colleen."

Virginia huffed a sigh. "I'll talk to Colleen."

Marney squealed with delight and wrapped her bony arms around Virginia in a tight hug. She was immersing herself in this to stay busy, Virginia thought, and to distract herself from the break-in, the danger they were all in. But that didn't mean it wasn't a good opportunity to repair some of the damage she'd done.

"WHERE ARE YOU GOING?" The officer in front of Virginia's door looked up from the game he'd been playing on his phone. The game plinged in the background, and he glanced down at it, then back at Virginia.

"I need some air." How, at eighty, had she found herself having to explain her comings and goings like a small child? "I'm going down to the porch to sit in one of the rocking chairs. Your colleague can radio you to confirm. I'm sure he'll be able to see me from wherever he's posted out front."

Satisfied, the officer gave a curt nod and turned his attention back to his phone. Virginia made for the elevators and then straight out to the wide porch adorning Breeze Village's main building. The sun had long set, the November evening coming early, but the Southern fall was still mild. A light sweater was all she needed, and the breeze felt decadent. She knew there was still an officer watching, protecting her from the unseen person who could slip into Breeze Village undetected to leave threats and who would have brazenly stabbed Colleen in a crowd of people, but she couldn't see them. She felt like she was alone. Herself and the night sky and Adam, somewhere. It was time to give him a call.

The phone rang six times before Adam answered it. She nearly hung up. Virginia had imagined the conversation at least a dozen times, picturing him confessing that he was after Colleen or denying everything but giving away a key piece of information that moved her investigation along. But in her head, she'd always jumped to the meat of the conversation. When he answered with a simple "Hello?" her heart froze, and her brain along with it. How was she supposed to get from *Hello* to *Yes, I'm the killer you're looking for, and you can find me at this address?*

"Adam?" Her voice shook, a tinny wobble in the great wide evening. She sounded old.

"Yes." He didn't give her an in. He waited for her to begin the conversation. She'd called him, after all.

Virginia counted to three in her mind and then came right out with it. "I'm calling because I am a friend of Colleen's and was hoping to speak with you."

"Colleen?" He sounded genuinely perplexed and entirely unfazed. Not the stunned, scared reaction she was hoping for.

"Colleen, err…" What was Colleen's last name? "The psychic." *Your would-be next victim, until I came along and spoiled your plans.*

"What's this in regards to?"

Virginia had two choices. She could be bold. Make a brazen accusation and see how he handled it, what his tone gave away. Or she could try to be clever. Adam didn't seem like he was going to give anything away based on how he'd reacted to hearing Colleen's name, but Virginia didn't trust herself to outsmart him trying a less blunt approach. Before she had the chance to make a decision, a figure stepped out of the shadows, and Virginia let loose a scream and dropped her phone to the floor.

"We need to talk." It was Colleen.

An officer came running from the corner of the building, weapon drawn. Virginia held up her hands and gasped out, "I'm fine." But she was glad to know he was there.

Virginia's breathing wouldn't slow. She held up a

finger to Colleen to signal for her to wait a minute. Then she looked at a point in the distance and tried to breathe in and out to a count of four. When she'd finally slowed her heart enough that she could hear sounds beyond her own body, she turned to where Colleen had taken a seat in the next chair over. "Let's talk."

"You don't want to forget that." Colleen pointed down at Virginia's phone lying on the peeling paint of the wooden porch. With a mumbled thanks, Virginia picked up the phone. The call had ended. She wondered if Adam would have called the police. Would he have been concerned for her or would he have brushed it off? What would he have even told the police? "A stranger called me and then screamed, and I have no idea who she was or where she might be?" But she didn't buy that he couldn't have figured out who she was.

"So," Colleen began. "You know about Adam."

"I know Adam exists," Virginia said. "I know you call him, or he calls you. I know he wants something from you. I know you're not delivering, and I know he's frustrated about it. I know his initial was carved into Irene Pushton and Herman Walsh."

Colleen let out a laugh, and Virginia flinched, still on edge. "Adam didn't kill those people," she said.

"Is Adam your son?"

Colleen laughed again. Virginia felt anger color her cheeks. "In a way," Colleen said. "Not like you're thinking. And he's not trying to kill me."

"Are you—?"

"I'm sure." Colleen let out a deep sigh and turned her gaze to the indigo sky before going on. "Adam is my friend's son. She was in an abusive relationship, and she didn't want the father to find out about him. She asked me to keep her pregnancy and Adam's existence a secret, so I did. For his whole life. Something he doesn't exactly thank me for."

The anger dissipated as quickly as it had arisen. Virginia pictured Marney and Dylan when she'd first seen them at the playground. She saw the way Dylan always seemed on edge around men growing up and thought about what a peaceful life she could have had if Dean had never known of her existence.

"Adam resents not having a father. He has two kids of his own now. Their mom left. Seeing her leave like that, just opt out of parenthood… It hurt him. He couldn't get past it. He's angry at her on his own behalf, of course, but also on behalf of his kids. He's angry about the relationship they won't get to have with her. And it brought back all the anger he had toward his mother and me for denying him his father."

"But he was abusive. It was for her safety. For Adam's safety."

Colleen nodded like this was something she'd heard or even said herself a thousand times before. "I know that. Adam doesn't know that."

"She never told him?"

"She didn't want to poison his mind with ideas about where he came from, who he's made up of. She didn't want him to question himself. For a long time, she told him his father had died before he was born. When he got older, he wanted to know more. She told him his dad had been a firefighter, a brave, strong man who died saving other people. Eventually, he got old enough to see through the lies. Penny got the fake names mixed up or messed up a date. I don't remember. But Adam was furious.

"He was about to take a DNA test a year or two ago. His wife left, and all that anger came right back to the surface, and he decided he was going to see what he could find out on his own. Penny begged him not to. I bribed him. The money was enough to hold him off, but that's the problem with a bribe like that. He can always raise the price or decide not to play anymore."

"So you've been paying him off this whole time?" Virginia thought back to the conversation she'd over-heard. "You told him you couldn't send him any more money right now. Have you paid him everything you made from your entrepreneurial success?"

"Heavens, no! But I can't let him think the tap is unlimited."

Virginia felt relieved to know her friend wasn't financially ruined by this twisted family secret. "And you're sure he's not… I mean, he's blackmailing you. You're sure he wouldn't…"

"Am I sure he wouldn't kill me for money and kill two other people I have no connection to for a reason I can't fathom?" Colleen asked. "Pretty sure. He's not in my will. I took him out of it the moment I made the first payment to keep him from taking that test, and I told him so, too."

The two rocked back and forth on the porch, the creaks of their chairs on the floorboards joining in the night symphony alongside the rustle of leaves in the wind and the calls of an owl in the distance. Virginia let her head fall back against the back of the chair as she rocked, eyes still wide open. Somewhere, unseen, the officer who'd rushed in at the sound of her scream was hiding with his weapon. Three others watched the building from other angles. Another still sat outside the door to her room. Five armed reminders that there was a predator out there and Virginia was no closer to identifying them than she'd been before.

"Are you still being haunted?" Virginia wanted to know.

Colleen seemed to draw into herself a bit. "The hauntings continue."

"My shoes went missing this morning." Virginia extended her legs to show her mismatched pair. "A while before that, cake appeared in my fridge."

"The spirits are reaching out to you, too?" Colleen planted her feet to stop her chair from rocking and looked at Virginia with concern. "This isn't good."

Though Virginia wasn't convinced the hauntings were the work of spirits at all, Colleen's concern stirred up dread in the pit of her stomach. She pulled out her phone and opened up the picture she'd taken of the visitor log before holding the phone out to Colleen. "This is everyone who signed in at the front desk on Halloween, when you got your note. Do you sense any energy from any of these names?"

Colleen looked at the picture, closed her eyes, then opened them and looked again before closing her eyes a second time. She stayed that way, as if she were meditating, for a few moments. Finally, she handed the phone back and shook her head. "Nothing. Well, not nothing. I get the strong sense that someone's visiting grandkid toilet-papered a house after their visit. But nothing helpful."

Virginia hesitated before asking her next question. "I heard there was a resident once who tried to get you kicked out."

"Dead," Colleen said, interrupting her before she could even ask.

"Yes, but I wondered if he was close with anyone who is still at Breeze Village? If someone could be looking for revenge on his behalf?"

Colleen assured Virginia that no one currently living at Breeze Village had any connections to him, and Virginia felt herself grow another inch shorter as yet another theory fell apart before her. Colleen stood to leave, then turned back to Virginia. She held one finger in the air and pressed her other hand to her temple, eyes closed. "I'm smelling saltwater on you. Are you headed to the beach for a night swim?"

Virginia considered the possibility. It was where she did her best thinking. "Colleen, would you be willing to help me with something?"

Virginia bade the officer at her door goodnight as she entered, then loudly shut the door behind her. On cue, Colleen came by desperately asking for help just a moment later. She heard the officer shuffle away, then Virginia slipped out with her beach bag over her shoulder and quietly shut the door behind her.

Colleen wasn't finished yet. Virginia waited for her in the elevator lobby around the corner from her door. The two rode the elevator downstairs together before Colleen hurried out the front door waving her arms above her head.

"It's all right!" she hollered into the darkness. Clouds moved quickly across the sky, and beams of moonlight shone down for a moment only to be replaced by dark shadows the next. "Your friend was able to help me, and I figured it out. It was just a spirit."

Virginia waited until Colleen had walked almost to the edge of the lawn and she was sure the officers watching the perimeter would be focused on her. Then she made her move, walking swiftly and confidently to her car. The officer who had been outside her door was sure she was still in her room. These officers weren't expecting her to leave. All that was left was to drive away.

Colleen continued her performance, going on about how something had been wrong in her rooms but a kind officer had been willing to help her, and it turned out just to be a spirit haunting her so there was no need to worry. In fact, Colleen believed that the spirits haunting her were the very reason she ought to be worried, but she didn't like living under scrutiny any more than Virginia did, and she was more than happy to help Virginia sneak away for a quiet think at the beach.

Just under a half hour later, Virginia was alone with the ocean. She stripped down and ran into the water, yelping at the cold, then hurried back to the shore and bundled up before sitting on one of the large wooden swings. Her body shivered in the cold, but she couldn't stifle the grin spreading across her face. Virginia's favorite thing to do, as it turned out, was whatever she damn well pleased, and there were bonus points when it included pulling one over on someone.

The screech of an owl sliced through the night, and Virginia jumped. The quiet seemed more pronounced in the wake of the interruption. She suddenly felt exposed, and it occurred to her that no one save Colleen knew where she was. She wondered if she'd made a mistake.

The rhythmic coming and going of the waves calmed her heartbeat until Virginia was able to relax, certain she wasn't in the presence of a killer. It was just her, alone. She thought of her conversation with Colleen, how she'd ruled out Adam. She felt for the boy. He was a man, sure, full-grown and responsible for his choices, but the person taking money from Colleen in exchange for not taking a DNA test was a hurt, angry little boy in a grown man's body.

Is the killer's name really on that list? Virginia thought about how every lead she chased went nowhere. And chasing them just got her into trouble. She thought of Marney's face when she'd come to tell Virginia her cottage had been broken into. Not only had Virginia made herself a target, but she'd endangered her loved ones, the one thing she'd sworn she wouldn't do, not with a grandchild on the way.

While her brain had a blast revisiting her failures, she remembered that she still needed to call around to local grocery stores to see if she could get any answers on the con man for Eliza. "Earl," she said, looking out at the water, "I think I've made a mistake. I thought I could do this, and I was wrong. I don't know what I'm doing."

The piercing ring of Virginia's phone cut the conversation short. She looked down to see Marney's name across the screen.

"Hello?"

"Virginia, where are you?" Marney was panicked. Her voice was breathy, and Virginia could hear her footsteps. She was running.

"What's going on?"

"Dylan's been stabbed."

"Tell me again what happened, slowly." Virginia was running to her car while talking with Marney, her attention entirely on the phone call and on getting to her vehicle. If the killer had been standing there beside her, she wouldn't have noticed.

"Dylan was stabbed. In your room. You weren't there." Marney's voice had steadied. She wasn't running anymore. And she was angry.

When Virginia was in the driver's seat, Marney told her how Dylan had relieved the officer at Virginia's door and was told she was inside. She'd heard a noise inside, but Virginia hadn't responded. Dylan entered the room and the killer was there. She stabbed Dylan before taking off out the second-story window. While everyone was worried about Dylan being stabbed, they were also trying to figure out where Virginia was and if she was okay.

"You weren't there," Marney repeated.

Virginia bit her tongue to keep herself from protesting. She'd snuck out. This was her fault. Nothing she had to say for herself would help. Then she bit down harder to keep from saying the next thing that came to her mind: *Did you say the killer is a woman?* That was one piece of information they hadn't had before, a piece that dramatically narrowed down the list of possibilities. But again, this wasn't the time.

"Where is she?" Virginia asked. She'd drive to the hospital and be there with Marney.

"Don't bother," Marney said. "Just go home. Where you should have been all along."

The words felt like a slap in the face. First, because Marney was right. Virginia shouldn't have snuck past the people trying to protect her. But second, because if Virginia had been there in her room like she was supposed to have been, she may have been killed that night.

"Is she okay?" The words sounded desperate, Virginia begging for the answer to be yes. But Marney had already hung up the phone.

Virginia didn't want to return to Breeze Village, but she didn't know where else to go. She wasn't about to turn up at Lawrence's place and explain the situation, nor did she want to tell either of her children how her actions had led to Dylan being stabbed. Going anywhere besides Breeze Village involved telling people she loved that she'd let them down anew, and she could not bear that. Besides, she figured a crime scene was likely to be safer than anywhere else. Her room would be crawling with police, and the scene would be secured. If she was allowed in at all, she could be sure no one was coming to get her tonight.

* * *

By the time Virginia was allowed to return to her room, the sun was nearly up. She shut the window, shivering in the chill of the November air and the knowledge that the killer had gained entry through this window, planning to kill her only hours earlier. She fell asleep the moment her head hit the pillow, then woke less than two hours later, covered in sweat with her heart pounding like she'd just run a race. A peek out the window revealed the first pink tendrils of sunrise emerging from behind the trees.

Her stomach rumbled, but she didn't dare go down to breakfast. What if she saw Marney? Others were bound to have heard what had happened, too. She couldn't take the curious glances. Her phone chimed and reminded her that she had a shift at work that day. She called in sick. The thought of standing on her feet and scanning groceries made her feel woozy. She needed to know how Dylan was, but she didn't dare ask.

After pacing circles around her room for what felt like a hundred times and eating a breakfast of mini powdered sugar donuts—the only snacks she had in her room—she slid on her shoes, still a mismatched pair since she hadn't been able to locate the others, and hurried out the door. No officer outside, she noticed. She kept her head down when she reached the lobby and made a beeline for her car.

She wasn't sure where she wanted to go. She just felt the need to *go*. The need to move. The energy inside her was too much, and she needed a release. The moment she started the car, her body took over, and in the blink of an eye, she found herself on the streets of what had been Grove Park. The neighborhood where she'd lived her entire life was transformed. The houses were demolished, and the new apartments Bellemeade was putting in were coming along but not nearly finished. It was a full-on construction zone with men in hard hats and reflective vests operating heavy machinery. Dust coated her windshield as she drove.

Whatever her heart was seeking in taking her there, it hadn't found. The familiar, safe place she'd spent her decades was gone. She turned a corner and made for the other side of town, a pull on the wiper switch sending a stream of fluid over the glass and clearing away the construction dust. She drove aimlessly. She still couldn't stomach going to see Lawrence or the kids. She pulled through McDonald's to get a coffee, then circled the town twice. Finally, she couldn't take it anymore. She called Jan.

If she was lucky, she thought, Jan wouldn't have heard anything about Dylan's stabbing yet. It had happened late enough that a good portion of Breeze Village would have been asleep, she hoped. Without their hearing aids in, most of them would have slept through the sirens and commotion that followed. And if the news hadn't already reached Jan, Virginia would be able to get her talking and not have to answer a single question herself. The perfect distraction. Exactly what she needed.

Virginia was surprised to find Jan sitting with Kim Nguyen in the sitting room at Harbor Vale.

"Kim! I wasn't expecting to see you here."

"I'm here for probably another few weeks at least. I had a fall and broke my hip, and I've needed some extra help until I'm recovered and can move back home." Kim put quite a bit of emphasis on *move back home,* and Virginia was reminded of how Kim had expressed such disdain at the idea of moving into a retirement community. When she'd sold her house in Grove Park, she'd moved into a bungalow close to her kids.

Virginia smiled. Another version of herself would needle Kim a little, ask about her kids and how she ended up in Harbor Vale after putting up such a fight, just to see her squirm. But the Virginia there today didn't need that. "You have it made here. Jan told me there's an in-house nail salon. I thought maybe we could get our nails done."

Jan leapt at the suggestion, and Kim, though she looked unenthused, went along. The chairs were far enough apart that they didn't have to speak to each other, which took the pressure of conversation off. Virginia waited to feel some of her heaviness subside, but instead, she just found herself peering at her phone every few minutes, waiting to see if Marney would call with news about Dylan.

"They don't have this at Breeze Village, do they?" Kim asked when the three of them were finished and comparing colors.

"No, we don't. I also heard you all have a dedicated movie room? Like a little theater?"

"We sure do," Jan said. "Want to see what's playing?"

Virginia liked the idea of another activity that required no conversation, so she agreed. As they made their way there, Kim muttered about the shortcomings of Breeze Village. Her attitude seemed to be that she sure wasn't planning to stay, but if she had to live somewhere other than her own home, it sure as heck would have every amenity.

Kim shuffled into the movie room ahead of Jan and Virginia, and Jan pulled Virginia to the side with a furtive glance. "Between you and me," she whispered, "I don't think Kim is moving back to that bungalow. But she's having some trouble adjusting to the reality of life at our age and the fact that this is probably home now. I think having you come visit is helping, though. She's taking a little pride in the place."

The three of them watched the last half of *October Sky* before emerging, blinking into the fluorescent lights of the hallway. Kim looked over at Virginia. "Want to eat at our restaurant before you have to go back?" Jan looked at Virginia eagerly, and Virginia agreed, bracing herself to listen to a litany of Breeze Village's shortcomings over their meal.

As it turned out, Kim could have recited a list of the shortcomings of Breeze Village, Virginia, and everyone Virginia had ever loved, and Virginia would hardly have noticed. Staring at her from across the dining room was Ed. If he knew of Marney's plan to get him and his wife back together, he didn't support it. He stared daggers at Virginia through the entire meal, and between that and her guilt and anxiety over Dylan, Virginia was hardly present at the table with Kim and Jan.

"You alright?" Jan finally asked. "You seem a bit distracted. Is this about the investigation?"

Virginia winced. "No, I'm fine." She didn't sound believable. The denial was too fast, too vehement. She took a breath and tried to sound more relaxed. "I was just thinking about work. This guy came in a while ago and scammed one of our cashiers out of a hundred bucks. She's young, and it really upset her. I was thinking of maybe calling other grocery stores to see if they've had anything similar happen and if maybe they got better security footage."

Jan looked impressed. "A whole other investigation. Look at you go!"

If only you knew. "I actually need to be going. But thank you both so much for a lovely afternoon."

Virginia didn't wait for a response, and she didn't offer hugs goodbye. She grabbed her bag and hurried out the door at a trot, then broke down in her car. A wail escaped her, and she saw heads turn on the sidewalk. Wiping her eyes, she turned the key in the ignition and pulled away from Harbor Vale. There was nowhere else to go. She couldn't kill any more time. She had to go home.

VIRGINIA SPIED two officers as she pulled into the Breeze Village parking lot. She wondered how many others were there that she couldn't see. Now that an officer had been attacked, the department had an easier time approving resources. Virginia's throat clenched with guilt. A security guard, not a member of the Seaview Police but a private security firm, paced in the lobby. He tipped his head in greeting when Virginia entered. She wanted to ask if he knew what happened to the officer who had been stabbed, but she didn't. She took the elevator upstairs, noted the lack of an officer outside her door, and locked herself in her room.

CHAPTER 35

*V*irginia woke disoriented. Drool clung to the side of her face while her hair stuck up straight from her head. She looked around, trying to pinpoint what woke her, then realized there was a knock at the door. She shuffled out of bed, slipping one foot into the slipper the maybe-ghost maybe-intruder had left behind, then looked out the peephole to see Marney standing before her and Pancake tugging at his leash, desperate to explore the rest of the hallway.

In her grogginess, she'd forgotten, but everything came rushing back to her with such force she had to put a palm against the wall to remain upright. Her stunt, sneaking out to the beach. Dylan's stabbing. The fact that she'd been too cowardly to call or visit in the interim. She backed away from the door, shaking her head. She couldn't face Marney. It was her fault Marney's daughter had been stabbed, and she hadn't even called. She couldn't have this conversation.

Marney knocked again, harder. Virginia returned to

bed and pulled the covers over her head, willing time to turn back. She'd remain there and face down the killer and keep Dylan from ever being in harm's way. But time pressed forward, and Marney knocked again, harder still.

The knocking eventually subsided, and Virginia breathed a sigh of relief. She wiped tears from her eyes as she reemerged from the bed and looked herself in the eyes in the mirror.

Coward.

A key turning in her lock tore Virginia from her self-recrimination. She watched with terror as the handle turned and the door swung open, grasping behind her for a lamp or other weapon she could use. Her heart stopped for a moment as her eyes focused on the figure before her. It was Haley.

"Ha—?" Virginia couldn't form the full name in her mouth. She set the lamp down.

Marney bounded in behind Haley, Pancake hurrying beside her. "You're okay!"

"Of course I'm okay." Virginia tried to make sense of Marney's fear.

"Then why weren't you answering the door?" That fear turned to anger as Marney realized Virginia had been hiding from her.

Haley left Marney and Virginia together, and Virginia stared down at her feet, one clad in a slipper and one bare on the carpet, trying to swallow the lump in her throat. She didn't have anything to say for herself. She couldn't ask about Dylan after saying nothing for a full day after the stabbing. So she stayed quiet and bit her tongue to keep from crying.

"You're not going to say anything?" Marney asked eventually.

"I'm sorry. I'm sorry I snuck out. I'm sorry Dylan was stabbed because of me. I'm sorry I wasn't here, and I'm sorry I didn't call or visit. I'm sorry I didn't ask how she was, and I'm sorry it wasn't me instead of her. Are you happy?"

Virginia was crying now, opening her mouth wide to suck in air and try to calm herself.

"Am I happy? Of course I'm not happy! My daughter is in the hospital, and my best friend has spent the entire time since she was stabbed avoiding me. How could I possibly be happy right now? And don't pull this 'It should have been me' bull with me. You know I don't wish that."

Virginia swallowed hard, the lump unmoving. "I do," she whispered.

Marney wrapped Virginia in a hug, her arms steadying her as Virginia's body heaved with sobs. "Dylan's okay," she whispered when Virginia had quieted enough to hear. "She's going to be perfectly fine."

Hearing that was all she needed for the waterworks to start back up again, and this time, Marney cried with her. When they'd both recovered, laughing tentatively as they blew their noses and wiped their cheeks, Marney told Virginia which hospital Dylan was in.

"The stab wounds weren't particularly deep and luckily didn't hit anything vital. She's in some pain, but there won't be any permanent damage."

"I can't tell you what a relief that is."

"And she got a pretty good view of the killer. Apparently, she wasn't expecting someone other than you to open the door. Dylan said she just stood there for a second, shocked, before diving at her twice with the knife and taking off out the window."

"She just jumped out a second-floor window?"

Marney nodded. "Dylan saw her land, roll, and run off with a limp like she'd hurt herself. I don't think she was planning on making such a quick exit." They both grimaced, aware of what the killer expected to have accomplished that night.

"How'd she get in the window?"

"There wasn't a ladder or anything. Police think she climbed a tree and then shimmied across where the brick-work makes that little ledge until she got to your window."

Virginia considered this. *So she'd been watching and knew which window was mine.* "Doesn't sound like someone our age if she's coming and going through the window like that."

Marney shook her head. "Dylan said she looked younger. Definitely not Colleen's peer."

"I assume they're doing a sketch?" Virginia wanted to see the face of the person who'd been living in her head these weeks. She wanted to see who she was up against.

"I think so. I may have forgotten a few things because I was a bit distracted. Dylan had news."

Virginia perked up. What news?

"She's stepping down from her position as Assistant Chief. She's leaving the force."

"She's *what?*" If Virginia had had a hundred guesses, she wouldn't have guessed this was Dylan's news.

"She's seeing someone." Color rushed to Marney's

face. Her smile reached from ear to ear. "Another officer. Officer McNeil. She said that in the wake of being stabbed, she decided she wants to live life to the fullest, so she's stepping down so she can give their relationship a real chance. He has kids, Virginia. Two kids, a boy and a girl. She told me not to get carried away, but I can't help it."

Virginia reached out and took Marney's hands in her own, then gave them a gentle squeeze. "Kids," she echoed.

A SECOND SURPRISE visitor knocked at Virginia's door while she was checking all possible hiding places for snacks in her room. She was still avoiding the common areas until the gossip around the stabbing had a chance to dissipate, but she was hungry. Virginia eyed the door with suspicion, expecting Ronald or Gemma wanting information. She received the second-biggest shock of the day—only a hair less surprising than Dylan leaving the police force—when she looked through the peephole and saw her daughter looking uncomfortable outside her door.

"Lucy? What are you doing here?"

"I'm happy to see you, too, Mother." Lucy stepped inside without waiting to be invited. She kept her heels on, assessing Virginia's space with a schooled neutrality to her face. Finally, she looked her mother over. "Where is your other slipper?"

"A ghost took it." Virginia decided to leave out the fact that this ghost-slash-almost-certainly-human had taken one of each pair of shoes she owned. As it stood, Lucy was free to interpret the ghost remark to mean that Virginia had simply misplaced one of her slippers and was less likely to worry. "Did we have plans I forgot about?"

"I wanted to drop by and see how you're doing. Things have gotten downright scary, what with Dylan being stabbed. By the way, thanks for telling us." Lucy shot Virginia a glare that reminded her she hadn't told the kids. "Dylan called to ask me to pick up some of her things. She was surprised to find I hadn't heard that she was in the hospital."

"Lucy, everything's okay, but Dylan got stabbed in my room at Breeze Village. The killer was in there and expected it to be me opening the door. Just wanted to let you know."

"Funny, but I'm being serious. I can't believe you didn't tell us sooner. Jack is beside himself, by the way."

"Of course he is. But I've got it handled."

Lucy put her thumb and middle finger on either side of the bridge of her nose and closed her eyes. "You do not have it handled, Mother. The *police* have it handled, which I was very happy to see. They've got officers all over this building, and they're working hard to identify the suspect. I had to show my ID when I signed in at the front desk. That's new."

Virginia tried to remember when Lucy had been to visit before, that she would know whether the procedure had changed.

"Look," Lucy continued, "I'm sorry to be snippy with you. But Jack and I need to know you're safe. And from what I can tell, you are. If—and this is a big one—you stop sneaking around trying to do everything yourself."

Virginia wanted to hold out her pinky and promise. Instead, she avoided eye contact with her daughter. She knew herself too well to make that promise. "I know. And I will try."

Lucy let out an exhausted sigh but didn't fight. "Jack and Stephanie are doing well," she said, changing the subject. "Stephanie loves the blanket you made them."

Virginia's cheeks pulled up into a smile, but her stomach contracted with shame. She wasn't the mom who could gift strollers and cribs and big-ticket items for her grandchild. That was Sam. She'd had to make her gift.

"I'm serious," Lucy said, apparently noting Virginia's embarrassment. "It's gorgeous and personal. Stephanie mentions it every time we talk, which is honestly exhausting, but I thought it might make you happy to know." It did make Virginia happy.

"Dylan's quitting her job," Virginia said.

Lucy's eyeballs practically leapt from her skull. "What?"

Virginia nodded. "She's dating another officer. Wants to give it a go and can't do that as Assistant Chief."

Lucy cocked her head to the side. "Good for her." She looked at her mother with discerning eyes. "Are you scared?"

"What do you mean?"

"You're losing your inside man. Not that Dylan is exactly taking up arms to partner with you in your investigations, but she's your connection to the force."

Virginia didn't want to admit anything other than joy that Dylan was following her heart. But she didn't have to admit it, apparently.

"It's okay," Lucy said. "You can be happy for the ones you love while also being nervous about what their decisions mean for you."

"I don't think it's an *effective immediately* type thing. If I know Dylan, she'll stay on until they catch the person who stabbed her. That's personal now."

"It was personal the moment the killer threatened you." Lucy's eyes bored into Virginia's, and Virginia had to look away. She'd helped raise Dylan, but they'd never entirely seen eye to eye. There had always been tension. And though she loved Dylan like she was her own, she hadn't felt that reciprocated. Lucy's mouth drew down in a frown. "You don't think Dylan took it personally when your life was threatened? Mom, she volunteered to sit outside your door during her time off work to protect you."

The guilt she'd felt over Dylan's stabbing only compounded. Lucy reached out to take her mother's hand in her own. "Don't feel guilty," she said softly. "But stop sneaking around, like I told you."

Virginia pulled her hand away and took the few steps to the window. She looked out, biting her tongue and tipping her head back to keep from crying. This was too intimate a conversation to be having with her daughter. They didn't have this kind of relationship. Virginia didn't know how to act.

"I've got to go," Lucy said, taking the cue. "I'm serious about being safe. Jack will personally come and tie you up if he gets wind you're being reckless."

There it was, the relationship she was familiar with. It gave her purchase to turn and force a smile while she saw her daughter out. The fortitude to make it through those two minutes and not dissolve until she was alone again.

Her children were afraid for her, and seeing their fear made her acknowledge her own. She was being hunted. By someone who could climb through windows and sneak around unseen. And whether or not that person—that woman, Virginia reminded herself; they knew what she looked like—was successful at taking her life, she'd already been successful at taking Virginia's freedom.

CHAPTER 36

*M*arney showed up at Virginia's door at the crack of dawn with a duffel bag under each arm. She was breathing heavily like she'd hurried there.

"I'm running late. Are you still up for watching Pancake while I'm gone?"

Virginia ran through every recent interaction she'd had with Marney, trying to remember if she'd mentioned a trip.

"The crochet retreat," Marney said, trying to jog Virginia's memory. Virginia still didn't remember and gestured for Marney to elaborate. "I booked it months ago. I'll be back day-after-tomorrow."

"Are you sure you still want to go, given, well, the current situation?" *Your daughter in the hospital and a killer on the loose.*

"Dylan's coming with me."

"She's out of the hospital?" Virginia breathed an enormous sigh of relief. "That's wonderful."

Marney's smile looked less than entirely relieved. "She is. And she insists on accompanying me on this trip. She's got another week off work while she finishes recuperating, and she would not be dissuaded."

Virginia cackled and shooed her friend off. "You said you're running late. Go! I've got Pancake covered." *I'll set a reminder in my phone so I don't forget to have Pancake covered.*

"I asked Jane, too, so Pancake will be receiving double the love and attention while I'm gone."

Virginia stiffened imperceptibly. Sure, she'd forgotten her friend's original request, but she bristled at the idea that Marney felt like she needed a backup for Virginia's forgetfulness. Virginia vowed to herself to spend extra time with Pancake. She was going to be the best darn cat-sitter Pancake had ever known, and Jane would not be needed.

Jane, as it turned out, did not wait to be needed. When Virginia went to check on Pancake after breakfast, Jane was sitting on Marney's couch knitting the fuchsia sweater Virginia knew she was planning to give Marney for Christmas. She greeted Virginia enthusiastically. Pancake purred, curled up against Jane's thigh, entirely disinterested in Virginia.

"I just came to check on the little monster," Virginia said. "It looks like you've won him over."

"He wanted to play with my yarn, and now he's tired himself out."

Virginia didn't want to turn and leave, conceding her job to Jane, so she stepped inside and took a seat on the chair across the coffee table from the couch, then pulled out a book. "The sweater is coming along beautifully," she said.

"Do you think Marney is going to like it?"

Virginia's heart constricted. She didn't like sharing her best friend, but she loved seeing Marney be loved. "I know she will," Virginia said honestly.

The two passed over an hour in contented silence, reading and knitting with Pancake softly snoring next to Jane. It wasn't until Virginia was returning to her chair from the bathroom that something caught her eye. The corner of something, jutting out from behind the couch.

"What's that?"

Jane turned to look but couldn't tell any better than Virginia. Virginia walked over and gave it a tug. She and Jane gasped in unison when she pulled it from behind the couch. It was a bulletin board that looked like something out of one of those cop shows Ed watched too loud for Jimmy's liking. Virginia recognized pictures of Herman Walsh and Irene Pushton in the center. A photo of Colleen was pinned to the side. Red yarn connected the photos to bits of information Marney had written on scraps of paper and pinned to the board.

"What is this?" Jane's voice was equal parts awed and afraid. Pancake lifted his head but watched from the couch, unwilling to give up his spot to come see what they were doing.

"I think Marney was investigating the murders." Virginia saw her own name written in Marney's handwriting, pinned to the corner of the board. It was linked to Colleen with red yarn, and beneath Virginia's name Marney had written, *Revenge for Saving Colleen.*

She'd had no idea Marney had been investigating on her own. She sunk down to the floor, glad for Jane's presence if only because she knew she had someone to help her up later. But she couldn't hold herself up any longer to the weight of what she'd brought upon Marney and Dylan. Marney's cottage had been broken into. Dylan had been stabbed. All because Virginia had gotten in the killer's way. She was always in the way.

She took in the rest of what Marney had gathered. She had noted the link between Colleen and Irene, Jenson Haider, the attorney who had dated Irene and lost in court to Colleen. Beneath both Irene and Herman, she had abbreviated life histories. Where they'd been to school, where they'd worked, where they'd lived.

"Hold on a minute," she whispered, scrambling closer to the board. Herman had worked at *Publishers Weekly* briefly in the early '90s. Virginia hadn't found that in her research. Irene hadn't worked for any of the same companies as Colleen, but she'd represented Hearst Magazines in a lawsuit in 1991.

There it was. The connection.

Irene and Herman hadn't worked together, and they hadn't worked with Colleen, but they'd all been in the magazine industry in New York City thirty years ago. Virginia would bet her life that the killer had been, too.

SHE HAD IT. A clue. A lead. Something to help narrow down the identity of the killer. It wasn't anything to do with the ice cream business or the ghost hunting. And it wasn't a resident upset with Colleen. It was from way back. *Just like Colleen said.* Virginia grimaced at how hard she'd pushed back against Colleen's insistence that anyone who wanted her dead was from her distant past. She left an astonished Jane and disinterested Pancake and took off at a trot across the courtyard. She needed to find Colleen.

She'd been down the list. She'd go through it again. But she needed Colleen to think about whether there was anyone specifically from her time in magazines that she'd left off the list. Did knowing that the killer was from Colleen's time in magazines jog any other ideas?

She rapped at Colleen's door until her knuckles hurt. No answer. She was turning to leave, ready to go back to her room and pore over Colleen's list anew, when Harriet's door opened.

"Virginia." Harriet smiled, leaning on the doorframe as she poked her head out into the hallway. Virginia grinned back, surprised to have been remembered. "I heard my ghost talking with that Adam again."

"Oh?"

"She didn't sound very happy with him."

"I'm sure it's fine. Actually, Harriet, I'm in a bit of a hurry." She waited for Harriet to dismiss her, the two standing in silence until finally, Harriet gave a tiny nod.

"Come visit me again," Harriet instructed before ducking back into her room.

Virginia fumbled with the key in her lock, eager to get inside and have another look at that list. She inserted the key, withdrew it, flipped it over, and tried again. On the third try, she managed to unlock the door and flew inside. Then stopped dead in her tracks. The door slammed shut behind her, but Virginia hardly heard it. A photo stared up at her from the carpet of her floor.

CHAPTER 37

$\mathcal{A}$ roaring whoosh accompanied by a high-pitched ringing filled Virginia's ears. She knelt down to bring the photo closer, then gasped and tossed it back down. It was a photo of her and Jane, less than half an hour earlier in Marney's cottage. They were looking at Marney's bulletin board.

Virginia turned to look behind her, then scanned her room again. There was no one there. The window was closed and locked. The photo was too far inside to have been slid under the door.

The killer was watching them, and the heightened security didn't stop her from getting to Virginia's room.

She dialed 9-1-1, reaching back out and clutching the photo in a shaking hand.

"What's your emergency?" The dispatcher on the other end sounded so distant and calm. Virginia's mouth opened and closed, releasing unintelligible sounds as she grappled for a way to explain her emergency. Finally, she found words.

"This is Virginia Walker. There's an ongoing investigation. I, uh, I need to speak to an officer on my case."

"I'm sorry, ma'am, can you please repeat that? Do you have an active emergency?"

"Yes." The word landed more forcefully than Virginia repeated. "A break-in. There's been a break-in."

The dispatcher asked Virginia to repeat her name and give her location. Virginia remained on the line while heading downstairs. She didn't need officers arriving to make a report of the break-in. She needed officers on her case looking for the killer who had been on the premises in the last half-hour and would still be nearby. She ran out the front door waving the photograph in the air. Two officers were by her side in minutes. One spoke to the dispatcher and ended the call while the other talked with Virginia.

"When did you find this?" His voice was urgent, and his eyes flicked around the parking lot as they spoke. He leaned down and spoke into his radio.

"I think the killer worked in New York thirty years ago. In the magazine industry." The officer looked at Virginia like she'd postulated that the killer liked Fruit Loops. Suddenly she was back in the spring, trying to explain to an officer how she was certain Ruth's death hadn't been an accident. She had to get out of here.

Her first stop, when the officers dismissed her, was Gemma's cottage. If anyone knew where Colleen was, it would be Gemma. The officers said they'd pass along the information she gave them, search the area surrounding Breeze Village for a suspect matching the description Dylan had given them, and maintain their presence at

Breeze Village. Virginia didn't feel any safer than if they'd said they were calling off the entire investigation. With officers surrounding the building, the killer had managed to snap a photo of Virginia in Marney's cottage, then get into Virginia's room to leave it there for her to find.

"What's the emergency?" Gemma was holding a cinnamon bun the size of her head and looked upset to have her brunch interrupted by Virginia's frantic knocking.

"I need to find Colleen."

"What's the hurry?"

Virginia laid the photo on Gemma's counter. "That's me and Jane in Marney's cottage this morning. I found this in my room."

Gemma set her pastry down, a grave expression on her face.

"Where can I find Colleen?"

"I don't know where she is. When she wants to be alone, sometimes she goes to the art gallery downtown or to the bagel place on Kemp."

Virginia screwed up her face in disgust. "That bagel place is disgusting! Only tourists go there."

"That's how Colleen makes sure she won't run into anyone she knows."

The art gallery was closer to Breeze Village, and Virginia could go there without feeling obligated to spend seven dollars on a cardboard bagel with gluey cream cheese, so that's where she started. She noticed the unmarked car following her and tried to focus on feeling thankful for police protection and not frustrated at constant supervision.

Seaview's largest art gallery occupied an ivy-covered building downtown that was once a residence. It stood three stories tall, and a chalk sign on the sidewalk invited guests inside. The owners had knocked down walls and added doorways so each room connected to all its nearest neighbors. Almost every room had more than two doorways, and Virginia felt almost as if she'd stepped into a funhouse. No matter where she went, there were too many points of entry, and she couldn't watch her back.

In one room, she was momentarily transfixed by a painting of an egret. She stood watching it, unaware just for a second of the other people around. When she remembered herself and turned, a woman behind her was staring at her with such intensity Virginia nearly turned and ran, but she didn't want to expose her back to the woman. Instead, she pretended to be interested in the painting directly behind the woman until she'd left the room and Virginia was confident she wasn't about to be stabbed. She passed through the gallery as quickly as she could before making her exit.

At Best Bagels, Virginia felt herself relax when she walked beneath the bells jingling on the door and spied Colleen in the corner sipping a cup of coffee.

"There you are!"

Colleen looked up, surprised to have a visitor. "How'd you find me here?"

"Were you hiding from me?"

"Not from you, specifically. Just from everyone. I needed some peace. All the police around, the constant reminders that someone out there wants me dead. This is one of my sanctuaries." She gestured around at the small shop. Canvas prints of art featuring cups of coffee hung on the walls alongside prints with phrases like *Give me coffee and no one gets hurt* or *Mug life.*

A line of tourists stretched to the door. Best was only a block from the visitors' center and the starting point for trolley tours. Virginia figured at least half their business was tourists who'd popped over to the visitors' center and were advised that the next tour started in half an hour, but there was a bagel place down the street where they could pass the time. She wondered if Best Bagels and the visitors' center had some sort of arrangement in place.

"Yeah, I'm familiar with the feeling of having someone want you dead," Virginia said dryly. "That's kind of why I'm here. Marney made a connection, and we know the killer is from your magazine era in New York."

"That's good news." Colleen brightened slightly but still seemed more interested in her coffee and newspaper than in talking with Virginia. "That narrows down my list considerably."

"I wanted to ask you to think back on that time and see if you could think of any other suspects. Now that you know our killer is a woman and when in your life you must have crossed paths, I thought maybe it would help you come up with more possibilities."

Colleen waved her away. "I already told you. Anyone I could possibly think of who might want me dead is on the original list I gave you."

Virginia slammed her hands down on the table. "And I'm telling you to think harder."

Colleen, along with the rest of the patrons, was shocked by Virginia's outburst. Virginia gave them all an apologetic glance, then reached into her bag and slapped the photo from this morning down onto the tabletop.

"What is this?" Colleen asked, but judging by the way her face was devoid of all color and her eyes were terrified, she already guessed.

"This was in my room waiting for me this morning. It was taken less than half an hour before I found it." She gave Colleen a moment for her words to sink in. "All those officers and this woman can still come and go without detection. She's taunting me. For all I know, she could have followed me here." Colleen looked around frantically. "Make me a new list," Virginia commanded.

Colleen pulled a pen and pad of paper from the large, formless bag she carried with her. She began to scrawl names, pausing between each one to stare off and think. When she finished, she slid the paper across the table to Virginia, and Virginia's jaw dropped. This list was nearly as long as the original list.

"They're not all people I think want to kill me. I tried to think of anyone I could remember working with during that time of my life. I figured it's better to be overly inclusive than miss someone."

Virginia thanked her and tucked the note away, hoping she could start with the *A* names and not have to progress beyond those.

"You'll let me know what you come up with?" Colleen asked, reaching out and gripping Virginia's wrist.

Virginia nodded, then slipped out of the café and onto the street. She didn't notice anyone following her until she spotted the same unmarked car that had followed her from Breeze Village idling across the street. She gave the officer in the driver's seat a small nod of acknowledgment before climbing into her own car and pulling away.

* * *

"Wʜᴀᴛ's ᴛʜᴀᴛ?"

Virginia startled awake in front of the computer in the second-floor common area, knocking the mouse off the desk so it clattered to the floor.

"Sorry." Virginia turned to see who had found her. Patricia was standing behind her, looking contrite. "I didn't mean to scare you."

"I must have dozed off." Virginia had a moment of panic and then relief that Colleen's new list was still there on the desktop.

"What's that?" Patricia repeated.

Virginia considered lying. She hadn't told Patricia or anyone else at Breeze Village that she was the killer's target, though based on the security outside her door and Dylan being stabbed in her room, she figured people had probably figured it out. "It's a list of suspects."

"Why is Cece on it?" Patricia pointed to a name Virginia didn't recognize. Ashley Grummond.

"What do you mean?"

"I saw it on her paperwork when she moved in. Her real name is Ashley Grummond. She just goes by Cece."

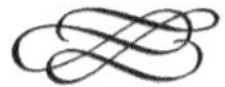

CHAPTER 38

"Cece moved in right before Halloween. Right before everything started. Her name—her real name—starts with an *A*." Virginia felt sick. "Why is she going by a fake name?"

"I've seen her on the stairs when the elevator was taking too long," Patricia said. "I don't think she's climbing in or out of any windows." Virginia also couldn't picture Cece stabbing anyone to death or carving her initial into them, but she didn't know what to think anymore.

"So she's got a sidekick! An accomplice!" Virginia closed all her open windows on the computer and carefully tucked the list of suspects into her pocket. "I've got to go confront her."

Patricia recoiled like Virginia had suggested jumping into a pit of snakes. "And what? Get stabbed like Dylan was? You need a plan."

She wasn't wrong. Virginia leaned over the computer

desk and bowed her head, trying to come up with something.

"Who are we confronting?" Ronald's voice startled both Patricia and Virginia, and they whirled to see him coming down the hall. "You two talk too loud. I sent Patricia to find you for a card game, and when she didn't come back, I figured I'd find you myself. Sounds like there's something more interesting than cards afoot tonight."

"Cece goes by a fake name. Her real name is Ashley Grummond, and she worked with Colleen in New York thirty years ago. I think she might be our killer." Virginia recounted the connection she'd made in Marney's cottage that morning, then showed them both the photograph. She tried not to dwell on the fear in their eyes when they realized how dire the situation was. She was being watched, and the killer wasn't discouraged by the police trying to keep her safe.

"Cece goes to arts and crafts every week," Ronald suggested. "She'll be there tomorrow morning for sure. I can keep watch while you break into her room like you did to Ed. Get whatever you need as proof and then call the police."

Virginia didn't want to wait for the next day. She wanted to move now. She knew she wouldn't get a wink of sleep knowing the killer was out there, undeterred by locked doors and armed guards.

"I'll stay with you tonight," Patricia volunteered, sensing Virginia's hesitation. "If you want."

Virginia didn't know Patricia that well, and here she was volunteering to stay with her overnight for comfort and protection. Virginia's heart swelled, but she shook her head. "That's very sweet of you, but I'll be okay." She wasn't ready to accept that kind of offer yet. Instead, she returned her focus to the operation at hand. "Your photographic memory has already helped. You don't happen to have any other hidden talents I don't know about? Lockpicking, maybe?" Marney wouldn't be back from her retreat in time to aid in their mission the next day.

Patricia shook her head. "I could read about it tonight, though."

"No need," Ronald chimed in.

"You pick locks?"

"I know someone who does." Virginia and Patricia waited with bated breath, and Ronald grinned, showing all his missing teeth, milking the moment. Finally, he pointed to the ceiling. "There's a rumor Colleen's neighbor was Picklock Paisley."

"Picklock Paisley?" Patricia scrunched up her face.

Virginia tried to recall why the name sounded familiar. "In Atlanta? In the sixties?"

Ronald nodded and grinned even wider.

"The cat burglar who terrorized the wealthy. No newfangled security system was a match for her. She'd be in and out with the jewels and cash before the homeowners ever knew, and the next day a women's shelter, soup kitchen, or other charity would receive a sizable donation."

Patricia looked awed. Virginia pictured Harriet and tried to reconcile the vision she'd had of Picklock Paisley from reading the papers and the image of the Harriet she knew. From the few glimpses victims got of her, all the police were able to ascertain was that the burglar was a woman. Virginia shivered at the similarities Paisley shared with her current tormentor.

"Harriet?" she asked. "I can't picture it."

"There's a peace that comes with the fading faculties of old age. The expectations get lower. People don't take you seriously. They underestimate you. Plenty of folks in here like that peace, and they want a taste of it before their faculties actually decline."

"You're saying she's not as out of it as she acts?"

"I'm saying, if she were my neighbor, I'd never assume she wasn't watching."

Virginia thought of Harriet calling Colleen her ghost friend. She didn't think Harriet was acting. But if Harriet was who Ronald thought she was, Virginia had never wanted to have drinks and hear the tales from someone's life as badly as she did now.

VIRGINIA, Ronald, and Patricia bickered as they approached Harriet's door. Virginia insisted that she'd be overwhelmed to be greeted by all three of them. Ronald insisted that all of this was his idea in the first place, and he wasn't going to be left behind. Patricia said nothing but didn't linger for a moment, not about to be the only one left out. Virginia glared at them both before knocking on the door. She heard a shuffling inside, the sound of the lock being turned, and then Harriet slowly pulled the door back and peered out at them. A grin broke out across her face. "Visitors!"

She ushered them inside. She only had two chairs, her recliner and a second armchair that looked like it rarely got much use. "Sit, sit," she said, pointing to the armchair before reclaiming her spot in the recliner. The three looked at each other, and then Ronald took the armchair. He gave them a wink that said *My plan, my seat.*

"You brought friends," Harriet said, fixing her eyes on Virginia.

Virginia squirmed a bit under her gaze, wondering what was going on behind those eyes that she had underestimated before.

"This is Ronald and Patricia." Virginia gestured to her friends.

"Why are you here?"

"Are you familiar with Picklock Paisley?" Ronald took a leaf from Harriet's book and got straight to the point. Her eyes flashed with recognition, and Virginia thought she saw the edges of Harriet's lips tug upward, though her race returned to neutrality almost immediately.

"Picklock Paisley." Harriet repeated the name softly. "I may have seen an article or two in the papers, back in the day."

"Articles, huh?" Patricia narrowed her eyes at Harriet, who laughed at the scrutiny.

"If I recall correctly, Paisley was a hero to the poor of Atlanta, those who needed her most."

"She was," Ronald nodded. "And now our friend Virginia here needs her."

It was Harriet's turn to narrow her eyes in suspicion. "I'm not sure why you're here talking to me, then."

"Can you still pick a lock?" Virginia asked.

Harriet didn't answer. She didn't have to. Her eyes were sparkling. Her fingers wiggled where he had her hands crossed in her lap. Harriet was itching to be back in action.

* * *

HARRIET WAS as reluctant as Virginia to wait until morning to pull off their burglary. They promised they'd come to collect her first thing, then Virginia spent the night tossing and turning, sitting bolt upright and grabbing the lamp on her nightstand every time something creaked in the dark. The metal lamp was warm from her grasp by the time the sun rose and illuminated the room.

"It's time." Ronald was waiting at her door when she pulled it open, ready to hurry down to his room. She wondered if the others had been as anxious as she had during the night. If she was right, they were breaking into the lair of a killer. Someone who had killed twice and was ready to do it again.

Harriet was dressed in all black when the three friends arrived at her door. "Let's do this." Her energy was infectious, and Virginia was practically bouncing with every step as the foursome took the elevator downstairs and started down the hall toward Cece's room.

Ronald peered in the window of the activity room and gave a thumbs up. Cece was inside, enjoying arts and crafts. They had another forty minutes until the activity would be finished and the yoga class would take over the space.

Harriet had the lock picked before Virginia could even

ask, "Will you be able to pick it?" She almost looked disappointed at how easy it had been.

"That was incredible," Patricia breathed.

Harriet's disappointment subsided. She glowed at the compliment. All four of them crept inside. Ronald flicked on the light.

"What the hell?" Virginia sputtered.

Cece's room could have been Marney's cottage. Yarn, crocheted objects, and half-finished works in progress covered every surface. Blankets piled atop Cece's floral upholstered armchair rose beyond the back of the chair, towering halfway to the ceiling. Stuffed animals in every color combination leaned against the wall. The only thing she was missing was a little tabby cat batting at the balls of yarn.

Virginia took a step forward and picked up one of the unfinished pieces. It was a gingerbread house, part of a Christmas village like Marney had been making.

"What is all this?" Patricia asked, a stuffed bear in each hand.

"Virginia?" A tiny, heartbroken voice sounded from the doorway. All four of them turned in slow motion to see Cece's crumpled face staring back at them.

"Aaargh!" Ronald charged at her, knocking Cece to the floor and pinning her down. Virginia thought that if she were the killer, she was easier to take down than Virginia expected.

"I'm sorry!" Cece cried out from beneath Ronald. He adjusted his position to keep her from squirming, but she only squirmed harder. "How did you find out?"

"Quiet!" Ronald commanded.

Cece brought a knee up and made contact with Ronald's gut. He let out a groan, and she was able to wiggle her torso out from under him. She gasped for air, then said, "I'll close my shop down. I'll share my proceeds with Marney."

Ronald froze. "What is she talking about?"

"Let her up," Virginia commanded.

Ronald moved off of Cece, and Virginia extended her hand to help her up. Cece took it warily. Patricia and Ronald both looked baffled. Harriet looked amused, like she'd won house seats to the best show in town.

"You're the competing crochet shop," Virginia said, holding up the gingerbread house. Cece bowed her head in shame. "How could you?" Virginia spat. She tossed the unfinished work down on the floor. "You stole her ideas. You stole her product descriptions and photos. You undercut her in price." With every accusation, she found herself stepping closer to Cece. She wanted to shove her. She wanted to tell Ronald to slam her back down on the floor. Instead, she asked, "Why?"

Cece avoided eye contact. She picked the crocheted gingerbread house up off the floor and picked lint off of it. "I saw the success Marney was having. I thought she was so cool. I wanted that for myself, and I've always knit and crocheted. I thought I'd open my own shop, make a little name for myself."

"But you didn't make a name for yourself. You opened a shop anonymously and stole from my best friend."

"I'm sorry!" Cece repeated. "I didn't know what to make, so I thought I'd take some ideas from Marney until I could come up with some of my own. Things got out of hand. It wasn't ever what I intended. I'll shut down my shop and give Marney all the money I made."

Virginia raised her finger, ready to lay in on Cece about how that would never make up for the distress she'd caused, but Ronald cut her off.

"I thought we were here to get proof Cece—or should I say *Ashely*—was a murderer?" he asked Virginia.

"A what?" Cece's eyes bulged, and she shook her head frantically. "I never..." She couldn't even finish the sentence.

"We were," Virginia told Ronald. "But I was wrong. She's not a killer. Only a lousy thief."

"But you worked in New York," Ronald said, still regarding Cece as if she were a viper ready to strike at any moment. "With Colleen, in magazines. You go by a fake name."

Cece released a breath slowly. "I left New York a long time ago. My husband was dangerous. I've been going by Cece for what feels like my entire life." Cece looked at them nervously. "I took cash jobs and avoided background checks, anything I thought might enable him to find me. I'm not a killer."

Virginia felt the sudden urge to squeeze Cece's hand, to comfort her.

"You're on Colleen's list," Ronald insisted.

"What list?"

Virginia's hand reflexively went to her pocket, where the list was nestled safely inside. "I have reason to believe the killer worked in the magazine industry in New York roughly thirty years ago. This was toward the end of Colleen's time in the industry. Both Herman Walsh and

Irene Pushton were there around the same time. We think the killer met each of them during that time frame and is enacting some sort of revenge plan now."

"After thirty years?" Cece seemed unconvinced. Virginia had had the same reaction when Colleen had first put forward her theories on who might be after her.

"They're clearly not a normal person if they're going around planting threats and toying with their prey instead of just taking them out," Patricia said. "This woman has been sitting in this anger for decades. She wants her targets to suffer. I'd imagine it's because she herself has suffered in the intervening time."

"Well, I'm not the killer." Cece crossed the room and nervously straightened a stuffed alligator.

Virginia pulled the list from her pocket and unfolded it gingerly. She paused for a moment, nervous to hand it over, then extended it toward Cece. "Do you recognize any other names on this list?"

Cece read down it, nodding. "She died ten years ago," she said, pointing to one of the names. An *A* name, Virginia noticed. "And Joy moved to California." Cece pointed to another name. She handed the paper back to Virginia. "I don't know anything about the others. It's funny Olivia Cooper isn't on there."

"Who's Olivia Cooper?" Harriet asked. Virginia had almost forgotten she was there. She'd quietly crept over to lean against the tiny counter of Cece's kitchenette.

"Colleen fired her."

CHAPTER 39

Cece had the full attention of the room. Colleen had fired someone. This was news. And if there was a motive to hold a grudge for thirty years, that sounded like a strong possibility.

"I only worked with Colleen once," Cece began. "I was a writer. There was one shoot where Colleen's team hadn't prepared. Things were really bad in my relationship at the time—this was only a month or so before I took off. Between that and how long ago it was, I don't know how much I can remember. I know I wasn't originally going to be there that day, but we were scrambling, trying to clean up Colleen's team's mess. I don't remember what happened, but Colleen came out on top. Saved the day, somehow. She cleaned up her own team's mess, and everyone acted like she'd rescued a baby from a fire or something. I just remember thinking, 'That's New York.' I wasn't loving the city.

"Anyway, everyone was on edge because Colleen had just fired someone the day before. It was a new girl, an intern. She'd caught Colleen's eye, and Colleen had taken her out to lunch. Everyone thought Colleen was going to take this girl under her wing, but then they got back and Colleen fired her. It was all anyone was talking about on that shoot."

Olivia Cooper. They had a name.

It didn't start with an *A*, but this was the best lead she'd had since she started the investigation, and Virginia wasn't going to let that get her down. "Thank you," she said, pulling Cece into a hug. The woman startled, not expecting the embrace, then relaxed and hugged Virginia back.

* * *

As soon as she was alone, Virginia called Dylan directly. She didn't want to talk with the officers. She wanted someone for whom this was as personal as it was for Virginia.

"Olivia Cooper," she said as soon as Dylan picked up the phone.

"And she is…?"

"Our killer, I think."

Virginia could hear Dylan shuffling around on the other end of the line. She heard papers rustling and the click of a keyboard. "You think this, why?"

"Colleen fired her. Publicly. She took her out to lunch as if she were about to take her under her wing and then fired her instead."

"Facebook says she moved to Charlotte. Not exactly close."

"Not exactly far, either," Virginia retorted. "No picture on Facebook?"

"No picture," Dylan confirmed. No way to see whether Olivia was the one who had stabbed her. "We'll check her out."

"Prioritize this. I'm telling you, Dylan, I've got a feeling."

Dylan sighed. "You always have a feeling."

Silence spanned the line. Finally, Virginia choked out, "I'm glad you're okay."

"I'm glad I'm okay, too," Dylan said. Virginia thought she could hear her smirking. "I'm going to hang up on you now so I can pass this along to my team."

"Right, yes, go!"

Hope thudded in Virginia's chest as she set down her phone. They had a name. The police were on it. Charlotte, she thought. Olivia's Facebook could say she was in Thailand, and she'd still tell Dylan to prioritize checking her out. She had a feeling. As she looked around her room, desperate for something to do, some way to move the investigation forward, it occurred to her that everything that had ever gone right for her was because she just had a feeling.

VIRGINIA'S own internet search of Olivia Cooper turned up very little. Her Facebook was devoid of any helpful information. She was the founder of a nonprofit in Charlotte dedicated to ending homelessness. The website did not include a headshot.

Her investigation was interrupted when Colleen knocked at her door. "I came home to my room this afternoon to find a visitor inside." Panic flooded Virginia's veins, and Colleen held her hands up to wave it away. "Not the killer. My neighbor, Harriet."

The roller coaster of panic and relief made Virginia feel woozy.

"She said there'd been a breakthrough, and I should come to see you."

Virginia nodded. "Olivia Cooper. Remember her?"

Colleen looked pensive, then nodded. "Intern. Bright girl. I haven't heard from her in a few years. Last I knew, she was starting a nonprofit."

Colleen had stayed in touch with Olivia? "You fired her, right?"

"I suppose I did!" Colleen laughed. "I forgot that was how our friendship started."

Virginia tried to make sense of what Colleen was saying. "Your friendship?"

"Olivia didn't want to work in magazines. She didn't want to live in New York. She was there because it's what her family expected of her and what she thought wanted. I saw a spark in her, and I let her know it. And then I cut her loose so she could pursue her passions."

"In other words, you fired her."

"And she thanked me for it."

Virginia remembered that the police were working on a sketch of the woman who stabbed Dylan. "Do you remember what she looked like? Have you seen her since New York?"

Colleen shook her head. "I haven't seen her in person

since I set her free, but I think I remember what she looked like."

Virginia pulled out her phone to call Dylan. She needed to get Colleen in front of that sketch. She needed to know whether Olivia was their killer. While the phone rang in her ear, she heard the tinkling of chimes outside her door.

"'Speak of the devil,' or something like that." Virginia's door opened and Marney stepped inside, Dylan right behind her. "We were just coming to find you. You called?" Dylan waved the phone by her face.

"You need to show Colleen the sketch of the woman who stabbed you. She'll be able to confirm whether it's Olivia or not."

"Precisely why I told Mom I'd swing by Breeze Village instead of having her drop me at the station."

"Wait, aren't you supposed to be at your retreat until tomorrow?" Virginia looked her friend over and realized she still had her two duffel bags with her. She hadn't even been by her cottage to set her things down.

"I was," Marney said, "but after your news, I couldn't very well stay put an hour away. And Dylan was itching to get back."

Virginia felt bad for cutting Marney's retreat short, but she couldn't hide her excitement that Dylan was here and soon they'd have confirmation that Olivia was the one they were after. Or they'd be back to square one.

"Wait!" Virginia called out as Colleen started to follow Dylan from the room. "When you think of Olivia, do you feel... energy?"

Colleen gave this a moment's thought, then closed her

eyes. Virginia, Marney, and Dylan looked between each other and Colleen. When she finally opened her eyes, Virginia waited to hear her say she felt the definitive energy of a murderer. Instead, Colleen looked perplexed and shook her head. "I don't feel anything."

"Nothing at all?" Marney asked.

Colleen frowned. "Nothing at all. Usually, I can feel some sort of connection to a person. However faint, I feel that little pull. We're all connected, however distant, to the spirit world, and I can usually sense that tie binding us all. But with Olivia… I don't feel anything."

CHAPTER 40

When Virginia had filled Marney in, Marney didn't like the idea of trusting the person who had made it her mission to destroy Marney's shop. "She stole all my ideas! And we're just supposed to work alongside her?"

"I'm not trying to work with her," Virginia said. "But her information checks out."

They walked to Marney's cottage to check in on Pancake and drop off Marney's things.

"When were you going to tell me you were investigating?" Virginia asked, pointing to the board she and Jane had left out. "I didn't realize you felt the need."

"What do you mean, 'Felt the need?'"

"I know I've involved you in these investigations before, and I know it's put you in danger. I just hate that because of me, you felt like you had to do all this work just to be safe."

Marney balked. "You think I did this because I was scared?"

Virginia blinked. "Didn't you?"

"I did this because it was fun! Like learning to pick locks. A way to feel empowered in retirement. I mean, of course, I'm scared. My daughter was stabbed, and my cottage was broken into. Actually... Was that even the killer?"

"What do you mean?"

"Cece stole all my patterns. How'd she get them?"

Virginia thought about it. "You said your crochet stuff was disturbed in the break-in?"

"That's right. I didn't think anything of it at the time." She looked at Virginia, a new emotion taking hold. "That bitch!" Virginia flinched.

"She promised to shut her shop down," Virginia offered. "And to give you the money she made off your work."

"I don't want her money!" Marney said. "I want her behind bars for intellectual property theft and breaking and entering."

"You'll have to work that one out with Dylan."

Marney nodded like that was exactly what she was going to do.

Virginia's phone chimed with a reminder that she had work in an hour. "Duty calls. They'll fire me if I call in sick again."

* * *

DESPITE THE PRESENCE of an undercover officer keeping a close eye on her, Virginia couldn't stop her heart from racing with every customer who came through her checkout line. Every woman anywhere close to Olivia's age looked to Virginia like she was about to pull out a knife and lunge across the counter at her.

Two hours into her shift, Eliza came in. "Sorry for my parents," she said with a wince as she passed Virginia's lane. "They're being crazy. You really do not need to investigate."

Virginia gave her a soft smile. "I haven't given up." It wasn't a lie. She hadn't decided to quit trying to find the man who'd conned Eliza. But she hadn't exactly done much work to that end, either.

Eliza perked up a little at Virginia's assertion. "What do you investigate, exactly? Like, you've solved a bunch of murders or something? The other cashiers were talking." She turned away as if embarrassed to have brought it up.

Virginia felt her cheeks turn rosy with her own embarrassment. "Oh, I just have a knack for being in the right place at the right time. And luckily, a knack for not winding up dead, myself." How easily things could have gone sideways any number of times.

Eliza took over the next register, flipping on the light and ushering the first customers into her lane. Virginia went back to work, breathing through the panic every time someone came through her line. After another hour, there was a face she was sure she recognized.

"Glass!" It took a moment to place him, but she was certain it was Lawrence's beau. She tried to remember when he'd said he'd be back in Blacksville and when he was returning to Seaview. "Glass!" She called his name again.

Glass's neck snapped around, and he made eye contact

with Virginia. He was holding a bottle of orange dish soap and started to back away. As he took a step backward, he tripped over an elderly man's grocery cart and took out an end cap of pumpkin cookies.

"That's him!" Eliza shouted, pointing. "The scammer!"

Glass was on his feet, running, but another cashier tackled him before he made his escape. A manager pulled the cashier off a struggling Glass, muttering something about a lawsuit waiting to happen under his breath. Glass started to take off again, but a group of customers had formed a wall with their bodies, blocking the door until police arrived.

"Glass?" Virginia's voice broke, and Glass avoided her eyes. "I can't believe it." All she could see was the look on Lawrence's face when she told him. And she knew she had to tell him. If Lawrence heard it from someone else, he'd never forgive her.

"You did it!" Eliza clapped Virginia on the back. "You weren't kidding about that knack for being in the right place at the right time."

It felt like a lightning bolt struck Virginia. In that moment, she understood the image of a lightbulb going off over one's head. She wouldn't have been surprised to find a glowing bulb floating above her own head. She couldn't dial Marney's number fast enough.

"Get everyone together," she commanded. "We've been at this all wrong, trying to find the killer. We need to get the killer to find us. Well, me, specifically."

CHAPTER 41

Marney didn't want to believe Glass was capable of stealing. "I wouldn't have expected to find him secretly donating all his money to charity, but to con a high school student at her job as a cashier? That's low." She looked as appalled as Virginia felt.

"I have to tell Lawrence," she said, her voice full of dread.

"You do," Marney acknowledged.

"But we've got something else to discuss." Virginia looked at the faces assembled at the table. They were in Ronald's room on the first floor. Marney had instructed them to stagger their arrivals in case they were being watched, and Ronald had drawn the curtains on his window.

Seated around his small table were Marney, Ronald, Patricia, Colleen, Harriet, and Cece.

"I just called Ronald and Patricia," Marney said, "but

then I ran into Colleen and thought she should come, too."

"And I saw Colleen leaving her room and asked where she was going," Harriet said. "She tried to lie to me, but I reminded her that without my lock-picking skills, we would have no idea who was trying to kill her, so I deserved to be included."

"And then I saw everyone going to Ronald's room," Cece said.

"So much for not being suspicious." Patricia looked around like it was everyone else, but not her, who had aroused suspicion.

"Besides, I'm the one who actually figured it out," Cece added.

Virginia looked to Colleen. She looked wan and sat quietly. "So it's Olivia? You saw the sketch."

Colleen nodded solemnly. "I saw the sketch. It's her."

Virginia paced, frenetic energy bouncing around under her skin. "Right. So." She looked back at her friends, all assembled to help her bring down a killer. Pride swelled inside her. "The reason I gathered you all. When I accidentally solved another case just this afternoon, I had a thought. A realization, if you will."

"Get on with it!" Ronald's grin revealed that he was happier for the chance to heckle her than frustrated at her slow pace.

"Everything I've ever gotten right has been because I just had a feeling and happened to be in the right place at the right time. Instead of chasing this killer trying to find her, we need to get her to find me."

Patricia gave Virginia a look like it was the dumbest

thing she'd ever heard. "She already knows where you are."

"I mean, we need to lure her out! We need to make me irresistible so she can't help but make a move. But instead of being caught off guard, we'll be waiting for her." No one said anything. Marney gave Virginia an encouraging look, and she went on. "We set a trap and use me as bait."

"I don't like it." Ronald stood from the table, shaking his head. "It's too dangerous."

"There's seven of us right here. Between all of us, we can outsmart her for sure," Virginia pushed.

"Lawrence will help, too," Marney said. She was right. Virginia knew there was no way Lawrence would let them go through with this without his help.

"This is how we get the upper hand. We let the killer think she's acting on her terms, when really it's on ours."

Virginia had herself convinced. One by one, the dominos fell and her friends began to nod their agreement, or at least their willingness to participate, even if they still thought it was a bad idea.

"We can't tell Dylan," Marney said. Virginia looked at her in shock. Marney had never suggested keeping something from the police in an investigation before. "She'll never let it happen." She was right. Dylan would shut their plan down without hesitation.

"So, boss," Harriet said, looking at Virginia with a sparkle in her eyes. "What's our plan?" Everyone else followed Harriet's lead and looked to Virginia expectantly.

Virginia thought about it. Where did they want to

draw the killer out? Where would the killer think Virginia was going to be alone and vulnerable?

"We go to the beach." Virginia hoped she sounded more confident than she felt. "We'll get Lawrence and Ronald to hide and take her down when Olivia shows up. Ronald has already proven his takedown abilities on Cece."

Cece blushed, and Ronald glowed with pride.

"The last time you snuck off to the beach, the killer didn't realize you'd left." Virginia winced at Marney's reminder.

"This time, I won't be sneaking. I'll go openly. She'll follow."

"Won't the police follow, too?" Colleen asked.

"We can cause a distraction," Cece offered. "We'll get the officers' attention, and Virginia can go."

Virginia nodded, then pointed two fingers toward Marney and Patricia. "Marney and Patricia will drop Lawrence and Ronald off at the beach, then leave, so there won't be a car there to tip off our killer. You go together, so neither of you is ever alone. Cece and Colleen engineer a distraction to buy me time. And Harriet…" She looked over at the woman. Her eyes had glazed over slightly. She looked less present. "We need everyone at Breeze Village to think things are normal. So your job will be to hold the fort here and make sure everything seems ordinary."

Harriet seemed satisfied with the role Virginia had made up for her. "I think I'm going to start by making sure everything is ordinary up in my room. If you'll excuse me." She made her exit, and the rest of the team huddled around the table.

"When do we act?" Patricia whispered.

"Tonight." Heads turned to Virginia, and she ignored her stomach doing flips. "The killer is close. I can feel it. We don't have time to waste."

Marney looked at Ronald. He nodded, then looked to Patricia. One by one, they nodded and looked to the next person over until the entire table was in agreement.

"Okay, then," Marney said. "We act tonight."

* * *

MARNEY DROVE ALONE to Lawrence's condo. Patricia and Ronald waited fifteen minutes before taking off in Patricia's car. Virginia wanted to go, too, but they all agreed she needed to stay put. As far as they knew, Olivia was watching her, and they wanted to avoid raising suspicion. As it was, everything looked normal. Now to keep it that way.

A text from Marney came through.

> Lawrence is in.
>
> Not happy about Glass, btw.
>
> I gave him the broad strokes. I told him you'd fill him in later.

Great. Something to look forward to.

Virginia stared at her Kindle, her brain reading the words but not processing anything on the page, entirely distracted by what was coming. The light coming in through her curtains dimmed until the sun had fully set. It was time.

Finally, another text.

Dropped off the boys.

She sent Colleen a message.

Go time.

Virginia didn't know what Colleen and Cece had in store. She just knew that she was to wait five minutes from sending her message and then make her exit. Her palms were sweating, and she kept wiping them down the sides of her pants. She watched the seconds tick by until three minutes had passed. She grabbed her beach bag and stuffed a towel and sweats inside as if it were a normal night when she wanted a little cold plunge followed by a think on the shore.

Four minutes.

She slipped on her mismatched shoes—one sneaker, one clog—and made a mental note that she would definitely not be outrunning the killer tonight. She said a silent prayer that Lawrence and Ronald were ready.

Five minutes.

When the elevator chimed and Virginia stepped into the lobby of Breeze Village, she was met with the shrieks of a bird alongside the unmistakable sound of Cece's voice. "Oh, Officer! It's on the bookshelf!" A terrible crash sounded in one the activity rooms, and Cece's scream was joined by Colleen's. A male voice cursed, and Virginia heard another squawk from the bird. It seemed their plan had been to bring a bird into the building. And judging by the sounds of an argument breaking out between officers on the best method of extraction, their plan was working.

Virginia made it to her car with no indication she was being followed. She only hoped she was. With her hands shaking so badly she almost couldn't get the key into the ignition, she tried to start the car. The engine sputtered but wouldn't turn over. "Come on," she begged, turning the key a second, then a third time. The car wouldn't start.

Movement outside the car window caught Virginia's eye. She yelped and jumped, and her hand made contact with the steering wheel, sounding the horn. She hoped everyone inside was still occupied with the bird.

Alone in the dark, Virginia grasped for ideas to salvage her plan. She needed to think, and she needed to think fast. Otherwise, she'd lured her protection away and given her stalker a perfect window to take her out without being seen. *Think. Adapt.*

The plan had always been to make the killer think Virginia was alone and have her friends take Olivia down. She'd just have to move the plan a little closer to home, she decided. It was time to call in reinforcements.

Virginia had a text half-written, ready to send to Dylan. The new plan would be for Virginia to take a stroll on the walking path at Breeze Village. Dylan and her team would be waiting, hiding in the trees alongside the path, and would take down the killer when she thought Virginia was alone. She didn't like it, but she didn't have time to come up with another alternative. She had her finger poised over the send button and was fully engrossed in the message when a rap at her window made Virginia scream for a second time.

CHAPTER 42

"You okay in there?" Virginia recognized the voice though it was muffled by the glass.

"Gemma?" She opened the door and nearly cried with relief as she wrapped her arms around her friend.

"What's going on?" Gemma's voice was distorted by the force with which Virginia was squeezing her.

"I'm just happy to see you," Virginia said, releasing Gemma to straighten her clothes and collect herself. "My car won't start."

"Where are you headed? I can take you."

Virginia looked around. She suspected the killer was watching, lurking behind a palmetto frond surrounded by the enormous oak trees that stood on the property. At least, she hoped she was. As she thought about it, she realized she wasn't sure what she was hoping for anymore. She wanted their plan to work. She wanted to be moments away from taking down a killer. But as her heart thundered in her chest, she also wanted to call the whole thing off.

"I was headed to the beach," she said finally. "I wanted some time to myself, and that's where I do my best thinking. Would you drop me off?"

If the killer was listening, she'd expect to be able to corner Virginia alone at the beach. Virginia didn't think she'd be able to resist.

Virginia had her eyes on the rear-view mirror throughout the half-hour drive through the marsh toward the beach. There were a few other cars on the road, but not many, and she didn't notice anyone following them. Her stomach churned, and after the third time she had Gemma repeat herself because she hadn't been listening, Gemma turned the radio on.

"You're acting funny," she remarked.

Virginia thought about how she would act if she weren't using herself as bait to draw out a sadistic killer. She couldn't come up with anything, so she grunted an acknowledgment and continued looking in the rear-view mirror. Gemma said nothing else about it.

Finally, Gemma pulled into a parking space. "How are you getting back?"

"Marney will take me." Virginia heard her voice wobble and break.

Gemma gave her a curious look but let it go. She waved, and Virginia watched her taillights shrink until they disappeared in the distance. She was alone.

The moon hung low in the sky, its white glow casting shadows that made everything look threatening. Virginia sat on her favorite wooden swing with her bag. On a normal night, she would strip down and run into the sea, then bundle up before sitting with her thoughts. Tonight, taking off her clothes felt like more vulnerability than she could handle, but she didn't want the killer to suspect that anything was out of sorts. She was preparing herself for the shock of cold air meeting bare flesh when there was a rustle in the trees behind her.

"There you are."

Virginia turned slowly as if the predator staring her down was a dinosaur who couldn't see her if she avoided sudden movements. She tried to remember the signal she and the gang had agreed upon. Was she supposed to make a birdcall?

Olivia stared her down with blank eyes. Her hands hung empty by her side. No knife, Virginia noted. Her hair stood in frizzy, tangled curls away from her face. In the moonlight, her facial features looked exaggeratedly sharp. Virginia thought she could see the bags under Olivia's eyes from where she stood. She looked like a woman untethered from their world.

Virginia opened her mouth and tried to make a birdcall. The strangled sound died on her lips. Olivia cocked her head as if studying Virginia, and Virginia started to try again when Lawrence and Ronald came barreling out of the bushes. At the sight of them, Olivia let out a laugh that sliced through the darkness and brought them all to a dead stop. Then she pulled out a gun.

The breath caught in Virginia's throat. This wasn't part of the plan. Olivia hadn't used a gun before. She was supposed to have a knife. They were supposed to stand a chance.

"So this was your plan?" Olivia sounded amused, almost impressed. Virginia thought she was about to go on, opine on how they'd taken her by surprise, but instead, Olivia rounded and raised the gun at Virginia.

Before Virginia could register the weapon aimed at her, Lawrence let out a guttural yell, and he and Ronald resumed their run toward Olivia. Then a siren sounded nearby, the explosive crack of a gunshot split the air, and Olivia vanished. The siren wailed ever closer as Lawrence, Ronald, and Virginia regrouped.

"Are you shot?" Lawrence asked, pulling Virginia up from where she'd fallen in the sand. "Are you okay?" He patted her down, searching for the warm wetness of blood, but found none.

"I think I'm okay," Virginia said, though her mind seemed to exist entirely outside of her body, and she couldn't have pinpointed a physical sensation no matter how strong.

"Where did she go?" Ronald roared.

The sirens converged until three police cars careened into the small parking area. Officers flooded out, surrounding the three. Virginia, Ronald, and Lawrence all put their hands up and raced to explain the situation at the same time.

"She's gone!"

"She disappeared."

"She ran away!"

Radios beeped as officers communicated with their partners elsewhere. Within minutes, two of the cars sped back out of the lot. Two officers remained with the group, and an ambulance arrived shortly thereafter. Paramedics looked Virginia over and confirmed she was fine. Police found a bullet lodged in the wood of a lifeguard stand a little way down the beach and concluded that Olivia wasn't a great shot.

"Thank heavens for that," Virginia breathed. Her pulse had slowed considerably, but she was still breathing like she'd just run a race.

Ronald took a seat beside her on the swing. "How'd the police know to show up?"

"I might know something about that." Lawrence held his phone up. "Marney sent us all a text twenty minutes ago."

"My phone was in my bag." Virginia reached for it.

> SOS MISSION COMPROMISED DYLAN KNOWS
>
> OFFICERS EN ROUTE TO BEACH
>
> She came to check in on me and asked where Virginia was. I'm sorry guys!! She cracked me like an egg!!

When the officers were finished processing the scene, they offered the three friends a ride home. "You'll have to squeeze in the back." Given that the alternative was waiting until Marney could get there, they agreed and piled in.

"That was a pretty dumb plan," the officer in the passenger seat commented.

"Dumb as rocks," the driver agreed.

None of the three in the back said anything. Virginia was heartbroken and reeling from defeat. Ronald was still fuming. Lawrence wasn't so easy to read.

Eventually, Virginia leaned over to her left to nudge his shoulder. "Sorry about Glass," she said.

"I'm over it." He wasn't, of course, but this wasn't the time or place to try to discuss it.

Over their radios, Virginia heard the police get a notice that the killer had gotten away. She wasn't surprised. As the adrenaline left her body, she just felt tired. She let her head fall to the side and rest on Lawrence's shoulder, and the next thing she knew, they were back at Breeze Village.

"Wakey wakey," Ronald teased.

"They didn't take you home?" Virginia was surprised they hadn't dropped Lawrence off sooner since his condo was so much closer to the beach.

"I'm going to stay here tonight. I'll sleep on Marney's couch. I want to be close by."

Virginia would have let herself cry if she didn't know it would delay being able to say goodnight and return to her own room. But desperate to crawl underneath the covers and sleep off their loss, she bit her tongue, put on a brave face, and said that sounded great and that she'd see him in the morning. She was so exhausted she almost didn't notice the figure sitting on her bed waiting for her when she walked into her room.

"Hello again."

CHAPTER 43

"Olivia." Virginia stood rooted to the spot. She saw a glint of light flash and noticed Olivia had her gun out. She remembered how Olivia had missed earlier. She wasn't a good shot. Virginia could run. But what then? When would it end?

"You could act a little more surprised to see me." Olivia's voice had a taunting lilt to it. She was the cat playing with the mouse.

"I'm tired."

Olivia nodded. "I suppose you are. I've put you through a lot, and you're not a young thing anymore, are you?"

Virginia wondered if there was anything she could say that would resonate with the woman. If she had any power in this situation besides the ability to flee.

"Should I cut to the chase, then?" Olivia asked. As she spoke, she gestured with her weapon. It cast little specks of light on the ceiling as she moved it around. Suddenly, Olivia raised it and aimed for Virginia's chest.

"Wait!" Virginia tossed her hands up in front of her and cowered, ducking behind the recliner.

"I thought you said you were tired!" Olivia put on a fake pout, then shrugged. "So I guess we won't cut quite to the chase, then. Very well. I've got all night. The police are looking for me a good thirty miles north of here. You want the story, then?"

Virginia nodded. If she could keep her talking, she could figure something out.

Olivia took a deep breath before beginning, as if she'd been waiting a long time to tell this story. "Three things happened to me that irrevocably altered the course of my life. Number one: I was forced to testify against my father in court. He was on trial for petty theft, and I was a witness. I lost my family that day. They never spoke to me again. My family is close-knit. My whole childhood and adolescence, I'd known the comfort and complete acceptance that was a loving family. That was gone in an instant. The attorney who subpoenaed me was Irene Pushton."

Virginia nodded, sensing where this was going.

"Number two: my long-term boyfriend Herman left me in my hour of need. Suddenly, I found myself without family and without a place to live, since I'd been staying in his apartment." Olivia lifted her eyes from where she'd been staring at the comforter and looked at Virginia. "You want to guess number three?"

"Colleen fired you," Virginia said softly.

Olivia nodded. "Colleen fired me. So there I was. Alone in New York, no family, no place to stay, and no job. I bounced back, eventually, of course. Made something of a name for myself. Started a nonprofit to try and ensure no one has to live on the streets like I did during that time. But you know what?"

Virginia tried to force a "What?" from her mouth. Her eyes darted from Olivia to the door as she continued to weigh her chances of survival if she ran.

"The city just released an updated snapshot of housing data. The homeless population actually increased in the last year. It has increased every year since I started my nonprofit five years ago. I work so hard." Her voice squeaked, and she took a breath to recover herself. "I have poured everything I have into this organization. I have done everything I can think of. And we haven't made a difference. I haven't made a difference."

Olivia stopped talking. From her stance behind the recliner, Virginia didn't have a clear visual, but she thought she heard the woman crying. She waited until Olivia reached up to wipe her face and then stood quickly, taking two steps toward the door before Olivia whipped the gun back up. "Stop." She gestured with the gun for Virginia to step back into the center of the room. "None of that."

"How'd you get in here?" Virginia wanted to know.

"I can pick locks." Olivia brushed the question off.

"How'd you get past security?"

"They're not as observant as they think they are." A twisted smile broke out on Olivia's face. "And if you look old, they don't look too hard."

So she'd worn a disguise.

"The hauntings," Virginia said. "Did you take my shoes or leave me cake?"

The woman squinted at her. "Did I what?"

"Okay, so it's not you, then. Someone's been haunting this place, and I didn't know if it was part of your game or not."

"It wasn't, but I like it."

Olivia stood from the bed and took a step toward Virginia. Only about six feet separated them. Virginia knew she couldn't run now.

"What about the initials?" Virginia asked, grasping for something to buy more time. "There was an *A* carved in Irene and Herman."

Olivia looked put out that Virginia brought it up. "I tried to make an *O* first, on Irene. It was harder than I thought, but I couldn't just leave the messed-up *O*, so I turned it into an *A*. She was dead anyways, so she didn't know the difference. Then I decided it was like a signature: uniquely mine, but didn't need to actually be a legible interpretation of my name. After Irene, I started signing my little notes with an *A*. For consistency, you understand."

Virginia shuddered. The way things stood, she was about two minutes from having Olivia's sick signature carved into her own body.

"People will hear that." She pointed feebly at the gun.

"And I'll be long gone when they come running and find your body," Olivia said, not concerned in the least. "I'm quick, in case you hadn't realized by now. Speaking of..." She looked at her watch, then back at Virginia. "It's time."

Virginia took a step back and tripped. Her arms circled wildly beside her as she fell backward, her back connecting with the side table before she rolled onto the floor.

A gunshot burst through the commotion. Virginia's ears rang as she tried to roll herself onto her hands and knees. As she lifted her head, she saw Olivia take aim a second time.

"No!" The door swung open, and Ronald burst into the room, shouting at the top of his lungs. Olivia's mouth opened in surprise, and Ronald leapt at her, grabbing her around the waist and knocking her onto the bed. A second shot rang out.

"Hands in the air!" The four officers who had been posted around Breeze Village rushed into the room, disarming Olivia and cuffing her.

Ronald helped Virginia up. "For a murderer, she's a pretty horrible shot."

Virginia grinned, then winced. Though the shots had missed, the table she'd crashed into had done a number on her back.

VIRGINIA AGREED to go to the hospital to be checked out. As she was escorted from her room, she turned back to where Olivia was lying facedown on the floor in handcuffs. "I have one more question." It had been nagging at her. "Colleen said you two were friends after she fired you."

"That's a statement," Olivia spat into the carpet.

"Were you?" Virginia asked.

Olivia's movement in response could be interpreted as

a shrug. "For a long time after I got back on my feet, I convinced myself she'd done me a favor. They all had. They'd forced me to leave the life I'd planned for myself behind and pursue something that mattered more. Colleen had given me an out, and thanks to her, I was doing something meaningful with my life. We both know how that went."

Right. Olivia was convinced her work didn't matter. And after long enough like that, she wanted revenge.

She turned back to the door and followed the paramedics outside, then rode to the hospital to make sure she hadn't sprained or broken anything in the fall.

Marney beat her to the hospital, worried sick. Lawrence's first words were an apology for letting Virginia go back to her room.

"As if I'd have let you stop me," she said with a smile. "I was so tired. I *am* so tired."

"We'll go," Marney said, though she didn't look like she was ready to go anywhere, firmly planted in the chair by Virginia's bedside. "I just needed to see you with my own eyes."

"Thank goodness for Ronald," Lawrence said.

"How did he get there so fast?" Marney asked.

"Apparently, he followed me upstairs and was camped outside my door. He planned to sleep in the hall that night in case anything happened." Virginia could hardly believe she had such devoted friends and thanked her lucky stars she wasn't the only one with good instincts.

"Thank goodness for Ronald," Marney said, echoing Lawrence's sentiment.

"Thank goodness for Ronald," Virginia agreed.

CHAPTER 44

Three days later, sitting around Marney's dining table, Virginia and Lawrence helped package orders for Marney's shop while Pancake batted a pompom around on the carpet. A levity had infected all of Breeze Village since Olivia had been arrested. The killer was caught, and they could all breathe a little easier. Colleen had promised to thank Ronald by taking him to an exclusive restaurant, appealing to his foodie side. He had been pleased with the offer and positively strutting his stuff around Breeze Village since his role in taking down a killer.

"Did you hear?" he'd say, walking from table to table in the dining room. "I tackled a murderer. Took her down all on my own." If the unsuspecting diners gave a polite "wow" in response, Ronald took that as his cue to recount the entire tale.

After Cece took her shop down, Marney's sales ballooned. Cece also formally apologized to Marney, and Marney was on her way to forgiving her.

The doorbell rang. "I'll get it," Virginia offered. She crossed the room, leaning heavily on her cane since her fall, and greeted Dylan at the door. "Come to tell us all about your exciting next chapter?" she asked.

"I didn't realize Mom had company. I didn't plan to stay that long. Brian and I have plans in just a bit."

"Officer McNeil?"

"The very same." Dylan gave her mom a kiss on the cheek, then regarded the packages the three friends had been preparing. "You've been busy!"

Marney absolutely beamed.

Over a glass of sweet tea, Dylan filled them in. She was still Assistant Chief through the end of the year. Then she'd be stepping down, and while she'd planned to take some time off to figure out what she wanted to do next, an opportunity had landed in her lap that she couldn't turn down. She'd be working as a victim's advocate at a non-profit focused on victims of domestic abuse. Marney's glow intensified.

Virginia left them all to go to Pilates. When the baby came along, Virginia figured she and Sam would be seeing more of each other, and this would give them something besides the baby to connect over. It was also her apology to Jack for deliberately putting herself in harm's way with her plan to lure out the killer. She agreed to keep up with Pilates to help improve her balance and coordination, and he agreed not to blow a gasket over her lack of instinct for self-preservation.

"Virginia!" Colleen caught her just as she was about to enter the activities room. "I just wanted to let you know that the hauntings have stopped."

"That's wonderful."

"I also wanted to thank you again. You were persistent, and without you—and Ronald, of course—I'd certainly be dead by now. You're a good detective."

"I wouldn't say that," Virginia laughed. "But I'll take the compliment."

Beside her in Pilates, Jane leaned over and whispered, "I heard Kim and Haley talking. There was a resident on the first floor, Martin. Actually, you might remember him. Marney once laid into him for being handsy with the nurses. Anyway, he died two days ago, right after your showdown with that murderer. They found a bunch of cash under his mattress and a stash of shoes."

"Shoes?"

"Mm-hmm. Weird, right?"

"Definitely," she agreed. "Did you know Martin?"

Jane shook her head. "He was friendly with Ed before Ed moved to Harbor Vale. Ed was probably his closest friend here."

Virginia nodded and forced down a giggle. She was pretty sure she knew who had been haunting her and Colleen and why the hauntings had come to an abrupt stop. She decided she wouldn't tell Colleen. For all Colleen needed to know, the spirits were satisfied with her safety and no longer saw a need to interfere in the earthly realm.

"All right," Carol said, her ponytail flapping behind her. She removed her YMCA fleece, fanning herself and giving Diana a thumbs-up, signaling she was ready to start the class. "We're about to heat it up in here. Who remembers those leg circles we did last week?"

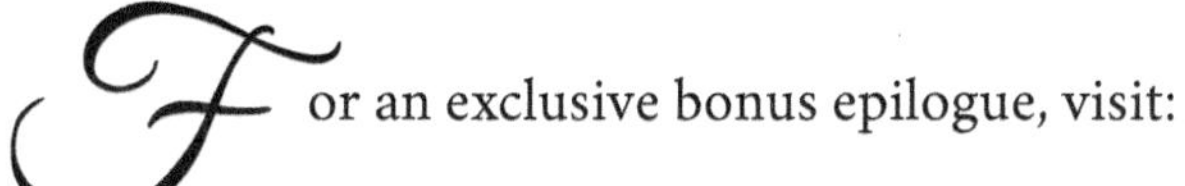

For an exclusive bonus epilogue, visit:

https://katemacleanbooks.com/tcl-epilogue/

291

* * *

IF YOU ENJOYED THIS BOOK, please consider leaving a review. It helps me tremendously.

ACKNOWLEDGMENTS

Writing this book would not have been possible without the support and encouragement of my friends, family, readers, and writing communities.

First, thank you to Tracy Mooring Liebchen, my editor. When I was convinced this book was perfect, you showed me that it wasn't, and then you helped me make it better. Thank you for your eagle eyes catching my mistakes and your kind words softening the blows.

Thank you to Sarra Cannon and the Heart Breathings Writing Community. Your support and co-working got me through every slump when I felt like I wasn't capable of making this book what I wanted it to be. Fri-YAY sprints and virtual retreats were a saving grace.

Thank you to the 20BooksTo50k community for your rising tide.

To every reader who has picked up Pension for Murder and Bingo, Bribes, and Alibis: thank you. I wrote them for you, and it is my greatest joy and encouragement to read your reviews.

And finally, thank you Ken for making this possible. Your love and support have been instrumental to my writing every one of these books.

ABOUT THE AUTHOR

A Georgia peach, Kate Maclean grew up in historic Savannah and spent much of her childhood reading Nancy Drew and Hercule Poirot mysteries on her backyard swing.

This lifelong lover of mysteries and crime dramas now lives outside Washington, D.C., with her husband and their cat. This is her third book.

9 789898 525002